LETTING STONES

Awakenings 5

Michele Zurlo

EROTIC ROMANCE

Siren Publishing, Inc.
www.SirenPublishing.com

A SIREN PUBLISHING BOOK
IMPRINT: Erotic Romance

LETTING GO 2: STEPPING STONES
Copyright © 2012 by Michele Zurlo

ISBN: 978-1-62242-076-6

First Printing: November 2012

Cover design by Christine Kirchoff
All cover art and logo copyright © 2012 by Siren Publishing, Inc.

ALL RIGHTS RESERVED: This literary work may not be reproduced or transmitted in any form or by any means, including electronic or photographic reproduction, in whole or in part, without express written permission.

All characters and events in this book are fictitious. Any resemblance to actual persons living or dead is strictly coincidental.

Printed in the U.S.A.

PUBLISHER
Siren Publishing, Inc.
www.SirenPublishing.com

DEDICATION

This is dedicated to everyone who sent emails and posted on my FB page asking for more Sabrina and Jonas. Without your encouragement (and some outright begging) this story would not have been written.

I especially want to thank Becca for her thoughtful e-mails/discussion and helpful critiques. And yes, the Samantha part was written for you.

Last, but not least, I want to thank my family. Without your support and understanding, none of this would have been possible.

Note to readers: Though this sequel stands alone as a story, I highly recommend reading *Letting Go* before reading *Stepping Stones*. If possible, also read *Hanging On* and *Two Masters for Samantha*. You will find *Stepping Stones* a richer, more rewarding read if you're already acquainted with each character's "how we got together" story.

LETTING GO 2: STEPPING STONES

Awakenings 5

MICHELE ZURLO
Copyright © 2012

Chapter One

Sabrina peeked out the window of her breakfast nook. In the distance, past the deck, the trellis bursting with tangerine and white roses, and a large expanse of lawn, the sun glinted on the water, beckoning her closer.

With the kids at her in-laws for the afternoon, she had some free time, and it had been a few days since she'd been able to get in a good, punishing workout in the water. She opted for a bikini—the hot-as-hell pool boy was due sometime today—grabbed a towel, and rushed to the pool.

As she got closer, she noticed the man with a long pole stuck into the water, and she slowed her pace. Too late. Now she would have to wait for the pool boy to finish cleaning it before she could swim.

With a sigh, she heaved herself onto a lounger and sent a baleful look in his direction. He wasn't supposed to show up until later, after she'd worked out. She had plans to pull herself, dripping wet, out of the water, throwing her hair back so that the sun caught some of the highlights. She'd squeeze away the excess, letting it drip over her breasts to draw his gaze to the gentle swells there.

He'd ruined everything by showing up early. There was so little variety in her life. She spent most of the day looking after her one- and three-year-olds, and the chance to put herself on display to torment the pool boy was one opportunity she hated missing. While her afternoon wouldn't be completely ruined, she did prefer to do things her way.

After all, a girl had to have fun, right? Her husband worked long hours and traveled all the time, so she had to get her kicks however she could.

"Good afternoon, Mrs. Spencer." He grinned at her from across the pool.

He wasn't wearing a shirt. She spent some time admiring the way his lithe, lean muscles bunched and strained as he methodically worked his way toward the far end of the pool. The tan darkening his skin testified to many hours spent under the punishing rays of the sun.

Her gaze traveled lower, taking in the way his shorts hung low on his hips. Too low. One tug and she'd catch an eyeful. The hipbones jutting forward were tanned as well. It made her wonder if his gorgeous ass enjoyed the same freedom.

"Armand, I thought I told you to not wear those shorts anymore. They're positively scandalous." She spoke to him in a tone that managed to be both haughty and lazy. "And put a shirt on. My husband will not look kindly upon you if he sees you walking around here almost naked."

He didn't respond. Nothing in the set of his shoulders or the tilt of his mouth gave her a hint as to his reaction, but she knew he had one. She knew he'd heard her. He hadn't stopped looking at her for a single second.

After forever, he extracted the vacuum from the pool and set it on the concrete patio. Ever so slowly, he rounded the pool, not stopping until his shadow loomed over her. This close, she could see the danger glittering from his olive-green eyes. They were hazel normally, but they tended toward green under most circumstances. When he was feeling amorous, they often turned topaz.

"Mrs. Spencer, your husband is half a world away. And you know as well as I do that you like when I wear these shorts. You think they're sexy. After all, you bought them for me." Like a cobra, his hand shot out. He caught the end of the string tied behind her neck to hold up her bikini top, and he tugged.

She felt the small pop that indicated it was no longer tied. She knew she should put her hands over the fabric to shield herself before he peeled the scrap of material away, but she was paralyzed by the hard expression on his face. The planes and angles that made up his face were what some might call handsome. She might think it, but she knew better than to say it to his face. And his lips were positively sensual. She imagined what they'd feel like traveling down her neck, sucking her nipple inside, and then slipping lower.

"Armand, this is highly inappropriate. My husband wouldn't like this."

The mask slipped away for a second, revealing Jonas's humor at her remark. They hadn't planned to role-play today. She knew he was pleased with her improvisation, and she loved how quickly he'd understood both what she was doing and what she wanted from him.

"He's a busy man, your husband. I'm doing him a favor by putting you in your place." With that, he tugged again, and the strings holding up her top came loose. "I'm going to make you beg, Mrs. Spencer."

Oh lord, she was moist. It only took one look from him to make her knees weak, and he was using it on her now. Thank goodness they'd stocked the pool house with the necessary equipment.

She'd wrangled her hair into a braid to make it easier to get under her swim cap. Reaching back, he grasped her by the long rope and pulled, urging her to stand up. He turned her around, so that her back was to his front, and he guided her back against him. Only then did it become apparent exactly how hard his muscles were. Before she could think to struggle, he banded one iron arm around her midsection.

Because she was half a foot shorter, her head fit neatly under his chin. He rested it on her now, another tool to keep her close. "Last chance, Mrs. Spencer."

"Really?" She didn't honestly think he'd let her off the hook so easily. Men as dominant and virile as this didn't take kindly to her haughtiness.

He chuckled, a low, sinister laugh. "No, not really. Your fate is sealed."

With that, he peeled away the fabric clinging to her breasts and squeezed one hard, his callused palm scraping her sensitive skin. She whimpered with the effort it cost to not beg for more.

He ground his pelvis into her ass, and she realized he was hard and ready. That could only mean one thing.

Without baring her further, he pushed her into the pool house. While he loved being an exhibitionist, she'd drawn the line when it came to overly graphic displays where their neighbors could see. Of course, he liked to counter that by saying their neighbors shouldn't be using binoculars to see into the backyard if they didn't want to see the kind of shows they put on.

In the cool darkness, she could barely make out his shape. The temperature difference made her nipples stand on end. She had to stop leaving the air conditioning turned up so high.

He ran his fingers through her hair, roughly combing out her careful braid, and then he pushed her to her knees.

"Hands behind you, Mrs. Spencer."

She complied, assuming one of the submissive positions he'd taught her. From their earliest days together, she'd loved pleasuring him with her mouth, and he never thought twice about taking advantage of her addiction. It worked well for them both.

One shove and those shorts fell to his ankles, proving her assessment correct. They were entirely too loose. He kicked them away, but she didn't pay much attention to them. Instead, she focused her gaze on his engorged cock. The thick purple head demanded the caress of her tongue.

She leaned forward and licked a path around the tip, widening her circles until she had him in her mouth. She sucked lightly, knowing it would drive him crazy until he was compelled to take over.

Until then, she took her time, exploring him with her lips and tongue. She loved his texture and the salty, musky flavor that leaked from the tip. After a few minutes, she heard him groan, and then his hands gripped the sides of her head. He set the pace now, fucking her mouth with long, slow strokes.

She relaxed her jaw and swallowed every time he came to the back of her throat, urging him deeper. His moans came faster and shorter. Crude language sprinkled from his lips.

"Fuck, baby. Take my cock deeper. Suck harder. That's right. Your little cunt is dripping, isn't it?"

She made a noise of agreement in the back of her throat. The vibrations shut him up for a second. He knew how much that kind of language embarrassed and excited her. Five years of marriage, and certain words still made her blush. Of course, that was why he used them. He loved to see her cheeks turn red.

And then he shouted and his hot semen shot down her throat. She swallowed to keep up with the supply, to keep every drop.

When he withdrew, she used the back of her hand to wipe away the extra saliva that coated her lips and chin. Giving head could be so very messy.

Always amused by her need for neatness and order, he laughed at her as he pulled his shorts back into place.

She lifted a brow. "Is that all you got, hot stuff? I expected more."

It was a dangerous move, mouthing off when he was in Dom mode, but she always loved the outcome. Jonas had a magic touch when it came to making her body sing in all the right ways. He didn't disappoint now.

The room upended and she found herself over his shoulder. The pool house wasn't large. It had a shower room that could accommodate four, and that was the main feature. Otherwise, it comprised two large rooms. One was a combination kitchen, living, and gaming area. The other was a bedroom. Shortly after she had it built, Jonas had turned it into a man cave. It housed so many electronics that she'd installed an alarm. She didn't mind, especially after the children were born and it became an escape for her, too. She'd even bought him a pool table.

He threw her down on the sofa. She landed on her ass, sinking deep into the cushion. It was too soft to provide any bounce. Knowing what was coming next, she scrambled out of the way, but he was too quick.

Before she knew what had happened, he had her face down over his lap. He threw one leg over her knees to hold her in place, and he placed one firm hand on her lower back.

Knowing she would be eagerly anticipating what was about to happen, he lowered her bikini bottoms slowly. She squirmed a little bit more now, trying to get him to slap her ass to make her stop, but he was too smart to fall for her ploy. He halted his actions completely.

Seconds ticked by. Her half-naked ass waited. He'd positioned her so that she was up a little on her knees, her ass presented prettily, her legs spread wide enough so that he could spank her pussy if he wanted. It didn't take long for her to give in. "Please, Armand. I'm sorry. I'll be good. I promise."

"Ask for it, Mrs. Spencer."

The moment she took his name, he'd begun calling her 'Mrs. Spencer' during most of their games. He used it often as a way to stake his claim. She didn't mind. She liked belonging to him.

"I've been bad, Armand. I need to be spanked."

"That's not asking." He rubbed his palm over her flesh, a little fresh incentive.

"Please spank me. Please? I need a good spanking. My husband is away and I'm going to be very bad."

His hand stilled. "You're *going* to be?"

"Yes," she said. "With you. I'll do anything you want if you'll just spank me. Hard."

The first time she'd gathered the courage to ask him for what she wanted, it had turned into the most blissful night of her existence. Since then, Jonas had steadily initiated her into the world of bondage and submission. And she'd discovered her inner masochist.

She could feel it already, the burn that would morph into a steady tingle, but he didn't deliver.

"Anything?"

"Anything."

A loud crack rent the air. He spanked her so hard her body scooted forward. The leg he'd thrown over the backs of her knees pulled her back into place, and she better braced her hands against the arm of the sofa. "I'll keep that for later."

Before she could process his comment, he delivered another blow. Knowing he wouldn't stop until she climaxed, she didn't bother to count how many times he spanked her. As he warmed her up, he rested between each smack, taking time to caress her heated flesh. Soon he switched up the rhythm, and she could no longer distinguish one blow from the next. It blurred together as an inferno coiled low in her abdomen.

And he stopped.

She wailed a protest.

He lifted her and set her on her feet. "I never promised you an orgasm. You begged for a spanking, sweetheart, and that's what you got."

Was he going to make her beg for a fucking, too? He'd never done that before. She was about to protest when he stood and moved into her personal space, thrusting his chest forward to bully her into walking backward.

Puzzled, she took one step after another until she bumped into an old, scarred table he'd owned for longer than he'd been with her. With a devious grin, he gripped her hips and lifted her on top. "A spanking only increases your attitude. You still think you're in control."

She didn't, not really. Sure, they had a safe word, which she could use if she needed him to stop, but almost nothing could induce her to call "onion." He could do pretty much anything he wanted to her, and she would most likely love it.

Automatically, she lowered her gaze. Though they didn't use titles, and Jonas typically didn't make her ask for permission before coming, he was as demanding, sometimes more so, as the Doms in those erotic romances she'd begun reading during her first maternity leave. And he always made her beg for an orgasm, so she really didn't see a distinction. She still only climaxed when he let her.

The coolness of the lacquer faded due to the warmth radiating from her ass. Somewhere between the lounge chair and now, he'd completely disrobed her. It hadn't taken much to get rid of the scraps of material that passed for a swimsuit, which wasn't something she'd wear for a serious workout anyway.

He shoved at her shoulders, and she found herself flat on her back. The tone of their encounter was set. Moisture pooled between her legs because she knew he wasn't going to be gentle.

With efficient movements, he buckled cuffs around her wrists and ankles. In short order, he used snaps to bind her arms above her head. The table might be ugly, but it served a purpose. It had hooks strategically placed along the legs and underneath the top. Jonas had modified it over the past five years to fit her body and all the positions he preferred to use.

Normally he would immobilize her legs next, but he threw her for a loop when he snapped the cuffs together. Then he pulled a chair over, climbed on top, and pulled a chain from behind a panel in the ceiling. It looked like he had modified a few things other than his orgasm table.

When he finished, her legs were stuck straight up in the air. She could lift her ass if she used her abdominal muscles, but those weren't as strong as they once had been, so she couldn't hold the position.

He stood at the foot of the table with his hands on his hips. Her legs hid half his body from view. "That's a damn fine cunt you have there. It's red and swollen from your spanking and dripping with juices."

She felt the swipe of his finger over those inflamed tissues, and she shuddered from the lightning it sent careening up her torso.

"I think you want me, Mrs. Spencer. Is that true?"

"Yes." No hesitation on her part. He'd denied her an orgasm and she was ready to beg. This was his favorite part. "Armand, please don't be cruel."

She knew he wouldn't be too cruel. Each of his personas had a distinct personality that had developed over the course of their relationship. Master J was cruel in all the right ways. Matt, the virgin she'd deflowered, was obsessed with a call girl. And Armand fucked like a marathoner. There were more, but these were her favorites. She'd signaled the terms of the scene with only the use of that name.

God, she loved this man. He made her dreams come true, and then when she thought up new dreams, he made those come true, too.

He rechecked her bindings before disappearing across the room. She heard evidence of him shuffling items around in a drawer or cabinet, but he had left her field of vision, and her position didn't allow her to shift.

She wasn't known for patience, and Jonas loved to exploit this weakness. Tugging with her arms, she tested the give of her wrist bindings. Then she tried to move her torso. In this she was more successful. However, it yielded no relief. The motion only made her more aware of her acute need.

"Armand." She breathed his name, a plea and a sigh. "Please fuck me. Please don't leave me here all alone."

He appeared on her other side, chuckling at her pathetic begging. Holding his hand over her body with his palm up, he paused. "You're going to stay still while I fuck you. This will ensure your cooperation."

She could see the glint of light from something silver. He tilted his palm, and a delicate chain slithered to land on her stomach. She recognized nipple clamps on a long chain.

From his other hand, he produced a ball gag. Sabrina wasn't a fan of the way it felt in her mouth or of the drooling mess it necessitated. She shook her head. "No, Armand, please. I promise I'll be good. I'll be silent."

He cupped her jaw and forced her mouth open. Wearing a gag made her feel more helpless than being bound. She struggled against it, but she lost the fight. She always lost these fights. He popped the ball between her teeth, brought the strap around, and buckled it on the side of her head.

Sabrina sank back against the table, feeling every inch of her body cede control to Armand. She didn't have the ability to just submit, and Jonas always knew exactly what he needed to do to force the issue.

"One more thing, and then you'll realize exactly how little control you have over anything, Mrs. Spencer. And then I'm going to fuck this tight, hot little cunt all afternoon. When your husband returns later today, you'll still be walking funny."

She tried to say something, breathe a shade of protest, but the gag turned her words into a whimper.

He pinched one nipple hard and twisted it viciously. Her back arched off the table, trying to ease the sudden pressure. No longer worried about making too much noise, she screamed against the sharpness, even as it ebbed into a pleasing sting.

He toyed with that tender bud, an arrogant slant to his lips as he ignored her desperate noises. When he tired of that kind of play, he clipped the clover onto her sore nipple and gave the other the same treatment.

Then he secured the chains to hooks on the underside of the table on each side of her body. Now her wrist and ankles were bound, and he'd used her nipples as the third point of security. If she shifted to the left, it eased the tug on that side, but it intensified the pain on the right side. A similar thing happened when she tried to wiggle to the right.

He watched while she tested the limits of her movement and the consequences of trying for something other than what he allowed. When he was satisfied with everything, he unbuttoned his shorts and let them slide to the ground. His tapered hips offered no resistance.

She watched as his body was revealed. The chiseled perfection never ceased to amaze her. He'd installed a workout room in the basement, and he used it regularly now that he didn't have a separate job as a Sadist/Dom-for-hire to keep his muscles as hard as iron.

His erection sprang from a nest of curls. If the gag hadn't been in her mouth, she would have licked her lips, inviting him to let her taste him again. As it was, he fisted his cock and pumped his hand up and down the length in slow motions that drove her insane with unsated need.

The thick scent of her arousal filled the room, her body's way of sending out insistent signal flares. She whimpered and wiggled. The pain brought a sheen of wetness to her eyes, forcing her to call upon the shallow well of patience that frequently ran dry. He would fuck her when he wanted, and she couldn't say or do anything to entice him closer, harder, or faster.

The topaz of his eyes betrayed the level of his desire and gave her hope. After an eternity, he rounded to the end of the table. She felt the nudge of his cockhead against her entrance. With her legs tied together, it was going to be a tight fit. She wouldn't be able to lift her hips or spread her legs wider to ease the way for him. He shoved inside roughly and abruptly, her plentiful cream providing all the help necessary.

She moaned and gave herself over to the conflicting sensations running rampant inside and outside of her body. Soon the climax he'd denied her loomed close. She fought the urge to writhe and was only half-successful. Each tug of the clover clamp on a nipple drove her further from reason. Behind the gag, she screamed out an orgasm.

Jonas—Armand—ignored her climax. He didn't slow down or take into account how sensitive her tissues became after an orgasm. A shiver wracked her body. Accepting her helplessness, she sank into a deeper level of submission. He hadn't asked for it, but he'd taken it just the same. Goodness, how she loved this man.

Another climax rocked her body. Tears streamed from her eyes. He just might kill her with pleasure. She felt bathed in her own juices, full, and thoroughly used. When she came again, he came with her.

She floated in a vast sea of blissful semiconsciousness for the longest time before fire ripped her from heaven. He'd removed one of the clamps. The other followed rapidly. If the gag hadn't still been in her mouth, the neighbors definitely would have heard her scream.

The fire lingered, growing and receding, pulsing in time with her heart. Jonas made no move to soothe it away.

He leaned down and nipped her earlobe. "I have a surprise for you." Now he closed one hand on her breast and plumped that tender globe.

She arched into his hold. That, coupled with the insistent moan she forced out from behind her gag, begged for more of his touch. Moving around the table to stand at her head, he gave her what she wanted. He remained on the gentle side, as though he knew she couldn't handle more right then.

His caress moved up her body, over her arms and to her wrists. She felt the slight tug and heard the scrape of metal-on-metal as he released her arms. He brought them down one at a time, massaging the protest from her aching muscles.

Then he removed her gag and wiped away the moisture from her face before massaging a reverent kiss across her lips. Now that her hands were free, she cupped his face and kissed him back. His submissive wasn't gone, but she had definitely grown bolder now that he had partly freed her from the restraints.

When the kiss ended, he drew a finger over her swollen bottom lip. "Let me untie your legs, and then we can talk about your surprise."

She'd thought the surprise was part of the scene, but it seemed she was mistaken. He moved down her body and stood at the end of the table that would give him a prime view of her exposed pussy. She knew what was coming next. The man was a stallion, and she knew he wouldn't be able to resist one more bit of torture.

He drew a finger along her dripping tissues. Her entire body flinched in protest, even though she knew this was the best part. When she was bruised and tender like this, it was the only time she could masturbate successfully.

The soft pressure of his digit on her flesh increased. He pressed her clit flat. In the absence of bindings on her arms, she gripped the edges of the table. "Armand, you're a beast."

With that, he plunged at least two fingers deep inside. He worked her into a fine frenzy, and when he reached up and twisted her nipple, she came hard one last time. It was a shorter-lived climax, intense and pulsing, but not lingering.

Then he used a cold, damp cloth to clean her pussy before releasing her legs from the hook on the ceiling. As he helped her stand, she resigned herself to the fact that she'd be walking funny for the rest of the afternoon. Her legs were rubbery at best, and her ass, thighs, breasts, and pussy throbbed with remembered pleasure and pain.

He helped her back into her bikini and carried her to the sofa. She slumped against him, resting her head on his shoulder, and closed her eyes.

"I love you, Jonas."

He kissed her forehead. "I love you, too, honey."

Chapter Two

With Sabrina asleep in his arms, Jonas settled back into the curve of the sofa where the back met the arm and enjoyed the weight of her body against his. The past five years were easily the best in his life. He cherished every moment from her surprise proposal—they hadn't even known one another—to the births of their two children.

From the first, she'd possessed an unwavering belief in him that still floored him at times. She trusted him fully, and she was game for anything he had in mind. Of course, this afternoon's role-playing had been a surprise. He really wanted to get the pool clean before their friends and family descended on them en masse for the small cookout he'd planned to celebrate her thirty-fifth birthday. And then he had a dozen other preparations to make, as did his beautiful wife.

The moment she'd appeared in that bikini, the one she never got wet because she didn't see the point in swimming in anything but a one-piece, he'd known what she had in mind. That's why he'd ignored her until she'd spoken to him.

She liked to play power-exchange games, where he started out as someone who worked for her but ended up in complete control of her body and her pleasure, and so did he. "Armand" seemed far sexier than a thirty-nine-year-old English teacher and father of two. He never voiced that thought because then he knew Sabrina would stop playing. She found him irresistibly sexy no matter what name she called him by.

And he lacked any desire to resist the classic beauty and understated charm of his incredibly lovely, intelligent, and thoughtful wife. She truly completed him. He'd always thought people were lovestruck or stupid when they said something like that, even though he'd seen proof of it in his parents' marriage and that of his best friend, Ellen, and her husband. Now he was lucky enough to understand the truth of that sentiment.

She stirred, nestling her cheek against his shoulder and inhaling deeply. He ran his free hand up her leg and over her hip. True to form, she shifted even closer. If they had time, he would take advantage of her again before anyone arrived.

But they didn't have time. He couldn't complain about the way they'd spent the afternoon even though they'd both be scrambling to complete the party preparations.

He continued his exploration. She opened her eyes when he exerted a small pressure on her breast.

"Sore?" He grinned down at her, knowing full well her breasts had to be tender after what he'd put them through.

She returned his smile. "Thank you."

"My pleasure, Mrs. Spencer." He closed his mouth over hers and devoured her kiss as another reminder that she belonged to him. Then he released her and spent a moment enjoying the dreamy slant to her eyes. "Let's get a shower, and then I need to get the grill going. My parents will be here with the kids soon, and your sister was supposed to come early with the cake."

Sabrina groaned as she sat up, a reflection of her reluctance to end their interlude. When his parents had picked up the kids that morning so they could get some work done, she hadn't been enthused to watch them drive away. She'd buried her face in his chest and said, "I miss them already."

It had made him a little doubtful about the gift he'd arranged for their anniversary, but her changed attitude renewed his faith that she'd absolutely love the surprise.

* * * *

The sound of a car door slamming had Jonas closing the lid to the grill he hadn't yet begun to light and jogging around to the driveway in front of the house. Rose, his three-year-old pride and joy, squealed and ran to him, her arms wide for an expected hug. Not one to disappoint the women in his life, he scooped her up into his arms and peppered kisses on her little cheeks. She giggled and squirmed, and her riotous blonde curls, a feature he felt looked much better on her than it did on him, tickled his face.

"Daddy, look what I made!" She held up a long scrap of flower-print cloth.

His mind moved at a million miles an hour to try to figure out what it was before she became affronted by his ineptness.

Luckily, his mother saved the day. Alyssa Spencer kissed his cheek and wiped away the lipstick. "She sewed that apron all by herself."

Rose's grin grew. "Nana only helped a little."

Alyssa helped spread the fabric, and he could now see the hemmed edges and the tie that would go around back. "She couldn't reach the pedal of the sewing machine."

"It's beautiful," he assured Rose.

Her hazel eyes reflected the green of her party dress, and they glowed with pleasure. His princess enjoyed dressing up. "Now I won't get so dirty when we plant flowers for Mommy."

Rose wiggled, her patience with being held at an end. A glance over his shoulder showed that she'd spied Sabrina, so he set her down and let her run off to greet her mother.

His father, Brandon, approached holding Ethan. At eleven months old, his son was starting to take after Sabrina in his physical appearance. The downy baby hair had darkened to chestnut, and it was growing in straight. Ethan regarded his father with serious chocolate eyes and held out his arms, all the while exuding an implacable patience. He liked to tell Sabrina that Ethan got that, and his stubborn streak, from her. She would laugh and shake her head, not bothering to voice what they both knew to be true. They were a family of stubborn people, and he wouldn't have it any other way.

He took Ethan and slathered his face with kisses until his son opened his mouth and bit his nose, his way of returning the kiss. They would have to work on that.

"Thanks for taking them. Were they good?"

"Of course." Happiness lit his mom's face, and she tugged at Ethan's foot. "Did you guys get everything done you needed to get done?"

That was open to interpretation. One might argue that he and Sabrina didn't get enough time alone together, and their scene this afternoon had been necessary. But they really hadn't finished any of the food prep they'd intended to have done by now.

Jonas shrugged. "Still a few things left to do."

His dad chuckled and slapped him on the back. "Good for you. When you have young children, you need regular breaks. Your mother and I survived having you three kids so close together because we could send you to your grandparents' houses every other weekend."

They didn't have a shortage of people willing to watch the kids. Tearing Sabrina away from them was a sometimes-painful process, and she'd only weaned Ethan a month ago. And he didn't really want to be away from them either.

"Does Sabrina know about the trip yet?" His mother whispered the question so Sabrina, who was exclaiming over Rose as she modeled her gardening apron, wouldn't hear. He'd arranged for his parents and Sabrina's mom to each take the kids for a few days. One or the other could have handled it alone, but he felt obligated to be diplomatic. Though Sabrina's mother had thawed toward him significantly since she'd accepted the fact that Jonas hadn't married Sabrina for her money, they still had improvements to make. Omitting her would have halted forward progress.

He shook his head. "I was going to tell her earlier, but I got sidetracked." *By the sight of my wife in a bikini.* He had no regrets.

Brandon rubbed his hands together. "What can we do to help?"

Jonas gestured to the backyard. "I haven't lit the grill yet."

His parents headed toward the back, and Sabrina meandered in his direction, Rose's hand in hers. He met them halfway. Sabrina leaned in and kissed a greeting on Ethan's cheek. He greeted his mother with a dimpled smile and a line of babbling that sounded suspiciously like a breakdown of how he'd spent the day.

She listened intently, nodding twice before he came to a close. "I missed you, too."

Jonas handed Ethan over because he knew Sabrina wanted a hug, and then he scooped up Rose and deposited her on his shoulders. Slinging his arm around his wife, he steered his family to the backyard. "Happy birthday, honey."

She smiled up at him. "One of the best so far, that's for sure."

Hours later, their house full of friends and family, Sabrina finally sat down and opened her presents. She wasn't very good at receiving presents, and she preferred to open them after people left. Jonas had let her do it that way once. She'd spent the time meticulously opening the wrapping as she wrote out thank-you notes, sucking the fun out of the entire occasion.

Last year, his best friend, Ellen, and Sabrina's sister, Ginny, had gone in on a complete set of new canes and floggers. Sabrina had peeked inside that box, turned bright red, and quickly closed it. As the person whose job it was to use those canes and floggers, Jonas had appreciated the present immensely. Sabrina had learned to love it as well.

Now, faced with a gift from Ellen, she studied the glittery wrapping paper with a frown. "Ellen, this had better be something I can open in front of children."

In addition to Rose, Ellen's five- and three-year-olds and several other kids were on the loose. They weren't paying much attention to the adults gathered in a circle around Sabrina, but that didn't matter much. Kids had an unerring habit of showing up at precisely the wrong moment.

Ellen tapped a finger on her lips. A gust of wind caught her dark hair and whipped it into her face, revealing the sham of her thoughtful pose. With a mischievous grin, Ellen shrugged. "It's just clothing."

With a knowing nod, Sabrina set the box aside. "I'll open it later."

Laughter rang out. Jonas noticed that his parents and Melinda, Sabrina's mother, seemed to relax on the heels of that pronouncement. Of course Sabrina would want to be courteous to their parents' feelings. Flaunting their sexual proclivities like that smacked of bad taste.

"That's probably for the best." Ellen, he noticed, did her best to hide a smirk. He had no idea what she'd given Sabrina, but he could guess. The Dominatrix in her loved to make Sabrina blush.

Sophia reached forward and moved her gift to sit on top of Ellen's. "You probably want to wait on that one, too."

Another Dominatrix who loved to make Sabrina blush. Sophia, however, could do that with a simple look. When he and Sabrina had nearly divorced toward the end of their first year together, Sophia had assumed the job of dominating Sabrina while they engaged in impact play. It rankled a little, but he'd left her high and dry, and that rankled more.

Sabrina gestured to the pile. "Anyone else need to withdraw something?"

A titter of laughter went through the group, but nobody stepped forward. The rest of the night passed without incident.

Later, when everyone had gone and he'd tucked his exhausted daughter into her bed, he found Sabrina in Ethan's room. She sat in the rocking chair, her eyes closed as she rocked gently back and forth with Ethan in her arms. A mountain of love welled in him at the sight of his wife and son. He crept closer and studied his son's sleeping face.

Sabrina opened her eyes and gave him a sleepy smile. Jonas lifted Ethan from her arms and put him in his crib. Then he pulled Sabrina to her feet and led her to their bedroom.

He closed and locked the door. Then he shoved her against the wall, lifted her dress, and ripped away her panties. All bleariness dropped from her eyes. Her breath caught even as her chest heaved.

Testing her pussy with one finger, he found her drenched. Inside, he grinned at the way she responded to him. It never ceased to amaze him how wet she became when he treated her roughly. She was so petite and dainty, and she oozed culture and refinement. Yet her cunt wept for him.

He kept his weight against her as he opened his jeans and shoved them out of the way. Then he lifted her and impaled her on his cock. She canted her hips forward and wrapped her legs around his waist. The softness of her skin heated him even more. He fucked her fast and hard, taking his pleasure without worrying about hers. It wasn't necessary.

Her pussy walls quivered around him, and she bit her lip to quiet the squeaks and moans she couldn't keep from making. He doubled his efforts, pounding her ass against the wall and lifting her a little higher with each thrust. She whispered his name over and over, a reverent mantra that became just the movement of her lips as a climax overtook her. He came next, following her over that cliff in less than sixty seconds. And to think, she'd never achieved an orgasm before she'd met him.

He was still proud of that.

After he withdrew and set her back on her feet, he kissed her softly, knocking her off balance by delivering tenderness after such a violent claiming. When he released her, she regarded him with a different kind of bleariness in her eyes.

"I love when you do that."

He allowed a cocky smile. "You're welcome."

She took a wobbly step toward her walk-in closet. "What did Ellen and Sophia get me?"

Jonas shook his head. "No idea." Well, he did have some idea, just not a definite knowledge. "I know what I got you, though."

That stopped her. She frowned. "I don't remember opening anything from you."

She wasn't pissed. He wasn't in the habit of buying gifts for her. He preferred to do things for her. Their first year together, he'd wanted to give her something beautiful, so he'd planted a rosebush. Sabrina had named their daughter accordingly, saying that he'd once again given her something precious and lovely. He really couldn't argue with that.

He lifted the mattress and extracted a folder, which he handed to her.

That frown deepened, and she regarded the folder suspiciously, but she took it from him and opened it up. He knew the moment she realized what it was. Her frown vanished, morphing to horror.

"No. Absolutely not." She shoved the folder back at him.

Shocked at her reaction, he took the folder from her. It contained plane tickets and a reservation at a private BDSM resort. Because they'd originally married for convenience, they hadn't bothered with a honeymoon. And when they'd renewed their vows a year later, she'd been nauseous the entire trip, a side effect of pregnancy. It hadn't been the trip he'd envisioned.

This was supposed to be another chance at a honeymoon. Before the astonishment could turn to anger, he harnessed his better sense. Perching himself on the edge of the bed, he folded his arms across his chest. Normally he'd enjoy the way her gaze followed the movement, lingering where his muscles bulged, but right now he had other fish to fry. Besides, he needed a little recovery time.

"You're saying 'no' to which part?"

Now she crossed her arms, a defensive gesture. "The being-naked-in-front-of-other-people part."

Without waiting for his response, she disappeared into the bathroom. Jonas didn't follow immediately. They hadn't been to a club since before Rose had been born. Afterward they'd both been too busy, and then Ethan had come along pretty quickly. They were finished having kids. His timing should have been perfect. While she wasn't an exhibitionist—that was his kink—she'd never objected to visiting a club or performing in front of an audience. She always said the crowd was inconsequential, only he mattered. He didn't understand her objection.

* * * *

Sabrina noticed that her hand trembled as she brought the wet cloth to her face to remove makeup. Not once in the five years they'd been together had she refused him anything sexually. He usually dictated where, when, and how. Even this afternoon at the pool, had he looked at her and corrected the name she'd used, that would have immediately reset the terms of the scene. Or if he'd smiled and ignored her attempt, then she would have known he didn't feel like doing a scene right then.

Giving over complete control to him was an arrangement she liked. He was never cruel or callous, and he was adept at manipulating her body to make it feel the most wondrous sensations.

She'd known this issue would resurface eventually. Jonas was first and foremost an exhibitionist, and he hadn't pressed the issue for almost three-and-a-half years, before she'd begun showing with her first pregnancy.

He didn't see the differences in her body, or if he did, then he had enough of a sense of self-preservation to not comment negatively. Once, she hadn't minded putting herself on display. She'd been younger and toned. The stretch marks that had appeared as her abdomen had expanded with Ethan hadn't been there. And her boobs hadn't yet given in to the call of gravity. They'd inflated with milk, stretching to accommodate the need, and when the milk had gone, the skin hadn't retracted. She needed constant support.

Sabrina didn't normally make much of a fuss about any of those things. She knew Jonas loved her and found her attractive. But she wouldn't have worn that bikini if anyone but him had been around.

The bathroom door opened, as she knew it eventually would, when she was in the midst of brushing her teeth. It was a long shot to expect him to just accept her refusal. She wanted to go. She wanted to surrender to whatever he had so thoughtfully planned. But she wouldn't enjoy it the way she once would have.

Without saying anything, he reached for his toothbrush and joined her, the way he did every night, at the sink. She studied him in the mirror, looking for little signs he was pissed off. Did he stand farther away than normal? Did he avoid those constant little touches in which he normally indulged? What color were his eyes?

If he noticed that she was extra nervous, he didn't let on. They prepared for bed normally. She shed her clothes and changed into a nightgown that fell to mid-thigh. Jonas stripped out of his shirt, but he left his pants on. Since he usually slept in his boxer briefs, Sabrina's nerves grew even more brittle.

He went to a storage closet off the bathroom in their master suite and took out the massage table. Normally this would make her body tingle with anticipation. He often followed up a massage with a light caning that left her body thrumming with need. And then he'd take advantage of her. He unfolded the legs and slid the little brackets into place to secure them.

"Take off your nightgown and get on the table."

Like the one in the pool house, this table was modified. It featured hooks to which snaps could be secured, turning it into a portable bondage table.

"Jonas, we already played today. I'm tired." And terrified. She knew she'd hurt his feelings. At the very least, she owed him an apology. Making it up to him was more appropriate, though, and she wanted to think of a way to do that before she apologized.

He nailed her with his topaz gaze. "There are two ways to do this, Sabrina."

The easy way or the hard way. She backed up, giving him a clear signal that she wanted him to be cruel. She deserved it for the way she'd rejected his thoughtful and heartfelt gift. He had every right to extract retribution.

With catlike reflexes, he pounced on her, cutting the chase off before it could truly begin. He was half a foot taller than her and a hell of a lot stronger. There was no contest. He lifted her easily and deposited her facedown on the cushioned table.

A series of quick rips opened the Velcro cuffs, and he secured her wrists and ankles. Then he tore her nightgown from her body. The satin stitches resisted at first, but like her, they gave in eventually.

She waited for the sting or thud of whatever consequence he chose, but it never came. He made no attempt to turn away from the table to retrieve their implements from a locked chest at the foot of the bed.

Instead he caressed her shoulders. The pressure of his forays grew until his fingers dug into the exact places where knots had formed in her muscles. In short order, he banished them. By the time he made it to her calves, she had relaxed completely.

She was also crying. The consequence she more than deserved never materialized. She could only speculate as to the depth of the pain she'd inflicted for him to forego any kind of response. Tears soaked the padded circle on which her face rested.

He released the cuffs, lifted her from the table, and carried her to bed. She tried to stifle her sniffles as she watched him fold the table and put it away. He disappeared into the bathroom, only to return seconds later in his boxer briefs.

Climbing into bed, he pulled her into his arms and pressed a cool cloth against her eyes. When her sobs died down, he took the cloth and threw it in the direction of the bathroom. Clothes on the floor drove her nuts. Wet things were worse. It landed with a dull thud on the carpet, and she didn't even cringe when he didn't get up to put it away.

He turned off the lights and snuggled down under the sheet, keeping her body close as he settled them both in for the night. In minutes, the steady rise and fall of his chest against her cheek told her he'd fallen asleep.

The lack of a consequence and his tender treatment left her feeling lonely and confused. Her signal and permissions had been clear. She'd run from him. Why hadn't he followed through the way she'd expected?

* * * *

Sunday morning usually meant an early wakeup call from Ethan because Jonas typically took Rose downstairs with him to make breakfast. When she woke to silence and an empty bed, she lifted her head to focus on the digital numbers on the clock. It was almost ten-thirty. She couldn't remember the last time she'd slept so late.

Throwing on clothes, she rushed through her toilette and scurried to the kitchen. It was empty, and the breakfast dishes had been cleared away. She stared at the clean pans in the drying rack with more than a little bit of dismay. What kind of game was he playing? She didn't like it one bit.

The back door opened, and Jonas strolled in with Rose on his shoulders and Ethan in his arms. Rose wore her gardening apron. Jonas and Ethan had dirt stains on their jeans.

Jonas smiled when he saw her, his expression radiating warmth and affection. "Good morning, honey. We let you sleep in. I put away a plate for you. Give me a second, and I'll heat it up."

He handed Ethan to her, bending to give her a kiss as he did so. Rose reached down for some love, but Jonas caught her before she tumbled from his shoulders. Her faith in her father to keep her safe ran deep. She giggled and squirmed until he set her down.

Sabrina cast a worried look at Jonas as he turned away, but Rose demanded her attention. She sat down at the kitchen table and pulled her daughter onto her lap so she could snuggle both of her babies.

As she ate, Rose and Jonas regaled her with the details of their morning. They'd made breakfast together, fed Ethan, and weeded an entire flowerbed. Jonas's flowerbeds were works of art, and it looked like Rose was becoming every bit as particular as her father about how they looked.

By the time naptime rolled around, Sabrina's nerves were once again stretched to the breaking point. She cornered Jonas outside where he was fiddling with one of the sprinkler heads.

"What the hell are you doing?"

He glanced up, lifting a brow at her unusually colorful language. She almost never swore when they weren't in a scene.

"Fixing the sprinkler head. It's watering the side of the pool house instead of the grass."

She stomped her foot, hating the gesture even though it made her feel a little better. "I mean last night. And this morning. If you're mad at me, I wish you'd just yell or spank me or something."

He rose to his feet, his lanky legs unfolding as he stood up, and wiped his hands on his jeans. "I'm not mad at you, Sabrina. You said you didn't want to go. I'm respecting your wishes. Last night you were strung so tight I thought you were going to snap. I knew you weren't going to fall asleep without help. And then when Ethan called for you and you didn't get up, I figured you were exhausted, so I got him out of his crib and we let you sleep."

No tension stiffened the lines and planes of his body. His olive gaze showed patience and a little bafflement. He truly wasn't upset with her.

She shook her head in disbelief. The resort was something he'd talked about on and off for years. "You didn't really want to go?"

He shrugged. "Doesn't matter. You don't want to go, and I would never make you do anything you don't want to do. I love you, honey. If we go, we go because we both want to be there."

Oh, but she wanted to be there. She just wanted to not have stretch marks or sagging breasts first.

"Sabrina, what's holding you back?"

Startled, she stared up at him. He'd always been able to read her. Sometimes that skill brought endless thrills. Other times it revealed secrets she'd rather keep to herself. Shaking her head, she said, "It's nothing."

"It's not nothing. You're about ready to cry right now, and that's not like you."

It used to be like her to hold in her emotions, swallow whatever bothered her and pretend like it didn't exist. She folded her arms over her chest. "I don't think people should see me naked. It's not a pleasing sight anymore."

His dark blond brows shot nearly to his hairline. "You're serious?"

Though she was easily one of the most attractive women on the planet, Jonas knew better than to argue with her. She required proof, not words. So he narrowed his eyes, took a step closer, and went with a different strategy.

"Why does it matter what anybody but me thinks?" He didn't add that he was her husband and her Dom, and his opinion was the only one that counted where she was concerned. There was no need.

Her eyes widened. Shades of brown swirled as she realized her mistake. She dropped her arms down by her sides and cast her gaze to her feet. "It doesn't."

Threading his fingers, grease and all, through the hair at the nape of her neck, he yanked hard to bring her gaze back to his. Tears prickled at the corners of her eyes, but they were the right kind. Her shoulders relaxed, and she gave herself over to his control.

"Clearly, it does. You're refusing to go on a proper honeymoon with me because you think other people might not find you attractive. If you think I'm going to share you, you're sadly mistaken. I will kill any man who touches you, Sabrina. Make no mistake, my opinion is the only one that matters, and I find you very attractive."

"No, I didn't mean that." She scrambled to reassure him, and he had to suppress a smirk at how well she responded to his reassuring taunts. "I meant—I—I—Damn it, Jonas. I have stretch marks all over the place."

He leaned down, not stopping until his face was inches away. "Each one of them proclaims to one and all that you belong to me. You're my wife. My submissive. The mother of my children. You will wear them proudly as the badges they are."

Perhaps that was pushing things a little far, but truthfully, he didn't think they stood out. Maybe they would if he held a black light next to her skin, but he had no intention of doing so. From his frequent and close inspections, he knew she had a few on her inner thighs, her ass, and across her stomach, and maybe one or two on her breasts and hips. They were parts of her, and he loved *all* of her. And he knew better than to tell her about the ones on her ass. She hadn't yet discovered them.

She trembled so hard he felt the shockwaves radiating across the small space between them. He knew she wanted him to treat her roughly, to make her forget about everything that was bothering her, but he refused to do that until everything was right between them.

"I'm just not as confident about this as you are." She touched his shoulders and traced the line of his muscles over the triceps and biceps. "You're still very toned and handsome. You can't possibly know how I feel."

The thing about being married to a smart woman was that she changed tactics mid-discussion. He resisted the urge to turn her over his knee. She'd like that too much. He knew she wanted to go. The brief gleam of excitement in her eyes told a different story from her mouth. If this was the only thing holding her back, then nothing was holding them back. He wasn't going to allow this to derail his plans.

Instead of responding to her statement—there was no way to win using that avenue—he nodded, indicating that he'd reached an inarguable decision. "I've arranged for your mother and my parents to watch the kids. We leave in one week."

"Jonas—"

He set his finger over her lips. "This discussion is over."

It was a risky move because Sabrina was only sexually submissive. Otherwise she was strong willed and highly opinionated. She was a brilliant strategist, practical and creative, and she ran a huge division of a marketing company. She commanded respect and obedience from nearly everyone around her. That was the woman he loved, and he wouldn't change her for the world. If she didn't want to go on that honeymoon, they wouldn't be going anywhere.

Her trembling ceased. She nodded, accepting his pronouncement.

His heart leaped with joy, but he allowed only the half-curve of a smile to grace his lips.

Chapter Three

The tiny plane barely bounced as it touched down on the runway. Sabrina gripped Jonas's hand out of pure excitement. Though she wasn't completely sold on being naked in front of strangers, the other delights promised by this exclusive resort located on a private island were high on her list of loves.

They exited the plane and were herded across the tarmac toward a small building. Sabrina barely had time to appreciate the tropical foliage before they were once again inside. Bright sunlight poured through high windows, but the walls went up too high for her to be able to see anything but sky.

"Welcome to Elysium."

In front of the six passengers from the plane stood a very tall woman. Sabrina looked from their greeter to Jonas and back again, visually measuring the height difference. The woman had to be three or four inches taller, which put her over six feet tall. She wore a colorful island dress with a flowing, uneven hem that fell just past her knees. Her tight black curls were cut short and tied back with a length of fabric that matched the print on her dress. Her wide lips were slick with ruby red gloss, and hoop earrings dangled from her lobes.

She radiated confidence, and Sabrina detected an edge of danger. The woman was clearly in charge.

"You may call me Mistress Hera. None of you have been here before, so there's a brief orientation before you'll be allowed ground privileges." She grinned widely. "Elysium was founded in 1947 by a group of people who found their lifestyles not accepted by polite society. They pooled their resources and created this heavenly escape.

Everyone here is involved in the BDSM lifestyle somehow. We don't require anyone to participate in anything, and we don't expect anyone to assume roles they haven't chosen."

Sabrina listened as Mistress Hera explained that they would find people at Elysium who participated in only the D/s aspects and others who were purely sadists or masochists with no interesting in being Dominant or submissive.

"There are two important groups to watch out for," Mistress Hera continued. "Employees of Elysium are not part of the package. They don't wear uniforms, so look for their badges. They're required to wear them at all times. They not only monitor public activities, but they're the people making your food and cleaning up your messes. Please be courteous and polite, but don't make the mistake of treating them as Dominants or submissives. While some of them identify that way, many of them do not."

A quick glance around the small welcome room showed several employees standing patiently near one door. They each wore badges on lanyards around their necks. Despite what Mistress Hera said about not having uniforms, each of the people waiting nearby wore colorful print shirts and khaki shorts. It was sort of a uniform.

Mistress Hera bestowed a smile on the group that seemed to simultaneously single each of them out. "The second group of people to look out for are the unattached slaves. These are guests who have chosen to come here in order to serve whomever they want in a multitude of capacities. They're easily distinguishable because they're either completely or mostly naked. They'll avert their gaze or drop to their knees if a perceived Dominant is nearby, especially one they wish to serve. If somebody drops to their knees in front of you and you don't want to play with them, just ignore them."

That seemed awfully rude to Sabrina, but she wasn't here to judge the customs. Jonas squeezed her hand and kissed the corner of her mouth, soothing away her unease.

"If you want to play with a slave, you may approach them. Observe standard protocol as explained in the releases you all signed, and be clear in stating what you want. Slaves will respond with permission or refusal. Refusals cannot be questioned. Supervised negotiation is required before you can play. All employees are trained to supervise negotiations, so you don't have to go anywhere special or do anything too complicated. Also if you witness misbehavior by a slave who is here alone, report it to an employee. Do not take it upon yourself to discipline them."

It seemed that slaves were well protected whether or not they came with a partner. That made Sabrina feel better. While she didn't identify as a slave, it made her feel better to know she could move around the island and not worry about random Doms or Dommes.

"If you have questions about protocol, ask an employee. They're very helpful." Mistress Hera swept her arm toward the three employees waiting patiently for her to finish her introduction. "I'd like to introduce Zorah, Draco, and Mayabeth. They'll see you settled and give you a tour if you'd like."

The three employees each waved as Mistress Hera spoke their names. Now Mayabeth came forward and extended her hand to Jonas. She was short like Sabrina, but her build was very slight. A strong wind could carry her away. She had dark eyes and long, dark hair that fell almost to her waist.

"Master Jonas, I'm Mayabeth. If you'll follow me, I'll take you and your submissive to your suite. Your bags have already been transported. They'll be waiting for you there." Her smile was genuine, and her gaze never left Jonas's.

Sabrina narrowed her eyes at the slight. The cute, petite woman wasn't flirting, but she completely ignored Sabrina.

Jonas let go of Sabrina's hand to shake Mayabeth's. Then he put his arm around Sabrina's waist. "This is my wife, Sabrina. We're not formal, and we only assume roles when in a scene."

Sabrina realized that Mayabeth's actions represented a misinterpretation of their roles, not an actual slight.

Mayabeth turned her smile to Sabrina. "Hello, Sabrina. Welcome to Elysium."

Good breeding dictated an appropriate response. "Thank you. It looked beautiful from the plane. I'm looking forward to seeing the island."

"It's incredible," Mayabeth agreed. "Would you like to freshen up before the tour?"

She'd rested just fine on the plane. Jonas had as well. He rubbed his hand along her spine. "How about a tour that ends at our suite?"

"Very good." Mayabeth nodded. "We can begin at Persephone's Garden. From there, we'll proceed to Hades's Palace, The Fields of Punishment, The River Styx, and then we'll end up on the Isles of the Blest where your suite is located."

By the time they made it to their suite, Sabrina collapsed on the sofa, exhausted.

"This place is huge."

Jonas chuckled. "They're missing a place of judgment, Charon's ferry, Asphodel, and Tartarus for the truly wicked."

She'd forgotten he taught an ancient studies class. "Charon's ferry would make for a nice day trip down The River Styx. What about the Furies and the other characters who live in the Underworld?"

"That would be one interesting masquerade party. I wonder if they do something like that for solstices or on Halloween?" He flopped down next to her on the wide sofa and put a firm hand on her thigh. "I guess this is what happens when the Caribbean meets the Underworld."

She leaned her head against his shoulder. Her eyes were heavy, and she struggled to keep them open. Perhaps she wasn't as well rested as she thought. "A tropical version of Hell?"

"The place where the distinction between Heaven and Hell blurs."

He'd obviously thought it through. He might have said more, but she had fallen asleep.

A short time later, she woke to find herself in the bedroom. Jonas had drawn gossamer curtains across the wall of windows that overlooked a gorgeous waterfall and the crystalline pool below. The soothing sounds of water penetrated the thick glass, as did copious amounts of sunlight. The curtains cut the glare, nothing more.

No matter. She didn't want to sleep the day away. They had five days and four nights to enjoy this vast island paradise. Mayabeth had pointed out paths and named the parts and popular features of Elysium on the way to the room. Sabrina looked forward to taking a closer look.

She freshened up and went out to the main room to find Jonas on the balcony taking in the view. He rested his forearms on the wrought iron railing and leaned forward to look down. Sabrina joined him. He slung his arm around her waist and pulled her against the hard planes of his body.

She planted a kiss on his cheek before peering over the edge to see what he was watching. They were on the third floor, which meant they had a great view, but they weren't far from the action.

The object captivating his attention was located on the side of the pool's patio nearest the building. A woman was tied, naked and spread-eagled, to a lounge chair. A man sat between her legs. As he carried on a conversation with another man, he alternated between lazily fingering his submissive and pinching her nipples. The woman's quiet moans barely made it far enough for Sabrina to hear them.

In silence, she watched. Occasionally, the man sucked her juices from his fingers, openly savoring the flavor. Time passed. Not once did he speed up his ministrations or show an interest in bringing her to climax.

The lack of completion wore on Sabrina's nerves, making her hyperaware of Jonas's every move. If he inhaled faster, she jumped. When he shifted his position, she stiffened in anticipation.

But he made no move to touch her intimately. She was wearing a short, strapless sundress with nothing under it, and he never once tried to explore her outfit. At home, no matter what the occasion entailed, he always managed to snake a hand up her skirt or down her blouse before too long. He was a very tactile person.

She'd also elected to wear her hair up. While she liked to have it off her neck, Jonas preferred when she left it loose, and he frequently pulled the pins and clips from her hair without asking.

Below them, the scene shifted somewhat. The man standing next to the sitting couple casually conversing with the Dom gestured toward the woman. The sitting Dom nodded, withdrew his finger from her cunt, and stood.

The second man knelt at the foot of the lounger, stretched his torso over the footrest, and wiggled around until he found a comfortable position. Then he buried his face in the submissive's pussy. She sucked in a breath, and the volume of her moans increased. The first Dom pulled another lounge chair closer, sat on it, and played with her breasts. He alternated pinching and sucking. She arched her back off the chair, writhing as much as the ropes would allow.

Sabrina felt her eyes widen at the sight. Sure, she'd seen threesomes before, but the second Dom hadn't seemed like part of the scene until now.

Jonas pulled her back a little. "Easy, honey. You're about to go over. I have plans that don't include splitting your head open. Other parts of you, maybe, but not your head." He grinned at his own joke.

"Do you think they know each other?"

Jonas shrugged. "Hard to say. Elysium is a safe place to play. Everyone has to be tested for a battery of diseases, and there's a background check as well. Some people come here to play with strangers."

While that didn't appeal to Sabrina, she didn't begrudge anyone their kink. Sophia and her husband Drew would probably love it here. They could play with a different submissive every night.

She turned her back to the railing and cupped Jonas's erection in her hand. "So what are you planning to do with me today?"

His gaze remained on the scene playing out next to the pool. "Dinner at Hades's Banquet Hall. I hear the show is stimulating."

She lifted her eyebrow in a flirty, suggestive gesture that was completely lost on him, so she slid her hand down his shorts and pumped his shaft slowly. "How stimulating?"

His smile grew secretive. "You'll see. Now turn around. I'm going to fuck you while we watch them finish."

Heat pooled between her thighs, and the amount of cream already there doubled as she obeyed. Being watched was his kink, though she certainly didn't mind. She liked knowing she didn't have a choice in the matter. If she didn't willingly turn around, he'd force the issue. She trembled under the force of his power, and he hadn't done more than give her a command.

She gripped the rail. He lifted the skirt of her dress and smoothed his hand over her ass. "Bare-assed. Good. You're not allowed to wear underclothes here unless I specifically tell you to."

A response wasn't expected and too much excitement gripped her anyway. She kept her gaze focused on the trio below. He nudged her legs farther apart, lined his cock up with her entrance, and plunged deep.

She expected him to fuck her quickly, but after the initial thrust, he didn't move. Reaching around in front, he lowered the top of her sundress to expose her breasts. They had attracted a little attention, glances here and there as the spectators witnessing the woman's pleasure noticed how it inspired others, but nothing constant. That, combined with the distance, reassured Sabrina. Nobody could really see the details.

Jonas cupped her breasts, kneading and massaging the globes, pinching and rolling the tips. His cock remained motionless inside her, a throbbing, cruel length she wanted to feel sliding in and out. She whimpered a protest and pressed back to urge him into action.

"What's wrong, honey? Tell me what you want." His tone was laced with false sympathy, mocking her with his power to make her say whatever he wanted.

It only made her need more acute. "I want you to fuck me." Her whispered admission was caught by the wind and carried away. Even she barely heard it.

"Nice and loud, Sabrina. You can do it."

There was no way out of this. She took a deep breath, concentrated on the way he filled her core, and summoned her best presentation volume. "Please. I need you to fuck me."

More people looked in their direction, eager expressions betraying their anticipation. Below them, she watched as a man pushed down his wet swim shorts and another man knelt in front of him. More voices joined the cacophony of needy moans echoing from the stone and concrete courtyard paradise.

Jonas heeded her wish. He set a moderate pace, but she was already too far gone. She needed more, and she didn't hesitate to tell him that in the same carrying tone she'd used before.

"Harder. Please, do it harder."

He obliged. "Don't bite your lip or hold anything in. I want to hear you come."

Sabrina hadn't realized she was biting her lip, but he had, even though he couldn't see her face. She let the poor, tortured piece of flesh go, along with the rest of the inhibitions Jonas didn't allow. In seconds, she climaxed. Her long, high-pitched moan carried across the space and blended with the sounds of completion coming from the woman bound to the lounger and the man being sucked off.

Jonas withdrew and drew her back into his arms. He banded one across her waist and closed his other hand around one exposed breast. "I want you to wear Ryan and Ellen's gift to dinner."

Almost an entire day passed between the time she set it aside and the time she'd found a quiet moment, but she'd finished opening her birthday presents. When she'd called to offer dubious thanks for the gift, Ellen had chuckled and informed her that Ryan had picked it out. The white chastity belt was made from PVC and neoprene, and it had places to attach various vibrating and dildo-shaped objects, which he'd also thoughtfully supplied. Sophia's gift had been a set of matching wrist and ankle cuffs, and a collar with nipple clamps attached. It wouldn't surprise her to find out that Sophia and Ryan had conspired together. Or that they'd all known about Jonas's gift.

Sabrina nodded, not that she had a real choice. Though his command had been couched as a request, it wasn't one. Jonas rarely picked out her clothing or accessories. When he did, he expected his instructions to be obeyed. Never once in their five years together had she disobeyed anything he'd asked. Even if she had, nothing would come of it. Unlike some of the other Doms and Dommes they knew, Jonas didn't believe in delivering punishments. It just wasn't his style. She recognized and respected his authority. It was all the motivation she required.

"Will you put it on me?"

"Of course."

Of all the attachments supplied with the belt, he chose a curved metallic piece that fit snugly into the palm of his hand. It wasn't very narrow in the middle, and it flared out at both ends. Having played with the devices as she put batteries inside, she knew it was a very powerful vibrator.

Jonas slipped the remote into one of the many pockets on his cargo shorts. Then he took her arm and escorted her downstairs. She still wore the white, sleeveless sundress, though she had wanted to change. The stiff material that fit tightly over her breasts was supposed to provide support. Due to their interlude on the balcony, it had lost its shape. Now the bust line was a little wrinkled and kept inching downward. Unless she kept a close eye on the dress, her breasts were likely to make an unscheduled appearance.

They went to Hades's Palace for dinner. During the short walk, she let go of his hand to hike up the fabric three times.

"Leave it be." Jonas said after the third time.

"I should have changed."

"No, you shouldn't have. I like you in that dress. White is particularly becoming on you. If it falls in front and your luscious breasts fall out, I'll either put them back in or leave them out. It depends on what I want."

A small shiver ran through her body, and some of her cream wet the dormant vibrator resting against her intimate tissues. Nothing turned her on more than when he stripped away her choices. While being naked in front of other people didn't affect her the way it affected him, she had to admit she did like to see appreciative and longing looks cast in her direction.

However, when they were in a scene in public, she focused exclusively on him. When Jonas looked at her with that tawny color to his eyes, nobody else existed.

And so she pressed her free arm firmly to her side, hoping it would be enough to hold up her top.

Hades's Palace wasn't quite what Sabrina had expected. Surrounded by Persephone's Garden on all sides, it rose from the center of the sculpted garden, a huge, obsidian structure glittering in the waning sunlight. The place looked dark and foreboding, imposing yet inviting. The very architecture embodied sin and decadence.

The inside was filled with shops and restaurants, each oriented toward a particular kink. In the center, the ceiling rose five stories to the top of the palace where it terminated in brilliantly colored mosaics that cast countless hues everywhere. The beauty of it stole Sabrina's breath.

"Jonas, it's incredible. The pictures in the brochure didn't do it justice."

He finished his slow perusal of the place. "Nope. They didn't. We're at Demeter's tonight. I'm looking forward to seeing what the Goddess has for us."

A man in a brightly colored shirt and khaki shorts came toward them, his arms spread in a welcoming gesture. "I'm Chad. Welcome to Hades's Palace. Do you need some help?"

Jonas shook Chad's hand. "We have reservations at Demeter's, but I'm wondering what else goes on here."

Chad gestured to the atrium positioned above them. "This is the shopping district. You'll find stores that specialize in nearly every kind of kink, as well as regular shopping. We have a pharmacy right next to the doctor's office." Then he turned to indicate an archway to the left. "Through there are the private apartments of some of the senior staff. The dining rooms are to your right, and the south side of the palace, as well as the nearby parts of Persephone's Garden, are dedicated to sex. You'll find private and public rooms dedicated to pretty much anything you can think up. If you like, you can arrange a private room set up however you want."

The sheer size and decadence of the palace impressed Sabrina. Hades's Palace was on par with luxury resorts the world over. It had everything she could imagine, and it was only one part of the tropical island.

Jonas grinned when Chad mentioned sex. It was a wily look, laden with unspoken intentions that made Sabrina's stomach twist into anticipatory knots. The device trapped between her legs under the chastity belt hummed to life. The jolt combined with her reaction to his smile, and only Jonas's arm around her waist kept her knees from buckling.

Chad provided clear directions, and they found Demeter's without incident. The room was decked out in an ancient Grecian decor, complete with marble columns and long, low tables that featured animal legs to hold them up. She and Jonas shared a surprisingly comfortable stone bench perched on four lion's legs. The fine workmanship showed the fur and claws in startling, if stony, detail.

Sabrina rocked back and forth on her seat, trying to move the vibrator a little to the left in the hopes it would hit a spot a little better. In all the years they'd been together, she'd never successfully masturbated unless she was still sore from a scene or a rough interlude.

Jonas leaned close. "Uncomfortable?"

"A little. An orgasm would help relieve some of the tension." She managed a cheeky, suggestive smile, though she felt more desperate than anything else.

He got that look on his face that sent her pulse rocking. She recognized that her husband and the father of her children was gone, replaced by this handsome Dom who inspired both longing and a little anxiety. This wasn't a role he played. It was too substantial and real to be an assumed identity. This was a part of him that he'd kept hidden for most of the first year of their marriage. He hadn't been afraid she'd reject it. On the contrary, he'd been afraid she would like that part of him better than the rest.

While she loved this part of him, her affection for her Dom was equal to her love for all the other facets of his personality. She loved him too much to stick him into a simplified category.

He expertly removed the clip holding her hair in a neat twist at the nape of her neck and deposited it into his pocket. Then he ran his fingers through the strands until it streamed down her back and over her shoulders. She'd once cut it short, and he'd forbidden her from ever doing that again.

"If you're very good, I might remove that belt later. For now it stays put. You'll have an orgasm if and when I decide. Do you understand?"

She nodded, answering his unspoken question as well as the one he actually asked. No orgasm would be forthcoming any time soon, and there was nothing she could do or say to change that fact. He was in charge, and her body was his to use as he pleased. It only made her wetter. The vibrator slipped the smallest bit to one side, but it didn't ease her ache.

The tables were arranged around the periphery of the room. In the center, two steps took diners down to a place where pillows were arranged in small piles. Doms and Dommes sat on several of them. Slaves knelt on the floor nearby. Some of them fed their Masters or Mistresses and were fed in return. Others simply sat in their submissive positions, waiting for instructions. One female slave was being paddled by her Master as another slave looked on.

Sabrina gazed longingly at the paddle. Jonas almost never used one. He preferred to spank with his hand, or he'd work her over with his flogger. Sometimes he got out the massage table and lightly caned her. It wasn't the paddle she craved, but desperation for any kind of relief sounded good right about now.

A waiter dressed in the bright shirt and khaki shorts favored by the resort employees brought a bread bowl filled with lentil soup. He set two bowls directly on the table, deposited a napkin and spoon, and left. A waitress appeared on her other side. She set down terra-cotta glasses filled with water. No alcoholic beverages were allowed on the island, as kinky play required a clear head and clear consent.

Sabrina thanked both servers, and they melted away to serve the next couple. Jonas turned off the vibrator.

"In ancient Greece, they didn't have forks, but they did have spoons. The used bread to pick up finger foods and to wipe their hands afterward. Those pieces were tossed to the floor where the dogs got to finish them off." Jonas offered this information, she knew, because she had an issue with the fact the food was set directly on the table.

"Good. I'm not eating the bread on the bottom." The bowl wasn't huge. It was meant to be the first course.

The second course consisted of a salad. Feta, Kalamata olives, cucumber, chickpeas, sun-dried tomatoes, and baby spinach were finely chopped and covered with some kind of dressing. It tasted great with the flatbread on which it was served. She was getting over the plate thing.

By the time the main course came around, she was stuffed. The delicately seasoned calamari tempted her for two bites. The moment she gave up on eating, the vibrating began again. She groaned and leaned her forehead on his shoulder.

"You're enjoying this, aren't you?"

He snagged a piece of her calamari and popped it into his mouth. "Immensely. I love when the food is this good and I didn't have to cook it."

As a rule, he didn't let her near the kitchen except to clean up. Even then, they had a housekeeper to help out with those chores. Sabrina had become the senior vice president in charge of marketing for Rife and Company. It left her little time to attend to shopping and cleaning. When she wasn't at work, she devoted all of her time to her family.

"That's not what I meant and you know it."

He wasn't the kind of Dom who had a problem with attitude or a strong personality, so she didn't worry about retribution. Generally, he did whatever he wanted whether or not she behaved. The only thing he insisted upon was something that invariably made her blush. She did not like to use graphic language. He found this amusing, and it was the one thing he consistently held over her.

His shoulder shook slightly as he chuckled. "It'll get better."

Workers folded back doors on three sides of the cavernous room, and a warm breeze drifted through, carrying with it the perfume of tropical flowers. The sun sank low on the horizon. A million colors streaked above the beautiful gardens outside. It stole her breath, momentarily making her forget the need growing more acute by the second.

"I'm so glad you brought me here."

He didn't answer. When she managed to tear her gaze from the spectacular display of nature's resplendence, she found him watching her, an expression of infinite tenderness on his face.

He leaned down, and she shifted to greet his lips. What started as an expression of affection and love quickly heated. She opened her mouth, urging him to stake a deeper claim. He obliged, pulling her onto his lap to hold her closer. She melted into his embrace and rubbed her thigh against his erection. If he was as horny as she, then she had a chance of seducing him into taking off the belt and satisfying their desires.

She ran her hands up his chest and gripped his shoulders hard. Her fingers dug into his muscles, but she didn't bother to temper her reaction. This was no place to hold back.

It didn't take long for him to pry her hands away. He broke the kiss and held up his hand, motioning to one of the servers.

"Restraints, please."

"What kind, Sir? I have metal handcuffs and neoprene wrist cuffs with snaps." He spoke as if he were naming the dessert options.

Sabrina silently prayed for the wrist cuffs. Handcuffs dug in too much when she struggled against them. The neoprene might leave a red mark or two, but they didn't bruise or restrict her circulation.

In seconds, the server produced the softer cuffs. Jonas fastened them with the Velcro straps and snapped them together behind her back. The juices between her legs started coming faster.

He pushed the front of her dress lower, tucking it under her breasts. He closed a hand over one globe and fondled it lazily. Then he glanced up at the server. "This will do. Thank you. Is that baklava for dessert?"

The young man nodded. "We have six kinds. Would you like a variety platter?"

"Sounds great."

Though the exchange hadn't lasted for too long, Jonas had alternated kneading her breast and grazing his palm over her hardened nipple while they talked. Sabrina quivered in his lap. She was so wet she wondered if the vibrator might slip out.

Jonas might have had the same thought. He slipped a finger under the edge of the belt nearest her mons and pushed it back into place. Then he cranked it up a notch higher.

The server brought the baklava on an earthenware platter, thank the Gods, so she didn't have to worry about that lack. Not that she planned to eat. Food was the last thing on her mind. She rested her head against Jonas's shoulder and closed her eyes. It focused the sensation, but it was useless to ignore it right now anyway.

Jonas munched the baklava and struck up a conversation with the couple across the table. Sabrina had barely noticed them before. She'd taken note of the other people at the table, but she hadn't paid them too much mind. Part of what she liked about being the submissive in the relationship was the absence of the expectation that she would be outgoing. Jonas was the extroverted half of their pair. She liked that about him.

Just now it was driving her nuts. She wanted him to shut up and fuck her. If she told him that, especially if she insisted, he would not take it well. It was one thing for her to sass him when the conversation was between the two of them. It was quite another for her to do it in front of others, doubly taboo after he'd established their roles for the night.

So she suffered through an excruciating half hour while he caressed her skin, played with her breasts, and alternated changes in vibrator speed with brief respites. In time, the sunlight dimmed and servers fired just enough sconces to keep people from tripping over one another.

Jonas feathered his fingers through her hair one more time and turned her face to capture her lips. Sabrina moaned and accepted him into her mouth, but she didn't move. Her limbs were heavy with need, and her wrists were still bound behind her back. She felt drugged and damp, his puppet to control however he wished.

"Let's walk through the gardens on the way back. You've been very well behaved, honey. When we get to the suite, I'm going to tie you to the bed and make slow love to you."

"Yes, please." Her voice scratched in her throat and sounded husky with desire. She was a little surprised he didn't plan to take her right there, as more than a few couples were doing at that moment, but she wasn't about to argue with a scenario that left her mostly clothed in public and still guaranteed satisfaction.

He unclipped the snaps holding her cuffs together and helped her stand up. Then he lifted the hem of her knee-length dress and removed the chastity belt. His hands were cool on her skin. His fingertips brushed lightly against her, but he didn't seek more substantial contact. The warm air felt cool next to the heat trapped between her legs. She inhaled at the sudden temperature difference even as she luxuriated in that small relief.

She wanted to fix the top of her dress, but she knew better than to try. He wanted her breasts exposed. It was his way of flaunting his possessions, only she felt his sentiment was now a little misplaced. Her girls weren't quite as perky as they'd once been.

Her accessories disappeared into one of his many pockets. A fleeting wish that he would leave the curved vibrator out came and went. It would fit in the palm of his hand, but she wasn't in the mood for his hand. She'd had enough foreplay. She wanted to feel his cock filling her and his hips pounding against her thighs until she passed out.

He held her hand and led her on a slow stroll. Sabrina vaguely noted the statues and sculptures as they passed by. Most of them had ground lights strategically placed to illuminate the artistic detail. Muffled moans and cries drifted through the air, taunting her and making her anticipate the fulfillment of Jonas's promise that much sooner.

As they neared the place where the path split in three directions, Jonas came to an abrupt halt. Sabrina didn't think he was lost. The sign pointing to their building utilized reflective paint and a small floodlight. She turned to face him, her eyebrows drawn in confusion.

He shoved at her hip, forcing her to take quick steps backward to keep up with him. Her heart beat faster, and she recognized the dangerous glint in his tawny eyes. Cream trickled down her inner thigh. She couldn't say why, exactly, but when he got physical with her like this, she lost all control. He set off a primitive response she had long ago given up trying to master.

She followed his cues, blindly trusting him as she walked backward, until she came up against something solid, a hard line across her lower back. A brief glance over her shoulder showed it was one of the many statues. This one featured a servant holding an empty tray. From the way Jonas had positioned her, it looked like she was now on the menu.

He deposited her on the stone tray, pushed her legs apart, and pulled her body tight against his as he ravaged her mouth with a hungry kiss. He fisted a hand in her hair and squeezed hard, bringing a light sheen of tears to her eyes. It hadn't really hurt, but she didn't have control over anything, much less automatic, biological responses.

Then he broke away from her lips, trailing his mouth down the column of her throat and over her bare breasts. Back and forth, he teased her nipples by sucking them into his mouth in hard, brief bursts. Mindlessly she ground her pussy against him, offering everything he could possibly want.

"Please. Please. Please." She begged, hoping he'd take her soon. Reaching between them, she did her best to grip his cock. She rubbed her hand up and down his erection, unsatisfied that she couldn't get into his shorts for skin-to-skin contact.

"Please what?" He barely paused in his torture to ask the question.

She knew where this was heading. If she didn't say the words, he'd play with her. He'd keep her on the edge until she gave in. If he hadn't kept her in a state of high arousal all through the leisurely dinner, she would have played the game. She would have tried to see how long she could hold out.

But she had no willpower. "Please fuck me. Hard, fast, soft, slow, however you want. Only please fuck me."

He eased back, putting a little bit of distance between them, and allowed her to unfasten his shorts. "Guide me inside you."

Sweeter words were never spoken. She took him greedily and reveled in the way she felt whole and complete once he was buried deep.

"Lean back, honey. Rest your weight on your hands behind you."

She did as he commanded. The stone was smooth beneath her palms, a testament to how many couples had come this way before.

Then he lifted one of her legs and bent it, perching her foot on the tray to spread her wider and allow deeper access. He feathered a light kiss over her lips. "Hold on the best you can. You've been tempting me for the past hour, and I'll be damned if I'm going to be gentle now."

If she'd tempted him, it was his fault. But she kept that thought to herself. His declaration was a soothing song after a hectic day.

He didn't wait for a response anyway. He braced one hand on the tray next to her hip and wrapped the other arm around her torso. He rocked in and out a few times, testing his range, and then he hammered her hard. She met every thrust, pushing against him in a harsh collision every time just so he didn't move her back with the force of his passion.

In seconds, she shouted her release, but she knew better than to give in and enjoy it fully. He was far from finished, and if she abandoned her obligation to stay in one place, it would interfere with his pleasure. The guilt that would gnaw at her would take forever to assuage.

The hand he had placed on the tray found its way to her breasts, plucking and lightly pinching her nipples. With the other hand, he pulled her closer, sealing her stomach to his, and he picked up the pace.

The stars shone brightly, splashes of pale color in the vast blackness. They faded to pinpricks as all semblance of control left her body. Her legs and arms went numb. As always, he caught her as she fell, holding her close for those last two thrusts that sent them both into the stratosphere.

She let herself float along for as long as she could. When she came back to Earth, she found herself shivering uncontrollably in his arms despite the warmth of the night.

"Honey?" Jonas withdrew and held her back a little. He perused her body with a quick scan, but he didn't appear to be worried.

"I'm okay. That was intense." Her teeth chattered, stuttering her words.

He helped her down from the stone tray and fixed her clothes before attending to his shorts. "We'll go back to the room. Can you walk?"

It was slow going, due in no small amount to her sore pussy, but they made good time. As he unlocked the door, she caught the decidedly cocky slant to his mouth. He was proud of the depth of her reaction.

"Were you hoping I couldn't walk?"

He chuckled softly. "Don't worry. We have a few days. There's time for that." He tugged her hand, urging her into the room. "We'll go hang out in the hot tub for a little while, and then I'll put you to bed."

Chapter Four

She woke the next morning with her head still pillowed on his chest. The last time this had happened was before the kids were born. Usually she woke up alone or to the sound of a baby calling. Jonas tended to wake up before everyone else. Sometimes he would have sex with her—whether or not she completely woke up—before he started his day.

A glance up showed that she'd indeed awoken first. His lashes curved against his cheeks, and his breathing was slow and even. Since she almost never had the chance to study him when he wasn't aware of her perusal, she took this opportunity. He'd definitely aged well. Forty was just around the corner for him, a mere two months away, yet he remained easily one of the most handsome men she'd ever encountered. At rest, she could admire his high cheekbones, the strong lines of his jaw, the slight arch of his brows, and his firm lips.

He'd developed some light lines around his mouth and eyes, side effects of his almost constant smile. Even when he wasn't smiling, he still had a twinkle in his eyes that hinted at his vast well of internal happiness. Sabrina liked to think she'd given that to him.

He kept his long, lithe body in shape by spending time in the weight room he'd installed in the basement and from their activities in the pool house dungeon. Though he flogged her only a few times each month, he put in time with a practice dummy to keep his aim and technique true.

She looked at her arm, bent across his chest, and reflected that she could use some time in the weight room as well. Though she swam regularly, her workouts weren't as punishing or as frequent as they used to be, and she found herself struggling just to maintain her current weight. This wasn't an issue she'd ever anticipated having. It seemed the hormonal changes wrought by having children had tampered with her body chemistry. Her metabolism had slowed drastically. Now when her sister brought over award-winning confections, Sabrina often turned down her portion.

Jonas didn't seem to mind the added padding. He honestly delighted in her new curves. That was fine for when they were alone, but she couldn't seem to come to terms with showing her body in public anymore. When they'd first married, she and Jonas had traveled the world, visiting sex clubs where she was often naked or very scantily clothed. Her husband was an exhibitionist. It came with the territory.

Now she didn't mind performing with people watching as long as she could remain at least partially covered. Last night he hadn't pushed the issue. He'd exposed and played with her breasts in public, but he had kept the rest of her problem areas covered. When he'd taken her on that stone serving tray, the deep shadows of evening had obscured most of what he'd exposed. She wasn't sure who, if anyone, had watched them, but she was certain they hadn't seen much. The skirt of her dress had ended up bunched around her waist, but the sides hung down enough to hide the stretch marks on her thighs.

Beneath her, Jonas shifted. The muscles in the arm under her tightened. He pulled her closer as he rolled toward her. Now her head rested on his arm and his body pressed along the length of hers. His cock stirred against her stomach, and his hand moved over her hip.

Even though he didn't open his eyes, she knew he was awake. "Good morning."

He hooked his hand around the back of her knee and brought her leg up to drape over his hip. Then he reached around and lined up the head of his cock with her opening.

She'd still been moist when he'd put her to bed the night before, but now her body responded enthusiastically. Before he'd made it an inch, heated cream rushed to her pussy, easing the way. He slid home.

He thrust lightly, teasing her with a languorous rhythm. She hitched her leg up higher to give him more access. He opened his eyes at long last, revealing the topaz depths of his desire. Then he rolled her onto her back, pushed her legs up and apart as far as they would go, and pounded into her.

The deep thrusts touched her core, hitting that sweet spot just right each time. She tried to lift her hips, but he held her legs down with his weight, so the movement was futile. The delicious helplessness of her position raised the stakes.

Her climax built slow and crashed fast, triggered by hot jets of his semen. He collapsed on top of her, the thud of his heart beating against her chest. She held him in her arms, taking the opportunity to run her fingers through his blond, curly hair and to explore the hard lines of his back and shoulders.

When his heartbeat returned to normal, he rolled away. She inhaled deeply, replenishing her starved lungs. He wasn't too heavy, but she couldn't breathe normally with all his weight resting on top of her.

They lay there in silence, listening to the sounds of the ocean breeze and enjoying the quiet peace that followed their interlude, until her stomach growled. She hadn't eaten a full meal the night before. "How about a quick shower and we go get some breakfast?"

"We have a fully stocked kitchenette. I'll make breakfast." He sat up. "I'll take a quick shower first. You can take your time. We'll eat on the balcony."

That sounded much more intimate and romantic than her suggestion. She smiled and nodded.

* * * *

Jonas added sugar to the pineapple chunks simmering in the pan. He wasn't sure Sabrina liked pineapple too much. He'd seen her eat it, but she'd never gone out of her way to ask for it. At home when he made toppings for pancakes, he stuck to blueberries or strawberries, fruits he knew both Sabrina and Rose liked.

He tamped down a small pang as he thought of Rose. He missed his kids. Last night, he'd successfully kept Sabrina's mind off them. He wouldn't be so lucky today. The water sounds from the bathroom ceased, signaling that he had about five minutes before his lovely wife appeared. He opened up the laptop he'd brought and dialed his mother's Skype account. By the time Sabrina appeared, he had Rose onscreen. His mother sat behind her with Ethan on her lap.

Sabrina appeared wearing a wraparound peach dress that draped over her curves nicely. It fell to just above her knees. He wanted to unwrap her and feed her slow bites of breakfast from his fork.

He settled for something tame, as befit the moment. "Honey, come say good morning to Rose and Ethan."

Her face brightened, and she joined him at the table. They talked for a few minutes. Rose reiterated everything she'd done in the past day. Ethan squealed, his big brown eyes widening with excitement, and tried to come through the screen.

By the time they signed off, Sabrina seemed to have relaxed a little. As they ate a leisurely breakfast on the balcony, he observed that she was still wound tight. Being high strung meant she was successful in nearly everything she did, but it also meant she had issues with letting go. He didn't mind forcing her. It turned them both on.

"So I was thinking." He let his beginning drift between them, a warning of things to come.

She set her empty plate on the small glass top of the table next to her chair. Her gaze remained on the horizon. "Was it painful?"

He grinned. "It might be, but not for me."

Her focus moved closer. Now she played with the hem of her dress. Her anxiety betrayed her interest. "You want to visit the Fields of Punishment?"

They'd get there eventually. "I want your submission."

Her eyebrows knit in confusion, and she looked up at him. "You get that all the time."

Technically her statement was true. Whenever he initiated sex, she submitted to him. Even when she seduced him, she submitted to him. Before and after a scene, she didn't show a hint of submissiveness. He had a hunch that it cost her a lot to always show her strong, independent side, especially as life became more complicated and busy.

He wanted to show her that she didn't have to shoulder anything alone. He was more than willing to support her. Part of his reasoning for choosing to honeymoon at Elysium was to give her a safe place to explore that side of her nature. Perhaps if he hadn't felt the urgency of his age and let it drive his need to have children so quickly, they might have had the opportunity to travel this path earlier. He didn't regret the decisions they'd made, but it was high time for Sabrina to understand and accept the true depths of her submissive nature.

"Outside of a scene."

Wheels turned behind her eyes with amazing speed. She scowled at him. "You want me to kneel at your feet and call you 'Master.'"

He lifted his brows. "You can call me all the things you usually call me."

From the expression on her face, he had a hunch he didn't want to know what kinds of names she was currently considering. She leaned toward him. "I'm not kneeling outside of a scene."

He could handle that, mostly because he was proposing an extended scene. "Okay."

"I'm not going to ask your permission to do things. Well, not outside the normal realm of good manners. I'm not into the slavery thing."

In the past few years, she'd had more than a few glimpses into the world of sexual slavery. His best friend and her husband had opened up. When the kids were away and the adults got together, Ellen and Ryan frequently appeared in their preferred roles. Ryan very much enjoyed serving his Mistress. And his youngest sister lived with two Doms. Though they toned it down, they didn't completely drop protocol when Sabrina and Jonas visited. It had been a little uncomfortable at first to see his sister in that role, but she was blissfully happy, so he accepted it.

Sabrina thought it was demeaning to women, though she didn't seem to have an issue with Ryan in the same position.

Jonas knew that kind of life didn't appeal to Sabrina. It came as a relief because it didn't appeal to him either.

Submission was another thing altogether. He was wired to be Dominant. While he loved and admired her strength, he didn't like the toll it had taken on her in recent years.

"Yes, you will. While we're here, you will ask before you do anything. You won't be my slave, but you will defer to me in all things." He braced himself to face her wrath. While she'd improved in her ability to express anger, she still kept a lot bottled up inside. When she got mad, she tended to sputter, and she hated sounding anything but smooth.

The sharp inhale of breath indicating she was struggling to keep it together never came. She stood and rested her hands on the railing. "You mean I won't get a say in anything? I don't get to have an opinion?"

That she was considering his proposal so seriously spoke volumes about what she really wanted. Losing that much control would be very difficult for her. She liked when he overpowered her in bed, but she hadn't yet submitted to him in any other way.

"You will be given the opportunity to voice your opinion. I'll take it into consideration. Then I will make the final decision."

She touched her hand to her neck. "And I can't argue with it. I have to do exactly what you say."

He wanted to take her in his arms, but she would perceive that as a weakness right now. "Yes. No arguments. No bargaining. You do as you're told or you will be punished."

Punishment had never been part of their relationship. He had never even really disciplined her. He flogged her because it excited her sexually. He got off on it, too, so that was a win-win. Occasionally he caned her because the steady staccato beat relaxed her. They both enjoyed bondage, and he loved to torture her sexually.

But it was no longer enough. He'd always wanted more, though he'd been loath to push the issue. As the kids had come along, adjusting to having them in their lives had taken precedence over having his wife's submission. Deep down, he knew she wanted more.

"This could blow up in our faces."

It could, but he wasn't willing to give her an inch. She was too intelligent not to take the mile. "It's for five days and four nights. You did fine last night. I think you can handle it."

Half turning, she threw a cheeky grin over her shoulder. "Are you sure you can handle it?"

He came to stand next to her. Planting his hands on her shoulders, he turned her to face him completely. The conflicted expression in her bottomless brown eyes troubled him. "Sabrina, I'm not forcing you into this."

"I know." She dropped her gaze, focusing on his lips. "I want to do this. You usually have good ideas. I'm just afraid because what if I hate it and you like it? Where does that leave our relationship?"

He pushed a strand of her luxurious dark hair away from her face. He knew she'd worn it down for him. "Being your husband is the most important thing in my life. Nothing is going to change that. I'm asking for five days. That's all."

And they would have regular discussions. He didn't expect to get everything he wanted, and he needed to make sure she got everything she needed.

"Four days. Four nights. The fifth morning, we talk." She looked up again, meeting his eyes. "And I'm not going to be naked where other people can see me."

He gave her a crooked grin. "Looks like I've finally impressed upon you the importance of talking about what works and what doesn't."

She didn't smile. "Yes. Well, I have a feeling we'll have a lot to talk about."

They would, which was why he didn't love the idea of waiting until the last morning to talk. But he knew when he'd milked a negotiation for all it was worth, and he knew when to not point out that he'd ignored her last condition.

* * * *

Calypso music came through the trees. Sabrina held Jonas's hand as they walked along the path toward the sound. For most of the day, they'd engaged in vacation activities. He'd secured a tour on a glass-bottom catamaran. They'd gone sailing and snorkeling. They'd chatted a little, watched colorful schools of fish, exclaimed over the island's beauty, and enjoyed one another's company.

As dinnertime approached, he'd instructed her to remove her underclothes and put her hair up. She changed out of her skirted bathing suit and back into the peach wraparound she'd worn that morning. Thin straps crossing from front to back held it up. The fabric hugged her breasts and cinched around her waist, and then cascaded over her hips to fall unevenly down her thighs. His eyes had lit up when he first saw her in it, so she knew he liked the way it looked on her. It was one of the new outfits she'd purchased for the trip.

She'd wrestled her hair into a long braid that she twisted into an artful crown on top of her head. The night was warm, and as they emerged onto the beach, she spied a bonfire. That made her extra glad he'd wanted her to wear her hair up. She wasn't worried about getting singed, but she hated to sweat unnecessarily. It simply wasn't sexy.

Of course, Jonas liked to tease her that she seemed to find sweat sexy on him. That wasn't strictly the case. She liked the way he looked when he used his muscles, like when he worked in the garden or lifted something heavy, and those activities tended to make him sweat. She often pushed him toward the shower before she'd actually touch him.

The beach was set up with bamboo benches and tripods. Some benches were placed around the fire. Others were scattered in a haphazard manner. Smaller tiki torches lit the areas that were too far from the mountainous fire to benefit from its glow. The dark water stretched endlessly eastward. This beach would look beautiful bathed in the morning light, but just now the sun was setting on the opposite side of the island.

"It's incredible." She watched the other guests milling around to see what they planned to do with the tripods, but everyone seemed to be ignoring them.

Jonas sniffed appreciatively. "I love the smell of fresh barbecue. Hungry?"

After a day spent on the water, she could probably out-eat him. "Ravenous."

They snagged paper plates, but Jonas took hers and put it underneath his. "You won't need this."

Feeding one another never failed to lead to sensuous activities, even when it wasn't the intention. Many times Jonas had asked her to taste a dish when he messed with the recipe. They'd frequently ended up ordering out because the dinner had burned when they snuck away for a quickie.

But she was too hungry to think about sex just now. She was tempted to argue, but she remembered her promise to be submissive and kept quiet. Where that action would normally have made her feel anxious, she felt only peace now. Her life was in Jonas's hands, and she trusted him completely.

Together they selected items for the plate. Jonas piled the chipped pork and spareribs high, stacking them on top of steamed vegetables and a baked potato. He held her hand as he led her to an unoccupied bench. They sat, straddling the bench to face each other.

Jonas placed the plate of food between them and stabbed the single fork into the barbecue-slathered mess. Sabrina eyed it hungrily. She wanted to ask if he expected her to feed him or the other way around, but she held the question in check.

"Open your dress at the top so I can see your breasts."

The firelight gave her skin a red-orange glow, but it didn't show much, so she reasoned it was safe. Reaching to one side of her waist, she untied one of the strings holding it together. The bench caught the bottom half of the fabric and kept it from falling completely away. Then she tugged the string on the other side of her waist. The dress fell open enough for her to see her breasts when she looked down. She tucked it away from her chest just to make sure Jonas got the view he wanted.

He regarded her appreciatively. "Beautiful. Simply perfect."

A man in love had a warped perception of beauty. Sabrina might have voiced that opinion, but the raw admiration in his tone gave her pause. If she argued now, she would likely face a punishment. They hadn't discussed it outright, but she knew him well enough to assume he'd added that element to this experiment.

He picked up a short rack of ribs and held them out to her.

She wanted to hold them with a napkin, but he hadn't provided one. Hunger drove her to forget manners. If he wanted her sticky fingerprints all over his body later, so be it. She accepted the messy ribs. "Thank you."

Silence reigned for several minutes while she devoured the ribs. When she went to suck the sauce from her fingertips, Jonas grabbed her wrist. He nailed her with a fierce look. "Mine."

He cleaned her fingers with his mouth. His tongue laved heat and his teeth scraped her skin. Her breath caught. Now that her stomach wasn't empty, another hunger was growing.

She pried his fingers from her wrist and licked his fingers the same way he licked hers. Before long, he leaned close and replaced his fingers with his tongue. He swept into her mouth and mastered the moment.

Then he sat back and picked up a piece of steamed zucchini. "Open your dress the rest of the way."

She pulled the material back so that it hung from the thin straps on her shoulders. Her entire front side was revealed to his gaze. He could see the rise and fall of her breasts, the pebbled tips of her nipples, and the reflection of the firelight from the moisture in her bare pussy.

He fed her slowly, pausing to caress her body as she chewed. She tried to return the favor. He allowed her to feed him, but he didn't let her hands wander on the way back to the plate.

As they finished, Sabrina swiped her finger through some of the sauce left on the plate. She painted it on her nipples and grinned in decadent invitation.

He pursed his lips in thoughtful disapproval. "That isn't very submissive of you, honey."

Usually he liked when she took the initiative. She always messed up when they played this game. Keeping it up for four more nights and days was going to be very challenging.

"I'm sorry." She tried to wipe away the sauce, but he stayed her hand.

Standing up, he unzipped his shorts, shoved them down, and kicked them to the sand. His erection sprang forth, and she spied the pearly drop at the tip betraying the extent of his desire.

He grasped his shaft, moved closer, and used his cockhead to clean her nipples. The soft glide of his skin over hers sent waves of shivers up her shoulders and down to her core. Then he straightened his knees, and he was so close to her mouth. Suddenly she needed to taste him.

"Open for me."

For him? Anything. Submitting this way was much easier for her. She knew to part her lips and wait for him. Sometimes he just wanted her to be still and accept that he was fucking her mouth. Other times he wanted her to actively participate. This was one of those times.

He eased forward. "Take me deep and suck me until I come."

She started slow, wetting him with long swipes of her tongue. When he was slick enough, she took him in her mouth and wrapped her hand around the base of his shaft. With her other hand, she caressed the sensitive skin on his sac. He let her set the beginning pace, but after a few minutes, he took over.

She relaxed her jaw and sucked the way he liked. His grunts and groans were punctuated with exclamations and rough encouragement. Hot jets of semen squirted down her throat. She swallowed quickly, sucking harder to make sure she got every drop.

Jonas collapsed back to the bench, sitting so heavily on his half that it jolted her side. He moved the plate and pulled her onto his lap so that she straddled him, and he peppered lazy, sloppy kisses on her lips.

He pushed her dress from where it fell on her thighs and caressed her with long, slow strokes up her legs, over her hips, all the way to her shoulder blades. She returned the favor, taking off his shirt and tossing it onto the small heap containing his shorts. Then she pressed her bare breasts into his naked chest and gave herself over to the passion overwhelming her system.

His kisses drugged her, and his heat fed the fire within. If he didn't do something to quench the inferno soon, she'd combust. It wouldn't be a pretty sight, so she preferred he take care of the issue.

The slow, deep pounding of drums invaded her consciousness, pulling her from the bubble that had wrapped around them. Jonas broke the kiss and looked over her shoulder. She knew from the interested expression on his face that his attention had wandered, and she hoped it wouldn't be for long. When they had sex in front of an audience, the spectators disappeared for Sabrina, but Jonas was always aware of them. They fed his passion almost as much as she did.

She turned her head to see a crowd gathering around one of the tripods. When he tapped her hip, her hopes were dashed. His passion had been sated by her blowjob, and he was more than willing to make her languish.

Reluctantly, she eased back onto the bench. By the time she secured the ties on her dress, he'd already put his shorts back on. He zipped them as she got to her feet, and he frowned when he took in what she'd done. "I didn't tell you to cover yourself."

The tripod was set up near the fire. While the light would be better there, it was still pretty dark. She untied her dress and let it fall open. He took her hand and led her through the small crowd.

Mistress Hera stood next to one thick bamboo leg. She wore a colorful corset, a flame-red skirt, and matching thigh-high boots. A riding crop was nestled in the laces of her boots, easily accessible at her side. Sabrina imagined being on the receiving end of Mistress Hera's discipline. A shiver of longing ran through her. Jonas shot her a knowing grin.

"Welcome, my friends. Tonight I'm going to show you some of the ways in which you can utilize a tripod. These things look a little intimidating, and they do present some challenges, but they can also open up your play by making you rethink some of the regular things you're doing." The crowd tittered, and Mistress Hera smiled indulgently.

Yes, it was true. While sex play in the BDSM world was exciting, doing the same things over and over could make the most exciting thing mundane. Sabrina thought about how she and Jonas used role-play to keep things interesting. Even then, they ended up doing a lot of the same things or cutting corners because they only had so much time before somebody awoke from their nap. She loved what they did, but she wasn't going to turn her nose up at something new.

Mistress Hera ran her hand over one leg of the tripod in an overtly sensual manner. "I'm going to need a set of volunteers."

The murmurs grew. Hands went up all over the crowd. Sabrina wouldn't mind trying it out, but she wasn't too excited about the idea of doing it in front of a crowd. Seeing somebody else go through this first would be enough to satisfy her curiosity. Then if Jonas wanted to try it privately, they could discuss that possibility.

Deep red lipstick on Mistress Hera's lips glistened in the firelight. Her gaze roamed the crowd and stopped on Jonas, who hadn't raised his hand. She lifted a brow, and he stepped forward, pulling Sabrina along with him. Alarm bells went off inside her head. She recognized that she'd been set up. There would be no discussion. Jonas was in charge. Though they'd nixed the "obey" aspect from their marriage vows, she'd agreed to that condition for the duration of their vacation.

Calm followed the sudden panic, squelching the feeling before it had time to set up shop. As much as she didn't want to do this for the first time in front of a crowd, she trusted Jonas to make the experience special. He always did.

Mistress Hera offered her hand to Jonas. "Master J. Thank you for volunteering. Can you tell me what kind of experience you have using a tripod?"

He gave her a weird look, as if he expected her to know the answer. Sabrina realized that this woman and Jonas were acquainted through some connection that had nothing to do with the island. She frowned at him, but he shook his head, so she didn't voice her question.

"It's been a few years. I remember the basics. You go ahead and talk us through them, and I'll demonstrate using my sub." Just like that, he established himself as dominant over the woman in charge of the entire resort.

From her wry smile, it looked like she'd already known what to expect with Jonas. Sabrina was confused. Normally Jonas didn't have a need to establish himself as the most dominant person in the room. He enjoyed amiable relationships with a number of Doms and Dommes, where he seemed to employ a live-and-let-live approach.

He guided Sabrina to stand next to the tripod, outside of the three legs. One tug, and he pulled her dress completely away from her body. He handed it to a khaki-clad employee, who draped it over his arm.

Sabrina reminded herself that the fire didn't allow enough light for people to see the details of her stretch marks. Still she was nervous. While she didn't mind people watching her have sex, she'd never engaged in an instructional demonstration. Would she get an orgasm at the end? If he'd given her one five minutes ago, she probably wouldn't be so wound up now.

"Masters and Mistresses, pay careful attention. You'll need to purchase or create a harness. If you create one yourself, you want to use a static rope to avoid unexpected stretching when you hang up your sub."

Mistress Hera's voice carried through the crowd. Someone handed a neoprene harness to Jonas. He placed her arms in the loops and adjusted the fit of the straps so that they went around her breasts. She heard a series of snaps as he finished it off in back. Next he guided her into the leg straps and attached them to the thick belt. Again a series of snaps in back told her that he'd attached everything that needed to be linked.

Throughout it all, Mistress Hera described what he was doing. Several times she nudged his hands out of the way to highlight some aspect for the crowd. Sabrina found her body shifted and turned so that everyone could see every step. She felt like a fish in a bowl. This was not hot and sexy. She wished they were back on the bench.

Mistress Hera moved onto the next phase of her talk. She pointed out features of the tripod and how they matched up perfectly with the rings and snaps on the harness.

Jonas leaned close. He rested his fingertips on her waist. "You're doing great, honey. I know this is going a little slowly, but this next part will more than make up for it."

She wanted to ask one little question, but it wasn't exactly a question. It was a rebuke in disguise, and she already knew the answer. Since she couldn't find a suitable way to tell him that she would have preferred if he'd asked her if she wanted to participate in this demonstration, she just nodded and kept her mouth shut.

The way he held her—possessively, but so lightly—combined with the feel of the harness to reignite her blood. Now that her world had boiled down to just the two of them, she wanted him to take her, fuck her any way he wanted in front of everybody. The key to her desire lay with Jonas. With a look and a touch, he demanded her submission, and she gave it freely. The onlookers and the demonstration no longer mattered.

He moved her into position. First he secured the top part of the harness. Then he slid one arm under her belly and lifted her to secure the bottom section. Through it all, Mistress Hera talked about winches and cooperation as she addressed the concerns from couples whose tops didn't have the strength to lift their subs.

"Once the submissive is fully bound, she or he is completely powerless." Mistress Hera stepped closer to Sabrina's head. She waved her hand close in an approximation of a caress on Sabrina's face, but she was careful to avoid direct physical contact with another Dom's submissive. "Master J will now complete the binding."

Sabrina's arms and legs dangled down toward the sand. If she stretched her toes, she could probably touch it. The harness didn't dig into her ribs or thighs uncomfortably. She could get used to this, though she considered the inelegant position on the edge of humiliating.

Jonas tightened cuffs around her wrists and just above her elbows. Then he guided her arms back behind her back and folded them. She heard the *snick* of the snaps as they were fastened together. She could move her arms, but not far. Next he bent her leg at the knee and secured her ankle cuff. When all was said and done, her ankles were tied to the same O-ring holding her body aloft. It was an interesting position and one that provided no support for her head.

Jonas knelt in front of her and lifted her chin. Flames reflected in his eyes, both literal and figurative. The bonfire cast his tawny depths with an orange glow, bringing out the flecks of brown and gold. "What's your safe word, honey?"

He'd never asked that question before. She'd never been in this position before. When they'd played in public, it had always been as equals. Well, not quite equal, but she'd felt free to refuse to do something he asked, and he usually asked or somehow made sure she consented.

"Onion."

A hint of a smile crossed his lips. "Words cannot describe how beautiful you look right now. You're naked and helpless and mine."

She was always his, so that was nothing new. And he often had her naked and helpless. Beautiful? She'd have to see pictures to believe it. Jonas was nothing if not biased.

Mostly she felt exposed. She could feel the heat of the crowd's stare penetrating her most intimate tissues. They swelled and wept, humiliated and wanton.

She choked back a cry. "Jonas, I'm not sure about this."

He silenced her with a soft kiss, and then he pressed his forehead to hers. "I know, honey. I know. But I am sure, and you're going to have to find strength and comfort in that."

It seemed to Sabrina that she'd come to the point where she took the idea of trust for granted. She said she trusted him. She knew she trusted him, but what did that really mean? In the course of their daily lives, they had fallen into a routine where trust meant she knew he would take out the trash and cook dinner. She knew he would run to the store if she asked or change a diaper without a comment about whose turn it was. She knew he would tie her up, hold her down, flog her, and give her a series of orgasms that left her trembling.

But what about when it came to the unknown? They hadn't tested this situation before. Suddenly she understood exactly what he'd been asking when he made that deal with her. He wanted to push the boundaries of their relationship, deepen their bond.

She offered her bravest smile. "I do. Thank you."

The kiss he gave her this time ravaged her mouth and demanded much. The heat of the crowd, which had been an invasive thing, morphed to complement the fires Jonas set inside her soul and between her legs.

He stood up and stepped back a pace. She let her head drop into a more comfortable position, and relaxed her neck muscles as much as she could. From the corner of her eye, she saw Mistress Hera standing next to Jonas. Never had another person been involved in their scene. It was disconcerting, but she trusted Jonas to have it all under control. They must have planned this, but other than when she showered, she couldn't think of many moments when she and Jonas had been separated since their arrival.

"This position is good for a lot of things. You can manipulate the harness to change the elevation of your submissive, make sure everything is accessible."

Titters of knowing and suggestive laughter sounded in all directions. Movement at Mistress Hera's side caught Sabrina's attention. The woman extracted the very crop that Sabrina had been drooling over ten minutes before and handed it to Jonas.

Every part of Sabrina's body seemed to grow instantly more sensitive, as if her nerve endings were reaching out and begging for the sting of that leather flap. Jonas ran it along her side and over her hip, teasing those nerves.

He took his time, and she understood that his attention was completely on her. Yes, he was aware of the crowd. Their energy fed him like almost nothing else. But he was attuned to her every action and reaction.

She tried to take a deep breath, but the quivering of her lungs made that a tremulous undertaking. He moved a little closer, angling the crop underneath to tease the sensitive skin of her stomach and breasts. He did this to her whole body. Mistress Hera's voice became part of the drone of the crowd, and that all melted into the hiss and crackle of the fire and the swish of the waves as they lapped the beach.

Peace wrapped around her, cocooning her in its arms. The trembling of her body ceased as she sank toward oblivion. A sharp crack brought her back. Stinging shot through her nipple, so close to the edge of fire she enjoyed. The blow had been more sound than force.

More fell in rapid succession. He concentrated on her breasts, hitting the globes with a million taps before he let loose with one that brought tears to her eyes. She gasped aloud, a sound lost in the roar of the fire and waves.

He kept at it, showing no mercy even though her cries grew louder. Stray hits wandered lower, peppering her stomach and mons, occasionally even striking her clit. Those hits she both loved and dreaded. They hurt like hell, but they brought her the sweetest bliss if only she was patient.

Tied like this, she gave in to the urge to writhe and buck. She swayed a little, but his aim remained true. Heat and cold, pleasure and pain, desire and dread. Conflicting sensations stole her reason. She gave up trying to anticipate and rationalize, and surrendered to the inevitability of it all.

Just when she thought she'd reached the maximum of her endurance, everything stopped. She heard her soft whimpers as she struggled not to beg for more. Beyond that, she heard countless moans and pleas all around her as submissives responded to her heavenly torment.

A glance to the side revealed a man with his hand around his submissive's hard cock. He squeezed, and the sub's knees nearly buckled. To the other side, she spied a woman, her Master's arms wrapped around her body as he held her to him and his fingers worked in and out of her pussy.

Sabrina lifted her head, but Mistress Hera's curvy hips blocked her view. The woman spoke to the crowd, describing what Jonas was doing and delivering tips of caution. In all the years since Jonas had introduced her to impact play, Sabrina hadn't known much about it. She loved that Jonas knew what he was doing, that he knew when to push her and when to stop, exactly as he'd done tonight.

She never once stopped to consider that he wasn't operating on instinct alone. There were guidelines for safe play that Jonas followed, guidelines she knew nothing about. These were things she could probably find out with a rudimentary amount of research, but she didn't want to. She liked the magic and the mystery, so she closed her ears to Mistress Hera's lecture and concentrated on the sensations running riot over her skin.

She felt Jonas's hands, cool and knowing, on the places he'd just tormented. He played with her tender breasts, stroked down her stomach, and lingered between her legs. Her pussy was slick with her juices. It throbbed with longing. He circled and rubbed her clit.

She wanted to climax so badly, but the more attention he paid to her pussy, the more acutely she felt the gaze of the crowd on her exposed tissues. Because he stood at her side and not behind her, she was completely open for public viewing. Every quiver, every drop of cream that dripped from her wanton core was there for everyone to witness. The woman who used to close her eyes and wish it was over now displayed her desire for her husband for a hundred eyes, and she did it because it was what he wanted.

More than naked, she felt stripped to the core, almost too exposed. The safe word hovered just behind her teeth and tongue. Only one thing stopped her from uttering it. She'd promised to trust him.

Some of Mistress Hera's words penetrated the fog of desire and anxiety clouding Sabrina's mind. "Flogging in this situation presents some unique challenges. You must make sure the lines of the harness are out of the way, and you must have very good aim. Mind you, this isn't for everyone. When some of your falls hit the lines, it can cause them to fall in an unpredictable and uneven manner, which isn't safe. We're extremely fortunate to have the world-renowned Master J here to demonstrate. He's retired from the public circuit, so this is a special treat. Please enjoy, but pay careful attention to his technique."

Falls whistled through the air, a familiar and welcome sound, and landed on her ass in a sharp announcement of what was coming next. She didn't have time to wonder where he found a cat to borrow because he didn't pause between blows. They came steadily, and she recognized that he was using two instead of one.

A shiver racked her whole body, causing her to sway in the air. Jonas backed off a bit until Mistress Hera stopped the motion by holding the lines on the opposite side of his target. He reestablished his rhythm.

He'd done this to her several times, though usually he had her bound to a huge St. Andrew's cross they kept in a room of their basement he'd remodeled and called a dungeon. Sabrina thought that, to the undiscerning eye, it just looked like a workout room with some odd equipment. Well they certainly worked out in there.

The sting of the leather against her skin was nothing much. It was the steady and unrelenting pace that provided the real drama. Because she couldn't process the sensations, they blended together and short-circuited her brain. Before she knew it, she was floating high above, looking down on the woman hanging from the bamboo tripod, the man expertly wielding twin floggers, the woman holding the lines steady, and the crowd, undulating as if they were going to break into a mass orgy as soon as the signal was given.

One sting distinguished itself from the others, and it pulled her back into her body. Every few strokes, Jonas reversed his pattern. The falls would come from below and strike her exposed pussy. Then he would reverse again and concentrate on her ass and thighs. This new pattern threw her off. She realized she'd been demanding, expecting a certain something. Now she could only sit back and appreciate what she got.

Before long, tension coiled, fed by the heat of her skin and the hiss of the bonfire. It broke suddenly, sweeping her to another reality. She cried out with the enormity of it, and the floggers fell away.

His cock felt cool against her burning flesh. He pushed inside her quickly. She offered no resistance. The slick, pulsing walls of her vagina sucked at him with a welcoming rhythm. He took her up that cliff once more before he surrendered to passion.

Chapter Five

The next night, he took her dancing. They'd taken ballroom dancing lessons together in preparation for their second wedding. Since then, Jonas often swept her up in his arms when the music was right or the mood struck him. He didn't usually take their surroundings into account. The first time he'd done it at a dinner party at her mother's home, the always proper and severely uptight Melinda Morozov had watched in shocked amazement until Sabrina's stepfather, Dmitri, had followed Jonas's example. Her mother had immediately relaxed, following her husband's lead. The evening had been fun and memorable.

Elysium featured a formal dance hall in the Bacchanal Arbor. Jonas had chosen a short, white, strapless dress for Sabrina to wear. It tightened under her breasts in a wide, satiny band around her ribs. From there, it flowed over her hips and stopped just short of indecent. On her feet, he placed low-heeled white and wicker sandals. Under her dress, he allowed nothing.

For himself, he'd selected a white cambric shirt, which he paired with dark green shorts. He wasn't as dressed up as she was, a fact she pointed out.

He smiled patiently and held out his arm for her to take. "I'm not the eye candy, honey. You are. It doesn't matter what I walk in there wearing, everybody's going to be looking at you."

She wondered if anyone would recognize her from the bonfire. Probably, if she showed them her pussy. She wasn't sure anyone had gotten a good look at her face. The memory made her blush.

Jonas chuckled. "I don't think I'll ever get tired of seeing you do that. It makes you look even lovelier."

Sabrina grasped his arm and followed him to the Bacchanal Arbor.

A small orchestra was set up near one side of the dance floor. Surrounded by trees, the pavilion was open on four sides. Glass panels retracted into the many columns, ready to be pulled out if the need for a more fortified shelter arose. Island greenery and explosions of tropical color formed the backdrop for this incredible location.

They sat at a small table, just large enough for the two of them, and ordered drinks. One thing about being on an island, all the girly drinks with the decorative umbrellas that Sabrina loved were readily available, albeit in virgin forms.

Jonas grinned fondly when the server delivered the pink, frothy drink. He leaned forward and captured her left hand. "The first time I saw you, I knew you were the type of woman who would drink something pink."

She lifted an eyebrow at his soft appraisal. "Are you sure about that? I thought your mind went immediately to sex."

That grin grew. "I'm capable of thinking about two things at once. Maybe it was a prop in my fantasy, something soft and feminine with a straw for you to wrap those luscious lips around."

She laughed at his audacity. When they'd met, she'd been an executive in the company, and he'd been a new hire. He had been in awe of her, and so he'd been shocked when she'd asked him to marry her. They had never spoken before, but she'd needed a husband in order to gain an inheritance, and he'd been sitting right there. "So you first imagined me as a tease?"

"You teased me just by walking into a room." He played with her wedding ring, moving the band back and forth with the flick of his thumb against the diamond. It had been his grandmother's. "You tease me by wearing that sexy, micro-dress with nothing underneath."

It had been a while since she'd had the opportunity to flirt with her husband outside of a scene. Even though she felt soft heat rising to her cheeks, she loved the banter. "You're the one who picked out my clothes."

"But you're the one giving me that come-hither look." He turned her hand over and ran his fingertips over her palm. The lightness of his touch tickled, but she didn't pull away.

"It's been four whole hours since you've made love to me." She pretended to pout, but really she had nothing to complain about. He'd scheduled a trail-riding excursion. A guide had taken a group of them on horseback to explore the dense tropical forest that made up the interior of the island. Their destination had been a secluded waterfall surrounded by magnificent natural rock formations where a picnic lunch awaited them.

Jonas had made the most of the occasion, and she had found out firsthand how soft moss could be on her naked backside.

He released her hand and swirled his glass with the sparkling cider the server had brought when they'd been seated. "I do love you, you know."

She blinked at the sudden sobriety of his tone. "I know. I still like hearing you say the words."

"Five years ago, you made me the luckiest man alive. I may not have appreciated it for the right reasons at the time, and it took me a while to learn, and so I thank you for your patience and forgiveness."

Sabrina blinked. Thinking about parts of that first year still tore her up inside and left her feeling vulnerable. She opened her mouth to utter the appropriate response, but he wasn't finished.

"Four years ago, you made me the happiest man alive by agreeing to marry me after you found out how messed up I was. Three years ago, you gave me the most precious gift in the world, our daughter. One year ago, you did it again, making our family complete with a son."

The pang she'd swallowed at the beginning of his speech grew undeniably strong, and salty tears wet her eyes. Jonas had given her life purpose. He'd shown her what it was like to feel pleasure and pain, desire so intense it crippled her will, and a love she'd never imagined possible.

"I love you, Sabrina. I love you with every piece of my soul and every inch of my body. I would marry you again every single day for the rest of my life."

Now tears fell in earnest. She wiped carefully under her eyes, dabbing with the edged of her napkin. He never ceased to amaze her. She wasn't nearly as gifted with words as him, so she settled for a simple response. "I love you, too, Jonas."

After dinner, they danced slowly to the romantic strains of music they didn't need to hear. Sabrina was so lost in the feel of his arms around her and the clean, masculine scent that was uniquely Jonas filling her senses that she didn't notice anyone around them. She forgot everything. Though she noticed that Jonas had guided her outside to the patio, the change of scenery didn't register until he stopped dancing.

The breeze had turned cooler and the clear sky showcased the multitude of stars, making it a perfect night. She held Jonas's hand and followed him to the lawn. It didn't take long for her to realize it was made up of semiprivate areas, most of which were filled with couples. Dim lights glowed from strategic locations, providing just enough light to make out shapes but not much else.

Jonas led her to an empty place and pulled her back into his arms. Strains of music barely beat out the moans and whispers surrounding them. Sabrina smiled up at her husband. She couldn't see his face clearly, so she ran her fingertips up his chest and over the planes and angles of his cheeks and lips. He let her explore for a bit, then he captured her lips in a searing kiss.

He pushed her dress down and over her hips before undressing and thoughtfully spreading his shirt and shorts for them to lie on. She welcomed his weight and the forceful thrust of his hips as he buried his cock in her body.

* * * *

They helped each other dress, fumbling in the dim light to find buttons and orient their clothing. Sabrina giggled when they made it back to the patio to find that Jonas's shorts were on inside out.

The satisfied smile didn't dim from his lips. He shrugged. "One of the hazards of eschewing beds."

A pair of hands clapped together, not the kind of sound that heralded applause, but the kind that announced somebody was about to get down to business. Hopeful of an erotic public display, Sabrina whipped her head around. She was a little disappointed to find Mistress Hera standing nearby, and her attention was on them.

"Master J, do you have a moment?"

The question was also misleading. Sabrina read the undertones. This was the kind of minute that took hours. It was the kind of minute one would find at a staff meeting, the kind that sucked valuable time into the corporate vacuum. This was her vacation. Meetings were prohibited.

Jonas seemed to sense Sabrina's unease. He put his arm around Sabrina's waist, drawing her closer. "Heather, now isn't a good time. And please call me Jonas. Master J has retired."

Heather? He knew her real name. Sabrina had suspected before that they knew each other. Now she knew for certain, and that fact didn't settle well on her shoulders. The "Master J" thing didn't rankle as much. Before she'd met him, he'd earned a good living punishing the sass out of submissives who'd paid for the privilege at Ellen's exclusive club.

"Please? Jonas, it's important."

A little bit of desperation crept in, enough to tug at Sabrina's heartstrings. Otherwise, Mistress Hera didn't appear distressed. Her regal bearing screamed "Don't mess with me," and her expression remained impassive.

Jonas looked down at Sabrina, the question in his eyes letting her know he'd walk away if she wanted.

"Okay, but I'm coming with you." She hoped to hell it didn't take long.

Mistress Hera nodded. "That would be best."

* * * *

Heather's office was massive. Moveable floor-to-ceiling windows looked out onto a huge balcony. The furniture inside showed no small amount of opulence. Jonas noted the high-end leather furnishings and the upscale art. It was the kind of stuffy, overbearing room he'd find at his father-in-law's mansion, not one he expected to see at a resort.

As Heather closed everything up tightly and turned on the air conditioning, Jonas watched Sabrina, noting her reactions. She was patient now, but he had a hunch that was only because her curiosity had been piqued. No doubt she suspected last night had been a setup. It hadn't been. He knew Heather chose him because he guaranteed a good show and he knew how to use the equipment. Choosing from among unknown, untested guests could present a number of challenges. He'd simply made her job easier.

When they'd landed on the island, Jonas had immediately recognized the tall woman as his ex-wife's friend and sometimes Domme. He didn't have anything against Heather, but they weren't exactly friends. The night before, when she'd come close to touching Sabrina, he'd given her a few warning looks that she'd correctly interpreted. Since she'd stuck to touching only the harness and not his wife, he was a little more willing to hear her out.

"Sit." She indicated the long, curved sofa. "Can I get you anything to drink? I have a bar."

Jonas shook his head, declining for himself and for Sabrina. For Heather to offer alcohol, something strictly forbidden on Elysium to ensure informed consent, indicated trouble. "What's wrong, Heather?"

"Heather. Wow." She shook her head. "Nobody's called me that in years. It's a little weird to hear it again."

He blew out an impatient breath. Next to him, Sabrina started at his display. She still grew uneasy when he fought with Ellen or showed annoyance. They weren't moods he displayed often, especially since he knew how uncomfortable she was with confrontation. It knocked her off balance, and he had no reason to want her that way right now. "You prefer Hera, queen of the gods?"

She waved a dismissive hand. "Heather is okay in private, but I will ask that you don't use it when others are around. Nobody here knows my real name, and I prefer to keep it that way."

Sabrina drew back. She cast questioning glances at Jonas, but he didn't have answers. He had neither seen nor heard from Heather since his divorce.

"That's fine." He hadn't come to Elysium to do anything but celebrate his five-year wedding anniversary. He made an encouraging motion. If she didn't spit it out soon, he planned to head for the door. He had plans for the evening that included his wife, the hot tub on his room's balcony, and perhaps some restraints.

Heather took a deep breath, and though it made her breasts strain against the neckline of her bright red shirt, it screamed desperation. "The owners of Elysium are in the midst of a nasty divorce, which has apparently been going on for five months but I only heard about it yesterday morning. They've put a stop on all the accounts. I have enough left to run this place for the rest of the week, but only if I don't pay any of the employees. I can run a business, but not like this. I don't know what to do, and you're the only person here I know who won't try to take advantage of the situation."

He had no idea what she expected him to do. He taught high school English and a few basic business classes, but he'd never applied those skills to real life. Logic dictated that she should ask the owners to reopen the accounts. "Have you spoken to any of the owners?"

She shook her head. "I'm running into a wall of lawyers. I was going to send everybody home, but what if I panic today and they get their shit together tomorrow? I'd lose my job."

It sounded like she was already out of a job.

Sabrina cleared her throat, perhaps as a way to ask permission to speak. He hadn't anticipated a situation like this when he'd asked her to be submissive. He nodded, giving his consent.

"Have you contacted the bank?"

Heather shook her head. "I don't know what good it would do."

"The bank manager might be able to offer a solution. If not, you probably need to stop new arrivals and meet with the employees. They have housing here, and their basic needs are being met. Most of them probably don't keep a second home anywhere. They might be willing to keep working in exchange for the right to stay here until they're evicted."

Heather stared at Sabrina, no doubt appreciating the combination of beauty and brains that Jonas often admired. She blinked and nodded slowly. "You're right. I think I'm just freaking out a little too much to see the rational course of action. I was right to seek you out. Thank you."

Jonas refrained from mentioning that the opposite could happen. The employees could refuse to work, and they could elect to stay put. The island wasn't part of a country. The security teams were comprised of ex-military personnel, but if they weren't being paid, they had no reason to enforce anybody's will. Besides, he couldn't see Heather kicking anybody to the curb. She was a firm Dominatrix, but a softhearted fool when it came to people in need.

He rose to his feet and pulled Sabrina with him. "If you don't mind, we're going to make the most of the night, especially since it might be our last."

Sabrina offered Heather a sympathetic smile that had just a hint of superiority, but it took an experienced eye to ferret out the tinge of condescension. He waited until they made it back to their suite before he took her to task for her attitude.

It seemed she had the same idea. The moment he locked the outer door of their suite, she rounded on him, her pointed finger blazing a path straight to his chest and her eyes narrowed to dangerous slits.

"How do you know her? Why does she call you Master J?"

She deserved answers, but he couldn't reward her for the accusatory way she'd accosted him. As sexy as he found it when she lost her temper, he couldn't let her behave like a spoiled brat. She was better than that.

He would have given her a look that let her know she was in serious trouble, but he'd never punished her, not even verbally. Sure they'd argued, but those conversations had been emotionally charged and they always ended with sex. If he gave her that look, it wouldn't leave her quaking in her sandals. In truth, it was likely to just piss her off more, and then she'd be even more difficult to reason with.

And while they hadn't agreed on punishable offenses or suitable punishments, he thought this situation warranted something to calm her down and put her in her place. If she objected, he would deal with it. If not, then he knew he'd chosen the correct course of action.

He grabbed her wrist. "I think we can agree using that tone with me has earned you a spanking."

Digging in her heels, she tried to jerk her wrist away, but it didn't get her anywhere. He was much stronger. She punched him in the stomach, confirming his suspicion that she was uncommonly angry. The unexpected blow winded him a bit, but he didn't let that slow him down. Whirling her, he captured her in his arms, holding her arms across her torso to deprive her of their use. She struggled against him, but with her back pressed against his front, she wasn't going to get anywhere.

"Son of a bitch." She growled at him and threw her head back. It hit his chest with a dull thud. "Did you sleep with her?"

"What the hell kind of question is that?" Jonas recalculated his strategy. He needed to teach her how a submissive acted when she was angry or upset. Showing emotion and having opinions were two things he liked. It meant a two-way relationship. But there were certain protocols that needed to be followed, ones with which she was unacquainted.

He was still going to paddle her ass. For asking such an offensive question, she'd find out the difference between an erotic spanking and a punishment paddling.

She stopped struggling. Perhaps the outrage in his tone brought home the reality of what she'd asked. "I didn't mean while you were with me. I know you're faithful. I meant before you met me."

"Whether I did or not is irrelevant. I don't ask you questions about the men you introduce me to." The occasion had never presented itself. If they met a stranger for dinner or ran into one while they were out and about, it was usually one of her clients, and she always made sure to provide a proper introduction.

"She called you 'Master.'" Sabrina jerked her body again, trying to break his hold.

"Stop that. You're going to hurt yourself."

She yanked again, and he knew he was risking bruises on her wrists. He heard her teeth grind together as she growled again. "I don't care."

He tightened his arms around her body, pinning her arms in place and making it impossible for her to move. "I care. You belong to me. While I might like to see you with reddened skin, I don't care for bruises."

She stopped fighting him, but she didn't relax into his hold. Her body was one long line of tension, and she used it to draw a line between them. He was going to have to set her straight before he could punish her.

"I never slept with Heather. She was a Domme I mentored for a little while, back when I used to work the club scene." He needed to come completely clean. If she found out that he'd omitted information, it would be worse for him later. "She was a friend of Helene's."

"Your ex-wife?"

He didn't know any other Helenes, and neither did she. "Yes. I don't know if they're still friends. I haven't talked to Heather since before the divorce. She moved away, and I never gave her another thought."

Her body softened slightly, still rigid, but less pissed off. When Jonas had first introduced Sabrina to his friends and family, more than one of them had remarked on her resemblance to his ex-wife, and they'd said it to her face. Sabrina hadn't liked the comparison, and Jonas hadn't cared for it either. While they shared the same basic attributes, height, and coloring, they were nothing alike, either physically or in their personalities. Sabrina was a goddess, so no real comparison could be made.

"Didn't you recognize her when we got here?"

She wanted to know why he hadn't said something to her earlier. He could have, but it didn't seem relevant. This was their honeymoon. Nobody else mattered. "Yes, but she didn't seem to recognize me. It wasn't important for me to jog her memory, so I let it go. I realized last night that she knew who I was." Heather had pretty much goaded him with that smug, knowing look. She hadn't bothered to even pretend to consider any of the volunteers.

Now the fight went out of her. She slumped against him. "So you didn't prearrange that whole scene at the bonfire?"

"No, but it was damn hot."

She snorted at his pun. "Why did she choose you?"

He held her gently now, rubbing his hands up and down her arms in a soothing caress. "I think she was looking for a reliable volunteer, one who knew what they were doing and wouldn't need much guidance. It made her job easier. I was a means to an end. She must be truly desperate to ask me for advice."

For the first time, it occurred to him that Heather had felt safe in asking him because she bought into his ex-wife's deeply held belief that Jonas lacked ambition. Heather knew he wouldn't make a play for her job or try to usurp her authority. That sentiment wasn't true. He had plenty of drive. He just hadn't wanted the same things his ex-wife had wanted.

Sabrina turned in his arms. As if she knew what disturbing conclusions he'd drawn, she touched her fingertips lightly to his cheek in a tender caress. "She knows she can trust you. You have a strong moral compass, and that's apparent no matter how well or how little somebody knows you. It's one of the things that makes you so good at everything you do."

Instantly his resolve to punish her melted. This was the reason he didn't identify too well with the title of "Master." He knew how to take care of his submissive. He knew how to bring emotional and physical fulfillment to the woman kneeling at his feet, but he had no driving need to have anyone, much less his wife, falling to her knees at the sight of him. While he'd asked her to submit to him for the next three days, he didn't expect her to behave this way for the remainder of their marriage. He appreciated knowing her opinion, and he liked the way they'd divided the leadership roles in the house.

But lately he'd come to suspect that Sabrina needed more than what he was giving her. These five nights were as much a test of him as they were of her. The balance they'd once established wasn't going to work anymore, and he aimed to return home knowing exactly what she needed to be his happy wife.

He inhaled the sweet scent of her hair, noting how the aroma of grass and flowers now mingled with the perfume that was uniquely her. Then he released her from his hold. She hadn't disagreed that she'd earned a punishment, and now it was time to keep his word.

"Punishment time, honey. You can't growl at me and hurl unfounded accusations. If you have questions, you know I'm always open to having you just ask them. Remove your clothes and get on your knees." Perhaps he was explaining too much, but he figured he had to treat her as if she were new to the concept, if only because she was new to the idea of being punished.

Her lips parted as she stared at him. He knew gears were turning in her brain, trying to figure out if he was serious. Once she came to a conclusion about that, he waited for her to figure out whether or not she could accept this amendment to the role of submissive. While she'd played in the past, he was asking for the real thing now.

With a somber light in her dark eyes, she lifted her dress over her head and kicked off her sandals. When she knelt before him with all the natural grace and beauty in her arsenal, he was nearly undone. His instinct had been correct. She wanted this. Maybe this was why she asked to be spanked so often in their scenes. She subconsciously craved a real punishment. He'd known for years that she liked to be flogged until she reached subspace, but he hadn't known she wanted to remain mentally present.

While he circled her body slowly, drawing attention to her complete lack of power, he searched his memory, trying to pinpoint when the shift might have occurred, but he failed. She was simply too fascinating for his attention to wander elsewhere.

Standing behind her, he gathered her hair in his hands. She shivered and inhaled sharply. Part of the reason she wore it up so often was because having it down made her aware of her sensuality and her vulnerability. Forcing her to wear it down stripped away layers of protections that separated her from the outside world. Knowing these little things about her made all the difference.

As strands of her hair cascaded through his fingers, he decided it didn't matter when she began needing to be punished. It most likely had been a gradual thing, much as his need to have her submission. Now that he was aware of her need, he would make sure it was met. Tomorrow he'd take her to the Fields of Punishment to see how much she could take. Today, he'd keep her punishment private.

"Get on your hands and knees. Spread your legs as wide as your shoulders. Turn your hands so your fingers point in at a forty-five degree angle. That will help keep them from slipping out from under you."

In one fluid movement, she achieved the exact position he wanted. He'd watched her dive before, and she used the same grace here.

"Arch your back. Deeper. Like that. Hold that position no matter what."

It would be challenging to hold it, especially after he started the punishment, but he knew she would do her best. Sabrina greeted all trials head-on, and she never gave up. The fact they were still together attested to that. She'd kept her faith in him that first year when he hadn't given her a reason to do so.

He admired the view of her naked body and her vulnerable position before he crossed the room to the large armoire situated between the doors to the main bathroom and the bedroom. The room came equipped with everything. He tugged open a drawer and rummaged around for a suitable paddle. Various shapes and sizes filled the space. Some had words cut out so that they'd leave an untouched imprint in the midst of the red mark. Most were leather. A few were made from rubber.

He chose one that packed more noise than sting. He knew she could take quite a beating. Subspace wasn't the goal tonight.

By the time he returned, her body was strung tight. Bending down, he ran a finger down one of her luscious cheeks. She flinched. He chuckled. "Relax, honey. This will be different. Make no mistake about that. You spoke disrespectfully to me, and I will not put up with that. You're a better woman than one who resorts to bitchiness and wild accusations. Tell me how many you deserve."

She inhaled with controlled steadiness. "Ten."

He would have accepted seven or eight. It was her first punishment and her behavior had been uncharacteristic. "Ten it is. Count and thank me for each one."

Standing behind her had some drawbacks, but knowing her so well made up for that. "Two more for rolling your eyes."

When she didn't argue, he knew he'd guessed correctly. He swung hard. The sharp crack echoed off the floor tiles.

"One. Thank you."

She'd altered her posture. He realigned everything before continuing. If they had been playing, he would have drawn it out, increased the sexual tension. She counted out all twelve. By the time he finished, she quivered with the effort it cost to remain on her hands and knees. It wasn't a position she was used to assuming.

"Drop down. Rest your ass on your feet, your cheek on the floor, and put your arms back along the floor so your hands are near your feet." It was a good resting pose, and it would keep her in a submissive position, give her some time to think about what she'd done and how he'd reacted.

He set the paddle on the island dividing the gourmet kitchen from the living room. Tomorrow night, he decided, he'd make dinner for the two of them. If they were still there. He couldn't imagine how Heather would be able to make travel arrangements for all the guests and workers on the island.

Because she was unbound and on the floor, he left her alone while he went to brush his teeth. They'd spent the day trail riding and he was beat. He estimated five minutes before he returned to find her exactly where he'd left her.

He crouched down and put his hands on her hips. "I'm going to help you up. You need to tell me if anything's fallen asleep."

With his guidance, she rose slowly to her feet. She rolled her shoulders and flexed her feet. "I'm fine."

"How's your ass?"

A deep, delicious red crept up her neck and blossomed on her cheeks. Her gaze fastened on a point somewhere near his belly button. "It's fine. You've spanked me harder with your bare hand."

Using one finger, he lifted her chin until she met his eyes. "What did you think of your punishment?"

Pressed against his finger, he felt her chin tremble. "I hated it."

That much, he knew. "Why?"

"Mostly because I didn't like the fact I let you down. I was bitchy to you, and you didn't deserve it. Being punished wasn't the bad part. The fact that you had to punish me was the worst."

A tear glistened at the corner of one eye. He waited for it to fall so he could wipe it away. "Now that you've been punished, the matter is resolved."

Hopefully that would allow her to let it go. He didn't want another apology or to have to issue additional assurances. Sabrina carried too much guilt for things that didn't matter all that much to anyone else.

She nodded, a stilted movement. He didn't push the matter. She needed time to process what had happened.

"Go get ready for bed. It's been a long day."

* * * *

Sabrina lay awake in the dark. Sounds of the sea drifted through the slider they'd left open to let in the soft trade winds and their soothing breeze. A glance at Jonas showed that he was crashed. The last two days had been physically and emotionally exhausting. She understood that he was trying to push their relationship to a deeper level. She wanted the same thing, only she didn't know if his methods would work.

When he'd first brought up the idea of being submissive, she had agreed because she trusted him. While she didn't regret her decision, she'd be lying if she said she completely understood her reaction to total submission. She also didn't know if Jonas allowing her to have an actual conversation with Mistress Hera as an equal qualified as a submissive activity.

Gently, she shoved aside the soft sheet and slid from bed. One of Jonas's chain store cotton shirts was draped over a chair nearby. She slipped it over her head and went out to the balcony. With the questions whirling in her head, she wasn't going to get much sleep.

She paced to the other side of the balcony. It ran the length of their suite, so she didn't worry about disturbing Jonas. Her mind raced as she stopped at the railing and gripped the edge. Above her, the Milky Way spun in the infinite space, dwarfing her problems, but not diminishing them.

Two years ago, her sister Ginny had talked her into taking yoga classes. Sabrina had enjoyed it and Jonas had been supportive, but between work and spending time with her family, there had been little time to continue practicing. She'd taken to using the breathing exercises when she needed a moment alone to relax.

At her core, Sabrina was one of those people who stressed about everything. If she tackled a project, she made sure it ended up a model of perfection. When they'd first married, Jonas had taught her how to take a step back and trust other people to live up to her expectations. It freed up a lot of her time, but it hadn't changed the fact that she was an obsessive perfectionist.

Snapping at Jonas had been a very low moment. It wasn't the first time she'd gone off on him. He'd spent years goading her into losing her temper as a way to relieve stress. When that didn't work, and it frequently didn't, he would strap her to a spanking bench or the St. Andrew's cross and flog her until she broke.

She needed a good session on a pretty regular basis, and Jonas had been wonderful about giving her what she needed. While she didn't think he wanted to have fewer sessions with her, she did feel his frustration that they were almost always just to help her relax. It put a lot of pressure on him. He didn't seem to mind, but she sensed that he wanted to find other ways to achieve the same results.

Did she like being submissive? That was a difficult question to answer. She'd played the part in scenes, which she loved to do, and she was always submissive sexually. It was a formula that had worked well for them for the past five years.

And this was a vacation. How would being submissive work once they returned home? She had kids to consider now. Would seeing this different dynamic make them think women were lesser than men?

Pressure throbbed at her temples. As she rubbed them, she realized she'd let Jonas open up a clown car. It seemed so simple and compact, but one problem after another poured forth. Each of them brought more stress.

So she switched her strategy. Instead of thinking about the problems, she thought about what she got out of it. Being punished had been a little on the humiliating side. If she didn't love and trust Jonas so much, she never would have been able to accept the spanking. Compared to much of the impact play in which they'd engaged, the spanking had been nothing. Though the smacks had resounded from the tile in the room, she'd barely felt them. The horse had done more damage to her rear end than that rubber paddle had.

Of course, that was the point. Jonas had known the humiliation aspect would be the worst part of it for her. He hadn't felt the need for lasting physical punishment. Given the fact that she was a strong, opinionated woman in charge of multibillion-dollar marketing campaigns and a host of employees, she would have thought she would revolt at the idea of being a real submissive.

But that hadn't been an issue at all. In fact, the punishment had absolved her of all the guilt she would have felt if she'd simply apologized. That simple act, one she didn't have a problem performing, had never been enough. The way she beat herself up over those things definitely annoyed the hell out of Jonas.

One issue had been satisfactorily resolved. The others required more time and experience. She still had three submissive days left before their scheduled talk.

Since she still couldn't sleep, she sat on one of the cushioned wicker chairs and stared at the sky. If she were a few inches taller, she could stare at the ocean. Given how the stars stole her breath, she couldn't mourn the loss. Due to light pollution, this kind of clarity was only available when they visited the Lake Michigan sand dunes.

As she sat there, her mind cleared, and she realized that talking to the bank manager wasn't going to get Heather anywhere. If the accounts had been frozen, then there was nothing a manager could do.

After a quick trip to the kitchen to grab her tablet, she settled back on the chair and called Ellen. Jonas's best friend owned an upscale BDSM dungeon and the attached dance club. She might be able to shed a little light on the issue.

Ellen appeared on the screen fairly quickly. In the background, the room was dimly lit and Ellen's hair was a mess.

Sabrina covered her mouth with her hand. It was the middle of the night. Ellen and her husband, Ryan, were probably asleep. Or they had been. "I'm sorry. I didn't realize how late it is."

The pretty brunette laughed. "That's okay. We weren't sleeping. What's wrong?"

The fact that Jonas's friend was so good at reading her had initially disconcerted Sabrina. Eventually they'd developed a close friendship. She trusted Ellen implicitly.

She tried to smile, but it came out tired and a little sad. "It's that obvious?"

"You look a little worse for the wear, and not in a sated, good kind of way."

Sabrina took a deep breath. Heather had confided in them, but Sabrina hadn't promised anything except to listen. "It turns out the woman who runs Elysium is an old friend of Jonas's." She left out any mention of Helene. Just the name could set Ellen on a tirade. It made Sabrina feel a little better to know that Jonas's friends and family liked her much better than his first wife.

Ellen lifted a dark brow. "Oh?"

Shaking her head, Sabrina said, "That's not why I called. The owners of this place are in the middle of a nasty divorce. They've frozen all the bank accounts. There's an island full of guests, and no way to pay the workers."

"Or the bills." Ellen snorted. "I bet there was infidelity. I've met the owners a few times. They were both sluts. It doesn't surprise me that they'd screw over their entire staff like that."

Ellen looked over at something out of frame for a second. Her cynical smile disappeared, morphing into something tender and predatory. Sabrina realized why Ellen's hair was so messy. She probably had Ryan tied up and gagged. It was probably best to conclude the call.

"I was just wondering what kind of advice we could offer Heather about how to manage this mess."

Ellen's attention snapped back to the screen. "Heather McDougall? Tall, black, and beautiful? A Dominatrix?"

Sabrina nodded. "She's going by Mistress Hera here."

Ellen pushed a strand of hair behind her ear and grinned. "God I miss her. After Jonas trained her, she became one of my best. Then she left to work at a resort in France and we lost touch."

Now that she'd realized what was likely going on where she couldn't see, she wanted to get off the phone. If she were tied up in bed or anywhere else, she wouldn't be too happy if Jonas stopped to have a conversation. She tried to prod Ellen. "There's nothing she can do, is there?"

Ellen pursed her lips. "Let me think about it. I'll call you back in the morning. Not too early though. The kids are spending the night at Ryan's parents, so we're sleeping in."

Sabrina nodded. "Thanks, Elle. I appreciate it." She pushed the button to end the call.

"What're you doing out here?"

Sabrina's heart raced. She felt like a naughty child who'd stolen an extra cookie and snuck outside to eat it only to find the law waiting. She put a hand on her chest as if that would slow the thumping there and looked up at Jonas, who wore only the boxer briefs he'd had on when he'd fallen into bed. The dim starlight glinted from the ripples of his well-defined chest. When he looked that good, there was no hope for her heart rate.

"I couldn't sleep."

He held a hand out to her. She rose from the chair and went to him. The idea of refusing never crossed her mind. He pulled her into his arms and pressed a kiss to the top of her head. "You're worried about what?"

Because she wasn't close to figuring out all the issues she had and she had no idea how to resolve anything, she chose not to talk about that. "I asked Ellen if she had any ideas for helping Heather. I realized the bank manager won't be able to help."

His arms tightened around her for a second before he steered her through the door to the bedroom. The screen closed automatically. She set the tablet on an accent table as she continued to the bed.

Jonas settled in next to her, wrapping his body around hers in an unyielding snuggle. "There might not be anything we can do to help. Heather has connections. She can always find another job."

"I know. I just…She had to be desperate to ask us for help."

He nuzzled her neck. "Are you sure something else isn't bothering you?"

"Maybe," she said. With his arms around her, the tension was already draining from her body. "I'm not ready to talk about it yet. We agreed on Friday."

"We did. But that doesn't mean we have to wait until Friday. If you want to talk, honey, that can happen at any time."

She hugged his arms. "Just hold me until I fall asleep."

"Try to stop me."

Chapter Six

Ellen set the tablet facedown on the dresser next to her favorite flogger. When it hit the target, the black falls parted to reveal red ones. She had a thing for red. Not only did she look damn good in red clothing, her handsome husband was a redhead, and his fair skin bore the marks of the lash so well.

She shot him a look that used to be unreadable. Having been together for twenty years, there was no such thing as unreadable anymore. He was so in tune with her that he could interpret the smallest change in her breathing.

He watched her carefully, just as she'd trained him to do. She checked the cuffs binding his wrists and ankles to each post of their extra-sturdy bed. Ryan sometimes fought the restraints, especially when things got extra fun.

He followed her around the bed with just his pale blue eyes. The red ball gag in his mouth kept him from voicing the questions she knew he had about the call. Sabrina wasn't one to call late at night, and the fact that she'd called halfway through her anniversary trip to Elysium was troubling.

She and Ryan had visited the place almost two decades earlier for their honeymoon, and they'd bragged about it to Jonas ever since. They knew firsthand the wonderful amenities the resort offered. Sabrina should have been too blissfully sated to worry about anything else.

Drawing a fingernail over his scrotum, she checked his color. Earlier she'd put a double cock ring on him. One steel loop went around his balls, and the other restricted his cock.

"She's okay. I saw Jonas hovering in the background when we were finishing up. He'll take care of her." She picked up the leather riding crop. This was also red.

Ryan relaxed the slightest bit at her assurance. Even before she'd refused Jonas's gift, Ryan had predicted that Sabrina would have problems at Elysium. For years he'd maintained that she was more submissive than she was comfortable admitting. He was on the fence about whether or not he thought Jonas should force the issue. Ellen was of the opinion that Sabrina could handle it.

She drew the edge of the flap along his chest lightly before bringing it down hard on his nipple. His back arched off the bed, and he cried out behind the gag. She skimmed it across his pecs and ribs, over his lightly tanned stomach, and down his thigh where she administered another sharp blow. Back and forth, she peppered his chest and inner thighs with taps both sharp and dull. Not knowing which to expect drove him out of his mind. He flinched and writhed, moaning and pleading behind the gag.

When her target areas had turned a nice, hot shade of red, she set the crop aside and reached for the double pinwheel. She liked this instrument. It looked like a set of spiked balls with a skinny cock protruding from it that functioned as the handle.

Ryan's eyes widened and his entire body quivered with anticipation. She'd ensured that his endorphin level was sufficiently high. He was up for almost anything.

She started with the bottoms of his feet. She'd read somewhere that the feet were the sensory pathway to the entire body. It had taken scientists years to figure out what the S/M community already knew. She set the pins against his most vulnerable place, the arch, and rolled the balls up and down. Ryan's cock, already purpled and standing at attention, seemed to flex as if it was waving at her in an attempt to entice her closer.

As she experimented with pressures, increasing where his sole was tougher, his moans turned to whimpers. He tried to move his feet, to escape stimulation, but the restraints held firm. When she thought he'd taken all he could, she moved up his body, finding the extra-sensitive places on his ankles, calves, the insides of his knees. She even drew it over his scrotum and leaned down to lick the drop of moisture beading at the tip of his cock before heading to the underside of his arms.

By the time she finished that exquisite torture, his entire body trembled with need. She unbuckled the straps for the gag and popped it out of his mouth. The sharp tear of Velcro rent the room as she released him from the cuffs. Though his muscles were tense, giving him the appearance of a catlike predator, he knew better than to pounce without permission. Sometimes she gave him his head and let him do as he wished. This wasn't one of those times.

She undressed slowly, first loosening the tight red corset that plumped her breasts—Ryan was unequivocally a breast man—and reined in some of the extra curviness he seemed to like way more than she did. When she removed her black lace panties, he licked his lips, and she realized he wanted a taste of her.

Climbing onto the bed, she pushed at his hip. "Kneel at the end of the bed. I'm going to come in your mouth."

"Yes, Mistress." Desire, fevered and hot, gleamed from his eyes, and his voice dropped to such a low baritone that it was more vibration than sound. He scrambled to follow her command, his ringed cock bobbing and bowing as he moved. She didn't worry about cutting off his circulation. He was very good about telling her if it got to be too much.

She spread her legs slowly, knowing he would wait on his knees, watching her cunt until she gave him the signal. Ever the tease, she circled her clit with her fingertip, spreading her cream and masturbating a little. Ryan's fists clenched on his thighs. He wanted to be the one who made her climax. It was a responsibility he took very seriously.

Sitting up suddenly, she offered him her finger. His lips closed around the digit, sucking hard as his tongue wrapped around it. For the first time that night, he took his eyes from her. They closed, and his face shone with the same ecstasy he displayed after a thorough flogging.

Ripping her finger from his mouth, she pulled him to her and crushed his lips with a dominating and possessive kiss. Then she pushed his head down between her legs and settled back against the pillows. His hot tongue worked her clit, circling and crossing the bundle of nerves before heading down to fuck itself into her hole. He put a hand on her inner thigh, urging her wider to allow him more access.

She obliged, and he buried his face in her pussy, no doubt half-suffocating himself. He easily took her to that place of bliss, but he didn't stop licking until she yanked hard on his hair.

Even then he only lifted his face to gaze at her with a questioning eyebrow lifted. He was a marathon pussy-eater. Once he settled in for the feast, she had to force him to stop. That option had come pre-programmed into his psyche.

"Now fuck me."

"Yes, Mistress."

He entered her carefully. Once he was fully seated, she raked her nails across his back. Earlier she'd flogged his back and caned his ass. By the time she'd finished, his back was a beautiful mass of red marks. One thing she loved about his fair skin was the way it kept the evidence for so long. Marks that might fade in several hours on somebody else were often still around the next morning on Ryan. He was inordinately proud of that fact.

He froze, a tremor running from head to toe. She had originally planned to make him come without permission so she could discipline him, but after that phone call, she knew he wanted to know the details. His caring and compassionate nature was one of the reasons she'd married him.

"Start slow. I want at least two orgasms before you come."

"Yes, Mistress. Can I touch you?"

His weight rested on his hands so that he hovered above her. She treated his chest to the sharpness of her nails. "After you make me come."

He took her up that cliff slowly, varying his pace so that he could last longer, which not only drew it out for her, but it made the climax that much more intense. Though she'd banned him from touching her, she hadn't restricted herself.

Ryan had a magnificent body, tall and lean and strong. Every other month, she made him get a full-body wax just so she could better see the results of her efforts. She caressed his body, raking him with her nails and pinching the light welts on his ass. He whimpered and panted, trying to control the way the pain magnified his passion.

"You're doing beautifully, darling. Now go faster and harder."

He obeyed. Tight coils of passion low in her abdomen were suddenly too much to bear. She gave in and let the climax take her. Immediately Ryan's hands and mouth were on her. He kissed her neck and nibbled at her lips. She couldn't form words in this most vulnerable state. He was taking advantage of her momentary senselessness, but he'd asked first, so there would be no punishment.

He touched her breasts, palming them easily in his large hands. Every few thrusts he dipped his head down and took one nipple gently between his lips and flicked his tongue across the sensitive peak. The light strokes drove her insane, and she came again before she was fully recovered from the first orgasm.

Ryan followed her seconds later, his entire body shuddering as he lost his rhythm and buried his cock deep. He turned to the side and collapsed next to her with his head on her stomach. He held her close with one arm across her legs.

With the last vestiges of her energy, she twisted her body so she could reach his cock ring. Slick with her juices, it came off easily. She tossed it onto the bedside table and lay back down to enjoy the sea of serotonin flowing through her bloodstream.

She was nearly asleep when Ryan spoke. "That was incredible, Mistress. I love you so much."

Using sheer will, she lifted her hand and rested it on his shoulder. If possible, he melted into her even more. "I love you, too."

"Did Sabrina say what she was really worried about?"

"No. She told me that Heather was managing Elysium now. The owners are getting divorced. All the assets, including the resort's bank accounts, are frozen. Heather asked Jonas for advice."

Ryan caressed her leg. "I'm glad she's not insecure about Helene anymore. Jonas was right, you know. She looks nothing like her."

Ellen wasn't blind to the resemblance, but it had ceased to matter. "No, she's much better looking."

His forays expanded the tiniest bit. "I think you should buy Elysium."

All lethargy fled her body. "What?"

"You've always dreamed of owning a resort. It's an established business with a huge clientele. I bet the Mehlbergs will be looking to sell, so we can negotiate a good price."

The club her parents had left her when they'd passed away was completely paid off. As long as she kept it profitable, she made a good salary. Even if they sold everything, they wouldn't make enough money for a down payment on Elysium.

"We can't afford it."

He pressed a kiss just below her belly button, at about the place where she had a C-section scar. "Sure we can, if you go in on it with Sophia and Sabrina. You can be in charge of running the place, Sabrina can handle advertising, and Sophia can take care of the accounting."

"We have kids. It's not a place to take a three- and six-year-old."

His lips moved a little lower and his hand moved a little higher. "Lots of islands nearby. We can buy a huge house for us all to use. The kids will stay there when we visit the business."

She grabbed a fistful of his hair and yanked him up until his face was level with hers. "How long have you been thinking about this?"

He looked off to the side, calculating or searching for information. "Almost twenty years. The moment you told me you wanted to buy the place, which was the second day of our honeymoon, I started trying to figure out how to make it happen."

She kissed him hard, thrusting her tongue into his mouth, and she rolled him onto his back. By the time she straddled him, his cock was hard and ready. "I'll call Sophia tomorrow. You can see if your sister or your parents will watch the kids. And then book our flight."

He held his cock at her entrance. She sank down and leaned forward, resting her weight on his chest and achieving the angle she liked. What he proposed wasn't going to be easy. The situation was already messy. But Ryan was in her corner, her cheerleader and her rock. With his support, she could achieve anything.

She rode him hard, and they came together.

Chapter Seven

They took a windsurfing class that morning, and Sabrina surprised Jonas with her instant success.

"You've done this before."

He stood on the shore, his hands curled in relaxed fists at his sides. A cool breeze blew in from the east, making his shirt and loose swim shorts ripple across his body.

She leaned back and changed direction to steer the board to shore nearby. As she beached it, he reached out to help her but changed trajectory at the last minute. He snagged her at the hips and lifted her against him. His clothes were wet, evidence that this was his first time windsurfing. He'd fallen into the water repeatedly.

"A few times," she admitted. Though it had been a few years, she found it was like riding a bicycle. "It's fun."

He looked so disappointed at the fact he hadn't shown her something new that she gripped his shoulders to keep him close. "I've never been parasailing."

"Great. I'll schedule it for tomorrow. I hadn't decided between that and snorkeling. I assume you've been snorkeling before?"

She nodded. "But I'd like to go again if that's what you prefer to do."

He touched his lips to hers, but he didn't kiss her. "Spoken like a true submissive. You're getting the hang of this very quickly, Sabrina. I'm proud of you."

Confused, she drew her eyebrows together and tilted her head back to put some space between them. She hadn't felt like she'd given anything up. "That wasn't submissive. That was an honest statement."

He smiled softly, his face filled with love and affection. "Honey, that's what makes it real submission. You didn't say it simply to please me or make me happy. You actually want to please me. Deep down. In here." He tapped just above her left breast.

Yes, she did. She gained a vital pleasure from making him happy. "That's because I love you. You're just as willing to do things to make me happy. Does that make you submissive, too?"

Jonas shook his head. "I still make the decisions. You abide by them. It's working very well for us."

The decisions he'd been making weren't ones she wanted to argue with. He'd chosen fun activities for them so far, and she derived most of her pleasure from his happiness. An edge of awareness hovered just out of reach. She wanted to chase it, but Jonas demanded her attention.

"I do like when you make decisions." When left up to her, Sabrina often spent far too much time pondering anything. She stressed over which option was right. If he'd asked her to choose between parasailing and snorkeling—he hadn't—she would have constantly doubted her decision, even after they'd gone and had a great time.

He hugged her closer. "I know."

"But I don't consider that submission. If I don't like a decision you've made, I have no problem telling you so. I do have opinions." Strong ones. Right now, the way he'd pressed his pelvis to her stomach, she could feel his erection growing, and she really wanted to make him come. It was an empowering, heady sensation to know she affected him so strongly.

He stroked a hand down her spine. "But you'll still abide by my choice. You are allowed to disagree with me, just in a respectful manner and not in front of other people. I also frown upon arguing. Resistance will be dealt with appropriately."

Had he just threatened to spank her for arguing with him? The humiliation of her punishment the night before was still fresh in her mind. That feeling lingered though the guilt had gone. She wasn't sure she liked it much better, mostly because she couldn't decide how to feel about it.

She ran a finger just above the collar of his shirt. "You're the one who taught me how to argue with you. There was a point when I was neither comfortable doing so nor good at it."

From the start, he'd been able to fluster her rather easily. He got under her skin the way no man ever had. And he'd goaded her into overcoming that lack of confidence.

He lifted half of his mouth in a crooked smile. "Double-edged sword. I don't want you to be docile, honey. Just submissive."

And she didn't understand the distinction. There didn't seem to be one. Before she could ask, he captured her lips for a probing kiss that seemed to last forever. She melted under this gentle domination. He stole her breath and made her a creature willing to do whatever he wanted.

He ground his cock against her, right there in the middle of the beach. To the right, sunbathers were treated to the display. To the left, other windsurfers could watch the show. Sabrina knew her husband well enough to understand that he would take full advantage of the pro-exhibitionist environment at Elysium.

She'd never understood why people witnessing them have sex made him so hot. She couldn't count the number of times he'd tied her to something and made her watch while he masturbated. He was a bona fide tease, but he'd made her realize she was more of a voyeur. By the time he finished, she was always wet and wanting.

In a bold move, she tugged at his swim shorts and lifted out his cock. She cupped his balls as he thrust his silky steel into her hand.

At long last, he broke the kiss to nibble on her lips. "You little vixen. You want my cock, don't you?"

"Yes." She arched her back, pressing her chest against him and offering the sensitive places on her neck. "I want your cock."

He thrust slowly, savoring both the feeling and the attention. "Where?"

"My mouth." She didn't hesitate. Not only did she not want to take her clothes off on this bright, sunlit beach, she truly wanted to give him satisfaction. This wasn't about her. This was about pleasing him.

"Get on your knees."

She dropped and stared at his hardness as she awaited his instructions. Jonas had a magnificent cock. It was both thick and long, but not too much of either. He filled her perfectly, a predestined biological fit. Desire had turned him dark red, and that purple vein pulsed, an invitation she had a hard time ignoring.

"Use your hands and your mouth. Show me how much you love to please me." In true Jonas fashion, he managed to deliver his order in an affectionate and appreciative tone.

Love suffused her heart. She swirled her tongue around the sensitive line of his crown, treating herself to that pearly bead at the tip, and then she traced the sensitive line down the underside of his cock. By the time she gripped his base with one hand and hefted the soft weight of his balls with the other, she'd wrung a series of moans and groans from him. His sounds of pleasure drifted about her head like a symphony of bliss.

She took her time urging him up the side of that cliff and slowing down when he got close. Not only would his orgasm end up being bigger this way, it drew out the show. They'd attracted a crowd, and she knew how much that fed his excitement.

From time to time, she opened her eyes to find that even more men on the beach were enjoying having their cocks sucked as they watched. A few women balanced by throwing a leg over their submissives' shoulders to better grind their pussies against their subs' faces. It seemed Jonas had spawned an outbreak. Sabrina was determined to outperform every other sub on the beach.

She played for a long time. Jonas tapped her shoulder, his signal that he wanted her to finish him. With a small mew of protest, she quickened her pace. At the right time, she gave his balls a little twist.

He shouted and buried his cock so deeply in her mouth that she had to relax and swallow convulsively to avoid gagging.

Sitting back on her heels, she let him have a few moments to recover. He gazed down at her with bleary satisfaction clouding his emerald irises.

They held hands as they walked along the beach, enjoying the view of the endless water and the epidemic of oral sex they'd set off on the sand. Sabrina pointed to a pair. The submissive was on her hands and knees, and her Dom knelt to fuck her mouth. "Look at how you inspire people everywhere you go."

Jonas laughed and caught her up in his arms. He swung her in circles, kissing her face and neck and biting at her breasts through her swimsuit. She couldn't remember the last time she'd felt so joyous and carefree. The kids were in good hands—Jonas made sure to call them every morning and every evening—and so was she. Part of her wanted this feeling to never end.

When he set her down, they leaned on each other for support until the world stopped spinning. She buried her face in his chest and luxuriated in having his arms around her.

"Mr. Spencer?"

Jonas lifted his head from where he'd been resting it on top of hers. "Yes?"

Sabrina opened her eyes to see a resort employee waiting unobtrusively several feet away. He wore the requisite bright, patterned shirt and khaki shorts.

"Sir, Mistress Hera invites you and your submissive to join her for a private lunch."

Ellen hadn't yet called back with advice. Sabrina didn't know what to tell Heather. It was a sad situation, one that was out of her wheelhouse. If Ellen didn't come through, Sabrina would contact her stepbrothers. They were geniuses when it came to business ventures.

She glanced up at Jonas to see he was wearing his stoic expression. That meant he didn't want to have lunch with Heather, but he felt he had no choice. It was interesting how she could read what used to be an unreadable expression. She hugged him a little tighter, letting him know she understood his dilemma.

"Give us about an hour or so," Jonas said. "Where would Mistress Hera like to meet?"

"In her private apartment, Sir. I will give her your message." With that, the young man bowed slightly and backed away.

With his hand on her waist, he turned her in the direction of their suite. "I know you want to wash the salt off your skin. We'll shower and I'll pick out something pretty for you to wear."

She wanted to call Ellen, but she didn't think her friend would have stumbled upon a solution so quickly. She'd been occupied with other activities last night, and Sabrina was well versed with Ellen's single-mindedness.

"I want to call Alexei and Stefano. They have more experience with these kinds of ventures. I bet they'd have a better idea of what Heather should do." She looked up at Jonas to gauge his reaction. His relationship with her stepbrothers was complicated by the fact they were involved with Jonas's younger sister.

Lex and Stef were very possessive of Samantha, even around her own family, and that sometimes created sticky situations. It wasn't that they prohibited her from interacting with them, just that either one or the both of them were constantly at her side, holding her hand or playing with her hair or just looking at her. Sabrina knew them well enough to know they were still in shock over falling in love and settling down, but Jonas didn't always buy that interpretation.

Jonas nodded, but his mind seemed to be elsewhere. "Shower first."

Ten minutes later, Sabrina found herself alone in the shower. Somehow when he'd said they were going to shower, she thought he meant they would do it together. The tile structure was certainly large enough. It featured four shower heads on three walls and eight additional, adjustable spigots located at various heights.

Disappointed, she soaped up and washed the salt from her skin. When she was rinsing the last of the suds, she heard him enter the bathroom. The door slid open, and he stepped inside. She waited, uncertain as to whether he wanted her to remain in the shower or get dressed. After blowing him on the beach, she thought he would want to reward her with an orgasm or two. He didn't usually take without giving.

"Kneel." He pointed to a place at the side of the stall.

Because she hadn't fallen from her board, she hadn't washed her hair. It was up on top of her head where it wouldn't get wet while she cleaned her skin. If she knelt where he indicated, she would be in line with one of the lower spigots, and it would soak her hair.

Reluctantly, she obeyed his order. Jonas watched her get into place, flickers of amusement playing over his changeable eyes. He reached over her and twisted the nozzle to halt the flow of water. She smiled up at him, a little awed by how well he knew her. "Thank you."

He stood under the warm spray, letting it cascade down his head. She watched the stream of water contour to his neck and ripple across his well-defined shoulders. Following the flow downward, she admired his tight ass.

"Spread your knees a little more and link your fingers together behind your neck."

He hadn't looked at her to give the command, and he didn't glance down to see if she followed orders. Of course she did, but what good was it to follow orders when he wasn't paying attention? She pouted a little bit.

"Ellen hasn't called. I checked your messages and mine. I tried getting hold of her, but she didn't answer."

Sabrina didn't know if kneeling submissives were allowed to talk, but this was the kind of normal conversation they had when she was putting on makeup and he was getting ready for work. She took a chance. "That's unusual. She answered last night even though it was late and she and Ryan were in the middle of a scene."

Jonas chuckled. "Did you see the scene, or did she keep the camera turned away?" He turned to face her, one eyebrow arched.

She'd seen snatches of their play, and it always left her blushing. Sometimes when they visited, particularly when the kids weren't around, Ryan would kneel at Ellen's feet and call her "Mistress." During those times, he often wore a leather collar. It looked kind of sexy.

For the first time she realized they hadn't been playing. That's how they normally behaved. They just toned it down for company and kids.

That was what Jonas wanted from her.

He might not want to be called "Master," but he wanted to be regarded the same way and treated with the same reverence. And he waited for her answer.

She shook her head. "I realized what they were doing when I noticed that Ellen's hair was messed up and she was wearing a leather outfit. I tried to hurry the conversation. Who knows what she'd done to Ryan."

Jonas went back to washing his hair. "Nothing he didn't want or need. Or both." He rinsed his hair and then turned off the water. He shook the water from his head and held out a hand to her.

She rose to her feet slowly. Experience had taught her that her joints would be a little stiff and her knees a little tender, but those feelings diminished quickly as long as she was careful. Jonas never made her kneel for very long, so it worked out.

He toweled her dry slowly before seeing to himself. She didn't bother to dress. The fire he'd ignited in her on the beach still smoldered inside, and the erection he'd grown upon entering the shower pointed in her direction. She hoped he planned to satisfy them both.

The kiss was tender. Though she melted into him, pressing her breasts against his warm, damp chest, she detected no hint that he might unleash some of that passion soon.

He broke away to rain kisses over her cheeks and eyelids. "That's what I want with you, Sabrina." He grazed his lips across her eyebrows. "I want to give you what you want, and what you need." He peppered her mouth with tiny smooches. "Role-playing isn't enough for you, not anymore." Now he moved to her neck, caressing the sensitive skin there with his firm lips. "Between work and home, you're stretched too thin. Some nights I worry that you're going to snap."

Some nights she had the same concern, but she always managed to maintain her temper. She'd never say this out loud, but she'd even considered quitting her job or going part time until the kids were in school. Her mother had stayed home with her and Ginny, but Sabrina couldn't shake the feeling that she'd be giving up on her dreams. Had her priorities shifted so much that her dreams were no longer that important? She couldn't decide, but she didn't feel that Jonas should decide that for her.

Too much whirled through her mind, and his loving attention drove away those thoughts. This was what she needed, to let go and trust that he'd catch her.

"Jonas?"

He paused on his way to her breasts. "Hmm?"

"The night you gave me the plane tickets, did you intend to cane me?" He'd massaged the tenseness right out of her muscles, but it hadn't been enough.

Lifting his head, he speared her with his tawny gaze. "I wanted to. If I had, you probably wouldn't have been so on edge the next day. I want you to learn to put yourself and your worries in my hands, trust that I'll make sure you get what you need, even if it's not what you want."

She hadn't wanted a caning because she knew it would break down too many barriers, and she hadn't wanted to expose herself to that vulnerability. "You're asking a lot. I don't know if I can do that."

"I know it's a lot, but I also know you're strong enough to do it."

The deal had been five days. It had been only three, and he was already talking about implementing this change to their relationship in a permanent way. She shook her head. "Friday. We'll talk about it Friday."

She wondered what would have happened if she hadn't designated Friday as their day to debrief. No doubt Jonas would have forced her to talk about her feelings and reactions every single day. He was like that, which she found odd for a man, and then she chastised herself for being so sexist. Of the two of them, she was the one reticent to talk about her thoughts and feelings. Jonas was the enlightened one.

He planted a hard kiss to her mouth, a warning of the difficult conversation coming, and let her have the evasion. "Tonight, my dearest darling, I'm going to take you anally."

Her heart raced. She wrung her hands until she noticed what she was doing. This was a subject they'd never discussed. Ellen had urged Sabrina for years to bring up the topic with Jonas. Every few months, Sabrina, Ellen, and a few of their friends got together for a ladies' night out. Though Sabrina listened whenever somebody brought it up, she had been too chicken to broach the idea to Jonas. Half of her was curious. The other half wanted to avoid unpleasantness.

With her entire being, she was glad Jonas hadn't chosen this opportunity to use foul language. She crossed her arms to avoid looking weak. "Are you sure about that?" He'd never brought it up before, either. There must have been a reason.

He skimmed a hand over her hip and up to her ribcage, urging her to drop her protective facade. "It's time. You need to know there's no part of you that doesn't belong to me, and you need to understand that you don't have a choice in the matter."

Except she did. They had a safe word, which she could use to stop him. She could end this experiment, and she knew he wouldn't hold it against her. Deep down, she didn't want to stop what they were doing. She recognized a need for the things he described. She only doubted her ability to submit in the ways he wanted.

Part of her wished he would demand her submission, give her no choice, steal it from her so that she wouldn't have to live with the fact she'd willingly given it. But he didn't operate that way. He demanded, yes, but only things she consented to give.

She let her arms fall to her sides, giving him complete access to her body. "Will you be gentle?"

His grin turned wicked. "Since when do you like gentle?"

Her anxiety level rose so high that she had trouble catching her breath. "When I'm tied up." And after a thorough flogging. Or while wearing clover nipple clamps.

She knew he recognized her apprehension, but he did little to ease her mind. Perhaps he wanted her on edge. "Go to the counter. Bend over, resting your upper body on the surface, and press your hands against the wall."

He'd said he was going to take her that way tonight, not now. She pleaded with the panic in her expression, but he only lifted an eyebrow, promising a punishment if she chose to disobey. Reluctantly, she did as he ordered. The cold marble made her nipples pebble painfully. Even her belly contracted to protest the contact. She placed her palms on the tiled backsplash and splayed her fingers, focusing on the sensation of grooves and grout underneath.

Jonas stood behind her. "Spread your legs wider."

She scooted them so they were shoulder-width apart.

"A bit more." He kicked at her instep, guiding her even wider. "That's it."

Though she'd been naked in front of him for years, and she'd delivered two children in front of him, she'd never felt so exposed. It was one thing to be in this position and know he was looking at her pussy. It was quite another to know he was checking out that puckered rosebud nobody had ever touched.

"Close your eyes. I want you to concentrate on feeling. No thinking allowed."

In the best of circumstances, she needed subspace to turn off her brain. He wasn't offering it. In lieu of that, she kept her silence. What he didn't know wouldn't hurt.

He drew his fingertips up and down her spine, traced the curve of her ribs, and palmed each ass cheek. "Relax, honey. I'll tell you when I'm going to touch you."

His hand slid between her legs, and he found her clit, still wet and wanting. He pressed and rotated. He circled and teased. Gradually her muscles relaxed. She hadn't realized how tightly she'd been clenching everything from her jaw to her calves. Squeezing her ass cheeks made sense. She had a natural inclination to try to keep him away from there.

Using her cream to ease the way, he inserted three fingers inside her tight channel. This is what she'd wanted since she'd sucked him dry on the beach in front of all those sunbathers and windsurfers. He fucked her masterfully. The sweet tension tingled throughout her body, a testament to how edgy she had been. When it got to be too much, she asked for permission to climax. The plea came naturally and from the heart.

He increased the pace. "Yes, honey. Come for me."

As she cried out, she thanked goodness something was holding her up. If she'd been standing, Jonas would have had to catch her. Waves of release, pure and gratifying, washed over her.

And when she was at her most vulnerable, she heard him murmur, almost under the roar in her ears. "I'm going to touch you now."

At the exact moment he uttered the word "touch," he rimmed that tight muscle, smearing the cream from her pussy all over it. The foreign sensation made her body want to tense, but the orgasm had stolen her ability to react quickly. By the time she gathered her wits, the feeling had normalized. While it still felt odd, it didn't feel invasive.

"That's it. Don't move. Just feel."

He pressed a little harder, and a curious awareness bloomed. Gooseflesh tingled on her scalp and the backs of her arms. It traveled down the outside of her thighs. He stimulated her this way for a few minutes. By the time he pulled his hand away, the fire inside had been rekindled.

She heard water running in the sink next to her. Opening her eyes, she saw that Jonas was washing his hands and a series of toys.

"Because you haven't done this before, I'm going to prepare you with a series of plugs. You'll wear the chastity belt for the rest of the day. Every hour I'll change out the phallus for a larger one. By the time I take you tonight, we won't have to worry about stretching you too far."

Judging from the size of the plug he was currently washing, he was preparing her to take something even larger than his cock. She wasn't sure that was necessary, but what the hell did she know? When it came to sex, she pretty much knew only what he'd shown her. She'd brought the ability to give awesome blowjobs to the relationship. He'd brought everything else.

He flicked open a bottle of lubricating jelly and poured it over the smallest silicone phallus. It wasn't much larger than his pinky. Then he spread lube over his fingers. She closed her eyes as he moved to stand behind her. He'd instructed her not to think, but she couldn't stop her brain from working overtime. Random thoughts winged through. She thought about hiring a housekeeper, changing the brand of juice she bought for Rose, a line from a song she'd heard on the radio. But none of those thoughts stopped long enough for her to make sense of anything.

As he'd done before, he massaged the tight ring of muscles, this time with the synthetic lubrication. "You're going to feel a little bit of pressure. Breathe out as I push in. Ready?"

Was he kidding? Nothing in the world would prepare her for this. Still, she inhaled.

"Exhale."

As she expelled air from her lungs, he pushed something into her. It didn't feel like much. Opening her eyes, she saw that he still held the lubricated plug in his hand, so she figured he must have inserted a finger. He sawed it in and out, turning it around, and she realized he was spreading the lube.

"Talk to me, Sabrina. Tell me what you feel."

The nerves he'd awakened clamored for more attention, but his finger was just too small to deliver. "It doesn't hurt. I can barely feel it. Earlier it felt good, made me want you to keep doing what you were doing. This is a little frustrating. There has to be more to it."

In response, he withdrew his finger. Her ass lifted automatically, seeking his return. She frowned at her reaction to the loss, but her confusion was short-lived. He returned with something larger, two fingers perhaps. It stretched her a little more. The snug fit stimulated the nerves that ran to her head and legs. "Better?"

"Yes." If nothing else, it halted the nonstop stream of thoughts she couldn't catch.

He threw the thin, lubricated plug into the sink and grabbed one with a larger circumference. He lubed it up with one hand, and then it disappeared behind her. Once again, she was empty. Thankfully this time it wasn't for long.

"Breathe out."

Just like that, he slid the thing past her entrance. She remained in position and watched him wash his hands and the unused plug. The tiled countertop had become warm from her body heat, and her nipples were no longer aroused.

But a new longing had been awakened. Energy coursed through her body, and she found it difficult to stay still. "Jonas?"

He halted the flow of water and dried his hands on a small towel. "Are you in pain?"

"No."

"Then you're fine. Some discomfort is to be expected as you get used to the feeling of having something there." His voice and his eyes had taken on a hard edge that thrilled her to no end.

"It's not uncomfortable."

He crossed his arms. "Stand up."

That's what she wanted. As she pushed her torso up from the countertop, she became acutely aware of having a foreign object lodged in her ass. The feeling was both oddly exquisite and disconcerting.

Before she could analyze it, he issued another order. "Go into the bedroom and lay down on the bed on your back, legs spread, knees lifted."

Usually when he gave that order, it meant bondage and maybe a flogger or a crop. Trembling with anticipation, she reflected that they might not make it to lunch with Mistress Hera at the time Jonas had indicated. Sabrina wondered if he was being a little passive-aggressive at her interruption of their vacation.

She positioned herself across the bed with her open pussy facing the door, just the way he liked. He hadn't said what to do with her arms, so she let them stay at her sides. Sometimes she thought about surprising him in that position, but she never had followed through. It didn't seem right to wait like this without having been given an order.

Jonas was in the room. She couldn't see him and he wasn't making any noises, but she felt the weight of his stare heating her core. He might have been fucking her with his gaze. It was that potent. Fresh juices rushed to her pussy, inviting him closer. She didn't dare lift her head to see if he stood in the doorway or if he'd come into the room.

After an eternity, she saw a figure at the foot of the bed. She turned her head the slightest bit to better see him. He would allow that small movement because he knew how the sight of him affected her.

He hadn't dressed. That was a good sign. He stroked his cock with one hand. That was a better sign.

Her vaginal walls spasmed in response, sucking at nothing. Suddenly she couldn't keep her arms still. Without consulting her better sense, she put one hand between her legs and stroked her clit. Perhaps she did crave punishment.

Jonas disappeared from view, and she stopped touching herself. It was never any fun when he wasn't around. A flush of humiliation washed over her. She hadn't enjoyed her last punishment. The concept took on a different meaning when they weren't in a scene.

He lifted her arm above her head and locked a leather cuff around her wrist, and then he repeated the action with her other arm. This bed had been designed for bondage. He threaded the line of a restraint through an eyelet just under the bed and hooked each snap to the D rings on her cuffs. A few adjustments, and her hands were trapped above her head.

Next, he lifted her head and put a leather strip underneath. Then he set her head down and buckled the ends of the strip together. It was a collar, something he'd never made her wear before. She'd once told him she thought such things were demeaning.

This, then, was her punishment.

"Except for hygienic purposes, you're not allowed to touch that cunt without my permission. It belongs to me, and you will only have pleasure if and when I allow it."

This was a complete reversal from the man who had encouraged her to masturbate when he wasn't around. She was rarely successful, so she'd didn't try very often. But to be forbidden from touching herself…that changed everything. Now she wanted to masturbate, and she was determined to be successful. She yanked on her restraints, but they held firm.

Restless energy zinged through her body. She shifted her legs to try to ease the aching need. His frown set her heart to racing. Damn! She hadn't meant to move.

This time when he disappeared from her field of vision, she arched her back to see where he'd gone. Not far. He'd set out a whole bunch of toys and tools on the dresser. Because she'd been intent on getting to the bed, she hadn't noticed them earlier.

He returned with more restraints. These he secured just above her knees. Then he attached lines that ran from them to the naked canopy. Sabrina could see now that the structure wasn't meant to provide a framework for a pretty covering. It was sturdy, meant to hold significant weight. Jonas checked the lines and the cuffs one last time.

"I know you're wanting a flogging right now, but you're not going to get one. Submissives who can't obey simple orders don't get what they want." He climbed onto the bed and knelt between her legs.

For the longest time, he stared at her body. His eyes, topaz with passion, traced paths up from her feet and down from her hands, always meeting at her core. She whimpered, a small, pleading sound in the back of her throat, and she fervently wished for a gag. If he gagged her, she couldn't humiliate herself further by begging before he told her to beg.

And somehow, having to do it from this position changed what had been a comfortingly predictable pattern. He'd always made her beg, but not like this. She was bound and helpless, a phallus stuck up her ass that somehow rendered her powerless.

Sabrina closed her eyes and accepted the fact she could do nothing. She moaned when she felt his finger outlining her clit. Though his touch was feather light, it had more impact than if he'd smacked it hard. Her entire body trembled.

"So responsive." He knelt over her and guided his cock to her entrance. "You were made for this, honey."

He traced his lips across hers, his tongue probing for an entry that she readily granted. As long as he used her body, she was happy. As he kissed her, he pressed his hips forward. The dildo in her ass made for a tight fit. It was a good thing she was so wet. He rocked deeper, not stopping until he filled her.

It wasn't a different feeling, just an amplified one. She felt the beginnings of a climax building even though he'd stopped moving.

He drew his thumb across her lips. "You feel fucking wonderful."

She wanted to touch him, but she'd ruined the opportunity by touching herself when she knew he wouldn't like it. The frustration built, fueling her climax. She needed him to move inside her. "Please."

His cock jumped, flexing inside her. "I love it when you beg, my sweet, sweet sub. Very soon, you'll even mean it."

She meant it now, but she knew better than to argue or to plead again. He waited until he was satisfied that she'd accepted his pronouncement, and then he withdrew almost completely. She didn't know if she could survive his absence. Sabrina dragged in a desperate, shaky breath and surrendered to her fate.

He played with her, thrusting deep only to withdraw and hold himself over her body, taunting her with his nearness. By the time he established a pattern, she was half out of her mind and seconds from having an orgasm.

"Please let me come." Her voice sounded thick and slow in her ears where the noise competed with the steady thrum of her pulse racing out of control.

When he shook his head, tears gathered in the corners of her eyes, a result of the strain of holding back the storm. She didn't know how long she could hold on. Because he'd bound her arms and legs, she couldn't shift her position to ease the fact that he hit her sweet spot every single time.

It was too much. "Please, Jonas. Please let me come." She heard it now, what he meant when he said she'd soon be begging in earnest.

"No." He pumped into her, harder and faster.

"Please!" She shrieked and tried to writhe, but the small amount of leverage she had in her hips only helped his cause. "I can't—" The words were barely out of her mouth when the climax stole her breath.

She didn't make a sound, not because she was trying to hide it. There was no disguising the feelings rioting through her system. Her back had arched and the top of her head dug into the pillow. The collar around her neck tightened enough to make its presence known. Every muscle in her body had gone stiff, and she couldn't have screamed if she'd wanted.

He doubled his efforts, pounding harder and faster against her pussy. The overload brought her back. She writhed back into position to find that she'd moved up a few inches. That gave her more leverage, but not enough to accomplish anything.

The tissues between her legs begged for a reprieve, but she knew it wouldn't be forthcoming. Jonas was in the mood to torture her. She recognized that he'd set her up for failure. There was no way she was coming out of this unscathed.

She remembered Samantha once telling her that Doms liked to play games like this to prove to their submissives that they have no real control over anything, not even their orgasms.

"Please, please, please." Though she had no idea what she begged for, she breathed the word over and over, a prayer that went nowhere.

He dragged her up that cliff again, proving beyond anything that he was the master of her body. And when she begged for release, he denied her, only to push her over the side. White patches blotted the edges of her vision, and still he didn't stop. He slowed down. He sped up. He swiveled his hips. He played with her clit and twisted her nipples.

Tears streamed from her eyes and her throat hurt from screaming words and phrases that made no sense. She lost track of time and space. Counting the orgasms was impossible because the sensations blended together. By the time he came, roaring so loud it echoed from the walls, she had gone numb.

She floated in the space between lucid dreaming and vague awareness of her surroundings. Jonas was nearby. It felt like he'd released the cuffs holding her prisoner, but she couldn't be sure and she didn't have the energy to move a muscle to find out.

Chapter Eight

Something cold penetrated the lack of feeling between her legs and a phone rang in the distance. She dimly recognized Ellen's ringtone for Jonas's phone.

The next thing she noted was the quiet murmur of Jonas's voice. He seemed far away, and that roused her from her fugue state. She needed him to be close, preferably lying next to her with his arms around her.

Sitting up slowly didn't stop the room from spinning. She found a bottle of flavored water on the nightstand. When she reached for it, something fell between her legs. Looking down revealed an ice pack. He'd put ice on her pussy. Even now, she could feel the heat radiating from that abused area. She wasn't sure she wanted to look. Generally she enjoyed the aftereffects when he left her sore. It made for optimal masturbation conditions. But that was forbidden now.

And she was too sated to muster outrage. She drank the water instead.

The door to the balcony slid open. Jonas tossed his phone onto a padded chair as he came in. "Ellen says she has everything under control, but she won't give me details."

Sabrina rose to her feet gingerly. The larger shift of her body made her aware of the plug in her ass. It no longer felt like much of anything. "That worries you, doesn't it?"

He exhaled a long stream of air and ran his fingers through the short blond curls on his head. "Yes. Whenever Ellen thinks she's being clever, I get worried. And Ryan won't answer his phone."

As she crossed the room, she noticed the way his gaze roamed over her naked body. He couldn't possibly be hungry for her again, yet it was there in the heat of his possessive stare. A glance at the clock showed they were more than an hour and a half late for lunch with Mistress Hera.

"Maybe he's minding the kids while she's at work." Ryan taught at the same high school as Jonas. He was off for the summer, which meant he had three months to be a stay-at-home father, and he loved every moment of it.

Jonas drew his brows together. "I talked to her on the home phone. I don't think she intended to answer, but Jake picked up."

Jake, Ellen and Ryan's five-year-old, had just learned which button to push to answer the home phone. Since mostly telemarketers used that number, they didn't bother to curb his enthusiastic shouts of "Hello!" and "All aboard!"

Sabrina ran her finger along the shell of his ear. "Are you deaf now?"

"I remembered to hold the phone far enough away." He lifted a wayward strand of hair off her shoulder. The careful knot from her shower had come undone. "Are you in the mood for lunch? You haven't had anything since breakfast."

"Yeah. Let me get dressed. Did you call Heather to let her know we were running late?"

He pressed his lips together, confirming her suspicion that he wasn't all that jazzed to spend time with his former acquaintance. "She'll figure it out."

Whether or not he wanted to have lunch with Heather was irrelevant. He'd accepted the invitation, and now he was being rude. It wasn't like him, and it tested the bounds of her patience. "Jonas."

He shook his head. "Don't, Sabrina. Not about this."

She dropped her gaze to the floor. "Does this have to do with Helene?" Every muscle in her face clenched at having to utter his ex-wife's name, but she managed to force it out.

"No. This has to do with the fact that it's my honeymoon and I didn't plan to spend it listening to other people's problems."

Someone who didn't know him would think he was being heartless. Sabrina recognized his aggravation. She ran a soothing hand up his arm. "It's just lunch. We'll listen and be supportive, but there's not much else we can do." Then something occurred to her. She shook her head. "I didn't call Lex or Stef."

"I did. They were both in meetings, whatever the hell that means. I talked to Sam. She's going to convey the message when they get home tonight." More frustration, but it wasn't as vehement. The way she caressed his skin was working.

"You tried. That's all you can do."

He shrugged, dismissing the problem. "I'll dress you. First we need to change your plug. Time for a bigger one."

She trudged into the bathroom and assumed the position. While she'd been semiconscious, he'd cleaned her juices away, so all he had to do was pop out the old one and insert the new one. The deed was done in a matter of seconds with zero discomfort.

Jonas scrutinized her when she stood up. "I thought you'd need much more stretching than this."

Sabrina shrugged, a perfect imitation of his. "I gave birth to two children. This is small potatoes by comparison."

Humor glinted from his eyes, which reflected the multitude of browns and golds in the various bathroom fixtures and finishes. "You know that was your other hole, right?"

"Whatever." She waved him away, but he caught her hands.

"Let's try a larger size."

It wasn't a suggestion. She settled back down on the countertop and chastised herself for being so blasé. If this hurt, then she deserved it because she'd shot off her mouth. He eased the current one out and tossed it into the sink. Because she was facing the right direction, she saw him grab the largest size. It was wider than his cock. She swallowed all the wrong comments that came to mind. She wanted lunch, not another punishment.

He worked it past that tight ring of muscle she was beginning to suspect wasn't all that tight, because it didn't seem to offer much resistance. It didn't hurt, but it definitely made its presence known. She wouldn't be sitting comfortably until he took it out.

When she wobbled with that first step, he caught her elbow to steady her. "Is it painful or uncomfortable?"

"I'm not sure I'll be sitting anywhere for very long." She gave a nervous laugh. Mistress Hera would either be wondering what he'd done to her or she would guess outright.

Jonas's laugh echoed hers, only it contained no trace of anxiety. "You'll be sitting at my feet. You're not going as a guest. You're going as my submissive. You will speak only to me and only with my permission. If anyone talks to you, I will do the answering. You may smile in greeting, but keep your eyes downcast. Only look up at me when you wish to speak. If I acknowledge you, then you may ask permission to talk. If I don't, then you can assume I've denied your request."

Her mouth gaped open. She knew this protocol was pretty normal in some circles. Sophia always required her submissives to follow these rules, though Drew, who was also supposed to be in charge of the subs they shared, treated the rules more like suggestions. Ellen used them sometimes with Ryan, but almost never when the four of them were together. She knew her stepbrothers were supposed to be badass Doms, but they almost never reined Sam in.

"Jonas, I—"

"Will find out what it means to be submissive. You're doing okay in private, but you have yet to master how to behave when others are around. Tonight is your first real lesson."

Without waiting for her response, he left the room. Sabrina stared at the open doorway, a million conflicting emotions slamming into her. This was the part of being a submissive she feared most. Being used as Jonas's sex slave was her fantasy come true. The idea of losing her individuality and personal freedoms left her cold.

But she'd agreed to five days. If she could get through today and tomorrow, she would be done, and she wouldn't let him down by reneging on their bargain.

Holding her head high, she ignored the fullness in her ass and went into the bedroom. He had the chastity belt in one hand and a towel in the other. When she entered the room, he smiled the way he usually did when she came into a room where he'd been occupied with something else.

"You're still swollen and tender. I'm going to put this ice pack inside your belt. You need to let me know when it's no longer doing its job. I can't have you out of commission yet."

She said nothing, but she did move closer so he could put the belt on her.

He regarded her warily. "When we're alone, you can speak normally unless I say otherwise."

But she had nothing to say. Her opinions on this entire experiment weren't settled. "Okay."

Grasping her chin between his thumb and forefinger, he tilted her face upward. "Sabrina, don't be bratty. I won't tolerate it."

"I wasn't being bratty. I just don't have anything to say. I feel so bad for Heather, and I'm afraid you're going to be rude to her. Well, more rude than you've already been."

"Ruder. Adjectives of two syllables or fewer generally form the comparative by adding -er."

When he started correcting her grammar, she knew he was annoyed. She wrapped her hand around his wrist in warning. "Jonas, don't start."

He narrowed his eyes. "I promise not to be rude to Heather, but you need to call her Mistress Hera. If you meet her away from here as equals, you can use her name. Here it's considered rude when you fail to use her title, whether or not she's present."

"Any other rules?" She congratulated herself on managing to make her question sound civil.

He shook his head. "Customs. I'm going to put a leash on that collar around your neck. Sometimes I'll use it. Other times, I'll want to hold your hand. That's my choice, not yours."

Her hand went to her neck, where the weight of that piece of leather increased a hundredfold. She'd completely forgotten about it. The thing had become a natural accessory, like a wedding ring, in a matter of hours.

"When we get there, you may nod a greeting, but you may not say anything. It's unlikely I'll give you permission to speak, so you just get to sit there and look pretty."

Her comment about his rudeness had brought out his domineering and irritable sides. Perhaps he should have rested with her. She pressed her lips together to stem the tide of argumentative comments piling up behind them.

"When lunch is served, I will feed you. Every morsel of food you consume will come from me. If it's not something you want to eat, tough shit. You'll eat it anyway."

Somewhere in the midst of her rising ire, a wave of peace washed ashore and swept the majority of it out to sea. If she couldn't speak to Mistress Hera, then she couldn't gush unwanted sympathy or come off as heartless and cold. She didn't have to worry about saying the wrong thing or giving bad advice because she wasn't allowed to say anything. This was a blessing in disguise.

She didn't worry about lunch. Jonas knew what she liked. She could spend an hour as a pampered pet. She preferred to be treated like a princess, but she wasn't going to complain.

"Yes, Jonas." The soft tone came naturally because she meant it.

The shock in his expression was quickly replaced with disbelief. "Two minutes ago, you were biting your lips to avoid telling me where to shove it. What happened?"

Sabrina shrugged. She couldn't explain it, not really. "I got over it. Are you picking out my clothes?"

"Yeah." He gestured to the chair next to the closet where he'd arranged a white, pleated skirt and a stretchy tangerine top. "Accessories first."

She held the ice pack in place while he adjusted the chastity belt. The small, thin towel he'd wrapped around the ice shielded her from the shock of something too cold. Next he produced a pair of nipple clamps on a chain. He threaded them through one of the rings on her collar and attached them loosely to her nipples. They pinched, but they didn't cut off her circulation, which meant they were more for show than enjoyment.

As she dressed in the outfit he'd chosen, she realized her shirt did nothing to hide the clamps. In fact, the scooped neckline emphasized everything, and of course Jonas didn't permit underclothing, so she couldn't wear a padded bra.

He clipped the leash to her collar and draped it over her shoulder. "You look incredibly sexy."

It was a compliment he paid often, so she didn't know why she flushed and bowed her head. He put his arm around her waist and guided her to the front door. As they left, she noted that he hadn't bothered to dress up at all. She'd tried to unpack his worn-out jean shorts before they left Michigan, but he'd just thrown them back into his suitcase. Paired with one of those cheap mall character T-shirts, he looked like a beach bum. On the surface, she looked ready for an upscale restaurant.

Not that it mattered. No doubt everyone would be looking at her breast features anyway and fail to notice anything else.

To her surprise, very few people seemed aware of them at all. Most were involved in their own activities. Unless they stopped and fucked in the middle of the street, which she didn't see happening with her chastity belt locked and the key tucked securely into Jonas's pocket, they weren't going to garner more than a passing greeting. That brought Sabrina no small measure of relief.

Mistress Hera's private apartment was located in the back quarter of Hades's Palace. They had to give their names to a guard and take a private elevator to get there. Once inside, Sabrina leaned close to Jonas, though they were the only people in the small car, and whispered in his ear. "It looks like she hasn't told anyone they aren't getting paid this week."

He lifted one corner of his mouth and shrugged. "Or she told them if they don't work, they don't get food and there's no way off the island. I've seen her be ruthless to get what she wants."

The elevator dinged, announcing they'd arrived at their destination, and Sabrina lost her chance to find out whether or not Jonas approved of that trait. He sometimes called Ellen ruthless. He'd uttered it as both a compliment and a complaint, so it wasn't a clear description.

Mistress Hera waited on the other side of the door. It slid open to reveal the tall woman clad in a flower print sundress that managed to be both stylish and modern. It dipped low, revealing lush cleavage, and it had a slit up the side to show off a generous amount of her shapely legs.

She held out her hands to Jonas, greeting him first with a kiss to the cheek. Since Jonas wasn't the kind of man who went around kissing his friends, Sabrina had to stifle her laughter at his discomfort.

Mistress Hera either didn't notice his standoffishness or she was used to it. "I'm so glad you could make it, even if you are two hours late."

Jonas lifted half his mouth in a sort-of smile that didn't reach his eyes. "Better late than never."

"Lunch is waiting." She motioned to the dining table in the open space to her left. "I had a feeling you'd be late, so I didn't call it in until you were on your way here."

Sabrina watched Mistress Hera closely, looking for cracks in her armor, anything to indicate that she found Jonas's hostile nature unsettling. She also wanted to know how the woman knew when they left their suite. But she crossed the room in a series of graceful steps, her bare feet making almost no sound as she padded over and pulled out a chair.

Because she was forbidden to talk, she didn't ask any questions. Instead she followed Jonas to the table. He had her stand a few feet behind a black, upholstered chair. The material looked like some industrial vinyl made to resist stains and tears. He snagged a large throw pillow from a pile behind Mistress Hera's sofa and tossed it onto the floor next to where he intended to sit.

He took his seat and motioned for Sabrina to occupy her place at his feet. Really it was to his right, but it was still on the ground. At least he'd provided a pillow. She didn't relish kneeling for an hour on the bamboo flooring. She folded her feet to one side and put her hand on his thigh, though she wasn't sure if he would approve of the fact that she wasn't kneeling properly. The larger plug in her ass gave her some discomfort when she sat up straight. This compromise allowed her to acclimate to the intrusion. She'd already accepted the presence of the ice pack. It soothed her hot and swollen tissues.

The answer came when he stroked a hand over her hair, which he'd let her brush before they left the suite, but he hadn't let her put it up or pin it back. The breeze had definitely impacted her attempt at fastidiousness, and she was sure she looked like she'd just rolled from bed. Technically she had, but nobody needed to know that.

"So I'll just dive right in and tell you that I asked you to lunch to thank you for coming over last night. Though I didn't get anywhere with the bank, the bank manager was able to contact the lawyer for Mr. Mehlberg who said he'd talk to Mr. Mehlberg today."

Sabrina didn't have to be a genius to know that assurance wouldn't get Mistress Hera or Elysium anywhere. The lawyer might know where the Mehlbergs were hiding, but he or she wasn't going to divulge that information.

The sound of flatware and plates clinked, indicating that Jonas was preparing to eat. She was hungry, so she hoped that meant he would feed her as he ate, not afterward. Mistress Hera made small talk about the food, and Jonas responded appropriately. At least he had remembered his manners.

His hand came down again, and he pressed something warm to her lips. The movement had been too fast for her to see what he had, and the angle worked against her as well.

She parted her lips. Delicate flavors popped in her mouth with the first bite. Lemon and ginger teased her taste buds. She guessed at shrimp. Jonas knew how much she loved seafood. Other wonderful bites followed—rice balls bursting with Asian spices, calamari, steamed vegetables. Every few bites, he would give her sips of water or fruit juice. It was a fresh feast, and soon Sabrina began to feel full. She rested her head on Jonas's leg and closed her eyes.

The whole time, Mistress Hera talked about the moral issues surrounding whether or not to tell the employees they weren't going to be paid this week and they needed new jobs next week.

"I haven't canceled any new arrivals for next week yet. I'm still hoping for a miracle."

Hearing a conversation without being able to see anyone's facial expression didn't bother Sabrina as much as she thought it might. It wasn't her conversation to have. She wasn't a participant, and both Jonas and Mistress Hera accepted her as an observer.

"Don't you think that's a bit shortsighted and dishonest? People deserve to know news like this no matter how bad it might be."

Mistress Hera had been talkative until this point, rambling on about costs and procedures and the hit Elysium's reputation would take for this fiasco. Now she was silent. With the table in the way, Sabrina couldn't tell whether Mistress Hera was thinking or if the silence was actually as heavy as it seemed.

"You know, I really didn't think you were going to bring that up. It's in the past. I don't even talk to her anymore." Mistress Hera's voice carried normally. Like her, it had a presence that demanded attention. But she uttered that mild rebuke so softly, Sabrina had to strain to hear it.

"I was willing to live and let live. You sought me out. You asked my advice, and now you're telling me you haven't changed a bit. You're still keeping harmful secrets. I don't give a shit whether or not you talk to Helene. I don't care if you're sleeping with her. I'm concerned that you're playing God with people's dreams. Were you planning to greet them with a speech about how the resort has no employees, so they're on their own when they thought they were buying an all-inclusive package?"

Sabrina lifted her head from Jonas's leg, the languor from her sated hunger fading fast at the mention of Jonas's ex-wife. She did note that he seemed more upset that Heather had no plan for being truthful than anything relating to Helene. In an abstract way, Sabrina felt sorry for Mistress Hera. It was never fun to deliver bad news, especially if denial is the first instinct.

"Look, I'm sorry I didn't say anything about what I knew."

Mistress Hera might have said more, but Jonas cut her off. "This isn't about that. It's been eight years. I would have thought you'd grown as a person since then. You're in charge of Elysium, a utopia for kinksters, people who hold honesty as a cornerstone for all encounters, and you're being dishonest."

While Sabrina couldn't see above the tabletop, she could see the way Mistress Hera worried the soft fabric of her skirt into a patch of wrinkles. The woman was under a tremendous amount of stress, yet Jonas cut her no slack. He wasn't actually being helpful. Sabrina's heart went out to the woman.

With no other recourse, she stroked what she hoped was a soothing caress over Jonas's knee, down his calf, and across the top of his foot. He did nothing to stop her, and she wondered whether he was in a holding pattern or if his attitude was softening.

"You're right, of course." Mistress Hera's tiny laugh was sad and self-deprecating. "I think that's why I chose to talk to you. I knew you would force me to do what's right. I'll call a staff meeting for tonight after the dinner shift ends. And I'll start making the guest notifications tonight."

Jonas settled back in his chair, and the tension eased from his muscles. "And call for a guest meeting tomorrow morning. You'll need to inform your guests as to which services will no longer be offered and what parts of the resort you'll be closing."

Sabrina realized that Mistress Hera hadn't been looking for a solution from Jonas. She'd known all along what needed to be done. She just wanted moral support, somebody to agree that the course of action was necessary. Last night Sabrina had only put off the inevitable with her offer of help. No wonder Jonas had forbidden her from talking this time.

As he and Mistress Hera continued to hash out the details, Sabrina tuned them out. It didn't concern her. She was here for Jonas. He required only the comfort of her presence and her obedience, which she was happy to give. Relieved, actually. If she had been a participant, she would have put pressure on herself to find a different solution, and she would be miserable because she would have felt so badly for Mistress Hera.

All that stress washed away, unnecessary and unused. Sabrina snuggled against Jonas's leg and let her mind drift. She missed her children. It would be time for their twice-daily video chat when they got back to the hotel room. Jonas's mother rolled her eyes whenever they called and told them to relax and enjoy themselves. She was under the impression that Sabrina was the only reason they were calling. Apparently she missed the eagerness in her own son's voice when he spoke to his children. Sabrina could only devote her time and attention to having fun if she knew her babies were safe and happy.

At least her mother, who had the kids for this second half of the week, understood. Her stepfather would smile with paternal pride and brag about all the things Rose and Ethan had accomplished since their last chat. Both her mother and Dmitri had been stern parents, but they'd turned into indulgent grandparents. Rose had an entirely new wardrobe by now, and Ethan was clutching a new toy every time she saw him.

When Jonas rose and held his hand down to help her rise, she hopped up, a happy smile on her face. She felt refreshed and carefree. Though she wished Mistress Hera the best, she didn't feel that she had failed the woman or that she needed to spend more time on the problem. And the plug in her ass shifted enough to make its presence known. It hadn't grown comfortable, and she no longer waited for her body to acclimate. She could accept the size, which had been the goal.

Mistress Hera walked them to the elevator. "Thank you for coming. I don't know what I would have done without that special kind of kick you're so good at giving."

Jonas smiled, and this time it was the genuine article. Sabrina reassessed her assumptions regarding why he'd been alternately grim and annoyed until after Mistress Hera had admitted what needed to be done. Had he been upset that his vacation had been interrupted with this unexpected wrinkle, or had he been dreading a conversation with his ex-wife's friend?

"You're welcome. I hope everything goes smoothly. There are no problems that won't eventually end. You'll move on to a new job. In a month, this will all be an unpleasant memory, and the Mehlbergs will have to deal with the fallout."

This time when she kissed his cheek as a farewell gesture, he softened a little. He didn't want the kiss, but he didn't openly reject it either.

Then she turned to Sabrina and took both of her hands. "You are one of the loveliest subs I've seen in a long time. Take care of this one. He's a good man."

A couple of snarky comments came to mind. She knew Mistress Hera saw her resemblance to Jonas's ex-wife. Like some of his other acquaintances over the years, she must also attribute the same personality characteristics to Sabrina. Helene had been a cold woman who had no problem giving her body to anybody willing to flog it first. Sabrina felt she had nothing in common with that whore.

Though her face was tight, she managed a smile she knew walked the edge of haughty. Jonas usually didn't have an issue with her giving attitude to other people, but so many of his expectations had changed that she didn't know if he'd take exception to a bit of rudeness she couldn't help.

"Thank Mistress Hera for the meal, Sabrina."

He didn't sound upset. She took that as a good sign. "Thank you for lunch, Mistress Hera. It was delicious."

As soon as the elevator doors closed he dropped her hand and pushed her against the stainless steel panel that made up the back wall. The handrail dug into her ass and gave the plug a push that jolted her insides. She took a moment to catch her breath.

He propped a hand on each side of her head. "That was one of the most condescending smiles I've ever seen you give, and I've seen you flash quite a few of those beauties."

Caging her like that produced one reaction no matter the circumstances. Heated cream rushed between her legs, and the scent of her arousal filled the small space. The breath she'd caught escaped again. She offered no explanation.

"Sabrina." A single-word warning.

Her breasts heaved, trying unsuccessfully to close the scant distance between their chests. "She implied that I don't appreciate you."

"No, she didn't. That was her way of apologizing to me. You see, she knew Helene was cheating on me regularly, and she never said a word. Doms are supposed to look out for one another, especially those they consider to be friends. When she first decided she wanted to become a Domme, I mentored her. I let her practice her flogging technique on Helene. She owed it to me to tell me what Helene was doing."

When they had been estranged, Sabrina had visited their friend Sophia in order to be flogged. She had come to need regular impact play in order to deal with the enormous amounts of stress in her daily life. Jonas hadn't been jealous, though he did take over that job once they got back together. Once in a while, he arranged for her to have a session with Sophia. No sex was involved. It satisfied her needs and it also let Sophia blow off some steam. She was married to a man who was neither a Dom nor a sub, so she did require another outlet to keep her happy.

Jonas was angry with her, not with Mistress Hera. That betrayal was in the past, a part of his life that no longer held him prisoner. Sabrina's behavior was in the present. She lowered her gaze. "I'm sorry. Would you like me to apologize to Mistress Hera?"

He shook his head. "I don't think she caught it. She doesn't know you well enough to read when you're being genuine and when you're being an ice princess. I'll punish you accordingly when we get back to the suite."

She knew he planned to cook for them tonight. As wonderful as the amenities on the island were, she was looking forward to a night alone. She nodded her acceptance. When the doors slid open, he grabbed the lead to the leash and motioned for her to exit the elevator. He was still a gentleman even when he was treating her like a pet.

The leash wasn't her favorite accessory. When he'd clipped it to her collar, she hadn't been too crazy about wearing it, but he'd draped it over her shoulders and left it alone. She could handle it if he just meant it to be for show.

Walking back to the suite was much worse than the trip there. This time, people's gazes not only lingered, but they smirked and smiled. Some called greetings, always to Jonas, but their eyes remained on Sabrina. She felt the heat of their judgment as it penetrated her shirt. In a betrayal, her breasts swelled and her nipples pebbled. The towel between her legs surrounding the ice pack was now soaked with her juices, and the liquid inside had long acclimated to her body temperature.

Had those people been present at the bonfire? Were they picturing what she looked like with her pussy spread wide as her Master whipped an orgasm right out of her? Could they still hear her cries of pleasure as he fucked her in front of them all?

Things that had bothered her a little now mutated into larger issues. She had made it clear to Jonas before they got on the plane that she hadn't wanted to be naked in public. Like a true Lord of the Underworld, he had charmed her, lulled her into a false sense of security so he could circumvent her hard limits and have his way.

Stepping into the coolness of their building's lobby had the same effect on her rising panic as a bucket of ice water. She was blowing things out of proportion. Jonas would have respected her safe word. He was the one who insisted on having it in the first place. He was the one who stopped their play every once in a while to remind her that it was there.

She breathed. In the elevator, she found the calm place inside and grabbed it with both hands. By the time they made it to the room, she had come back from the brink all by herself.

Jonas unclipped the leash after he'd closed and locked the suite door. "Strip."

With trembling hands, she lifted her shirt over her head and shimmied out of her skirt. Jonas unhooked the chastity belt and removed the ice pack. The belt dangled from the attachment in the back. He took a step backward and studied her.

She didn't know what he saw, but she knew what she felt like. Her insides were a raw mess and she was barely holding on to her sanity. Her exterior showed all the classic signs of arousal—hard nipples, wet pussy, heaving bosom.

"Remove the plug from your ass."

Sabrina stared at Jonas, waiting for him to laugh, for that stoic expression to slip, anything to show that he was joking. But nothing like that happened. He lifted one eyebrow, and she knew that if she didn't follow orders, she would be in line for another punishment spanking. That was not the fun kind.

Reaching back gingerly, she found the flat silicone base. It spread outward in a disc, which she supposed was so it wouldn't slip inside completely and get lost. That would kill the passion pretty quickly.

The first tug produced no result. She felt it sucking at her rectum, striving to remain in place. The awkward position caused one nipple clamp to slip off. The heat of embarrassment washed through her body, and her chest bloomed with color. Jonas smiled like a pleased stallion and removed the other clamp.

She tried again, yanking harder. It slipped a bit. She worked it out slowly, wiggling it back and forth to keep up the momentum. Shards of pleasure sparked through her body, traveling up her spine to tingle in her scalp. Her knees grew weak. She wished he'd positioned her so that something else was holding her up.

When it was completely out, she held it out to him.

He shook his head. "Go into the bathroom and wash it off with soap. Then clean yourself up. I'll check on you in five minutes."

Sabrina rushed to the bathroom. She needed some time alone. She needed to process the reasons she'd panicked just because he'd put her on a leash. It was demeaning. Humiliating. This from a man who had always treated her like a treasure. She didn't understand why he suddenly wanted things between them to change so drastically. Then she took a deep breath. Five days. Two nights and one day left. She could do this. It meant a lot to him.

Jonas knocked on the door, a fact she found surprising. He rarely observed the door as a barrier. At most it was a temporary inconvenience.

She'd finished washing, and she'd even managed to freshen her outlook. "Come in."

He looked her up and down, and then he took a clean cloth and wiped down the chastity belt that still dangled down her backside. "Your punishment will be twofold."

Though she could have used the mirror, Sabrina looked over her shoulder at him. "Wasn't the leash punishment?"

Throwing the cloth into the wicker laundry receptacle, he shook his head. "That was because I wanted to." He planted both hands on her shoulders and whirled her to face him. His eyes had taken on an olive-green cast that made them nearly impenetrable. "As your Master, it is my right to bind you however and whenever I want. Your job is to accept my will. You may enjoy it. You may revel in it. You may hate it, but you must accept it."

Part of her did enjoy it, probably the part that enjoyed bondage. Another part of her hated the public display that might have set the women's rights movement back half a century. It also regarded the part of her that enjoyed it with hostility. She sighed. "All right, Jonas. I accept it."

If he was surprised by her easy acquiescence or her reluctance, it didn't show on his face. "Spread your legs."

His fingers were inside her before she could widen her stance. She grabbed his shoulders for balance while he fucked her that way. Cream rushed to lubricate her walls, and he found her sweet spot. The ice had done its job, and her pussy was no longer swollen or sore. But it was still a little tender, which just made it more receptive to pleasure. She threw her head back and struggled to spread her legs.

She thrust against his hand, chasing that delicious release. Just when she felt the first stirrings of a climax, he withdrew his fingers and licked them clean, savoring every drop of her juices. He'd never hid his enjoyment from her, and she still found it fascinating how much he loved her taste.

He produced a small bullet vibrator. Its diminutive size didn't fool her. She knew how much power it packed. He inserted it halfway. "Clench, honey."

Holding it was easier said than done. Luckily she only had to keep it until he had the belt in place. For something that was supposed to ensure she didn't receive sexual stimulation, the thing so far had only been used to tease and torment. She might welcome an afternoon employing it for its intended use.

"This will add another dimension to your punishment. You came without permission four times this afternoon, and then you were rude to Mistress Hera. For that, you will remain on your knees for the remainder of the evening. This will remind you of your position." He traced his thumb over her collarbone as if the words he'd spoken had been loving and tender.

Sabrina gaped at him in astonishment. He'd forced her to climax all those times. She'd asked, but he kept refusing permission. Being bound, having the plug in her ass, and his finesse as a lover had been more than she could resist.

"Shocked the argument right out of you, haven't I?" He grinned, gloating even further.

"You bastard." She whispered the word, which was the most she could manage right now.

He wove one hand into the hair above the nape of her neck and squeezed. She winced at this unexpected violence, and her juices went into overdrive. He knew how to push her buttons too well.

Pulling down, he forced her head back. Tears pricked behind her eyes, and he bit her neck just below the black leather collar, sucking the skin there into his mouth. She cried out in pain as the bruise formed that marked her as his. She dug her fingers into his arms, no doubt leaving fingerprint bruises, but the action was in vain. It didn't counteract the sting and it didn't make him stop.

While it hurt, she wasn't tempted to call her safe word. He'd been like this only a handful of times before. Each time he put her through hell and sent her to the heavens. In moments, the force of his bite tapered off, and he released her neck with a loud slurp.

He lifted his head and studied his handiwork. The pressure of the fist in her hair eased. "Yep. I'm a bastard. Now get on your knees and crawl to the kitchen. You'll keep me company while I make dinner."

Chapter Nine

The rumble of deep voices coming from the direction of the front door penetrated Samantha's state of total concentration. Dropping everything, she ran from her studio overlooking the ocean to the front door of a house she considered obscenely large. Three people did not need this much space.

She skidded to a stop at the edge of the rug, suddenly remembering that she was dressed. Her oversized painting shirt was stained with a multitude of colors, and her washed-out jeans weren't much better. If she was going to greet her Masters wearing clothing, which was technically against the rules, she was of the firm opinion that it should be the sexy kind. Looking like an escapee from a painting crew didn't make her list of styles most likely to cause her men to drool.

"Remember when we used to have this wonderful submissive who greeted us at the door each day on her knees, wearing nothing but a smile?" Lex set his briefcase on a round table in the foyer whose only purpose was to hold flower arrangements. His back was to her as he spoke to his brother. "Long blonde hair, wide blue eyes, lips so luscious you had a hard time deciding whether to kiss or fuck them."

Sam heard the amusement in his tone, but it still stung. She took great pride in her submissive role in their relationship. Once again, she'd let them both down.

Stefano placed his case next to Lex's. He tugged at his tie. "You know how she gets when she's in the middle of something."

When her Masters were at work, which was most of the time, Samantha was free to do what she wanted. She could work on a painting or lay on the beach. The time belonged to her. When either one or the both of them were home, which didn't happen as often as she liked, her time belonged to them. She belonged to them.

"Sorry," she said, interrupting and drawing attention to her presence. She leaned against the doorway, gauging their reactions before she decided on the best course of action. "I was researching."

Lex turned toward the sound of her voice, moving in a way that gave her a clear view of both her men. They were tall, a couple inches over six feet, which she loved. Being a tall woman who was also submissive, she liked a larger, stronger man who could overpower her to exert his will.

Both had thick, black hair and startling blue eyes that could change from tender and loving to hard and demanding faster than she could process the transformation. She spent hours studying the way light played over the planes of their sharp cheekbones and the angles of their jaws. Their matching jackets hung deliciously from their broad shoulders. She loved how their bodies tapered to trim waists before flaring into powerful thighs.

Mouthwateringly handsome, charismatic, dominant, and sexy, they were identical in every way, save one. Being mirror images of each other, Alexei was left-handed and Stefano was right-handed. Almost nobody could tell them apart, but Samantha never confused them, not even when they were asleep. When she looked at her men, she saw the subtle differences, like the way Lex's gaze always lingered on her breasts or the way Stef defended her when he should have been preparing to punish her.

Stefano's eyes lit up when he saw her. He shed his suit jacket, throwing it on the table with his briefcase. "What were you researching?"

Lex also threw his jacket on the table, but he folded it first. "Painting I can excuse. Was the research related to painting? Were you looking up anatomy pictures? I told you I'd pose naked for you."

Laughing, Samantha shook her head. Though she had made somewhat of a name with her paintings of sunsets and sunrises, she had recently begun diversifying her subject matter. "It's nothing that can't wait until I take care of my Masters. We can talk about it later."

She tugged her shirt over her head and let it fall to the floor. Her bra and jeans followed. She hadn't been wearing panties. Stefano had shredded her last pair, and she hadn't been shopping since then. After sliding to her knees, she arched her back until her hands gripped her ankles. She was completely open to them, an offering of her body and her submission.

"I'm not sure, Lex. I think I might prefer watching the striptease to missing it." Stefano's shadow loomed over her, but she knew better than to move. "Sammy? Was your research related to the reason Jonas called us at the office today?"

Her brother had called her after he failed to get either Lex or Stef on the phone. He'd only asked if she knew where they were or when they planned to be home. Ellen's call had come afterward, and that had led to the bout of research.

"I don't know Master. Jonas only asked when you'd be home. I told him to call back after seven." She couldn't resist a tiny smile. She knew they were scheduled to be home by five.

Lex promptly reminded her of that fact. "Samantha, did you lie to your brother?"

"No, Master. I didn't think you'd want to talk to him the moment you arrived home. I simply told him to call when he had the best chance of reaching you when you weren't busy." That time might put the call smack in the middle of dinner, but she didn't worry about that.

A hand closed over her breast. Lex had moved from the visual to the tactile. He squeezed the stretched mound before pinching her nipple between his fingers. She gasped as the small pain brought a tingle of pleasure.

"Am I going to be busy?"

Another hand treated her untouched nipple to the same torture. Stefano wasn't as sadistic as Lex when it came to her breasts, but he did know the exact pressure that made her pussy clench.

"If you wish, Master." The words stumbled from between her lips as Lex's mouth closed around her throbbing nipple.

Stefano slid his hand up her neck to cup her cheek. "What do you wish, Sammy?"

Even at this angle, she didn't mistake the glint in his eyes. "I wish to please you, Master, however you want."

Lex trailed his mouth down her stomach, scorching her skin with his hot lips. He rimmed her navel with his tongue. She gasped as his hand traveled lower, lingering on her bare mons, inches from her anxious pussy.

Stef's tender caress disappeared. He removed his belt and unbuttoned his pants. She licked her lips as he pulled his erection free and shoved his boxers down his legs. They pooled around his ankles with his pants.

Though she couldn't see what he was doing, it sounded like Lex was doing the same thing.

"Kneel up. You're going to need both hands."

Being upright meant she got to see them both at the same time, which she liked very much. Lex stood next to Stef, and she could see that he'd discarded his pants completely. Two erections pointed at her, and her two men regarded her with expectant expressions.

This was better than painting. She wrapped a hand around the base of each man's cock. Last time, she'd started with Stef, so this time she licked the purpled crown of Lex's cock first. When it was wet enough, she prepared Stef the same way. Back and forth, she sucked one cock and then the other. It wasn't enough to bring either of her Masters to orgasm, but they both liked sharing her in this manner. It was foreplay. With enough practice, she was confident she could learn to coordinate her hands and mouth well enough to make them both climax at the same time.

When it got to be too much, they lifted her together, communicating almost telepathically to synchronize the timing. Lex had insisted the front living room have many ottomans of different sizes and shapes. They carried her to a rectangular one long enough to support her from ass to neck.

Her head dangled from one end. Stef positioned himself here. She closed her eyes and opened her mouth, accepting the passive role he required just now. He thrust his cock deep, but not enough to choke her. She swallowed as much as she could and hollowed her cheeks to maintain suction.

Lex straddled her chest. He pushed her breasts together, sandwiching his cock between them. Though they didn't need to, they thrust in tandem. Stef withdrew as Lex thrust forward, rocking her body into the natural rhythm of their pleasure. Before long, Stefano bathed the back of her throat with his semen. She swallowed convulsively, sucking even as he withdrew completely.

She didn't know whether the friction wasn't as great on her chest or if Lex drew it out because he loved to fuck her breasts, but he didn't appear close to finishing.

Stef kissed her, gently and reverently. "I love you, Sammy."

Tears wet her eyes as tender feelings welled in her heart. "I love you, too, Master."

With a shout, Lex finished. His ejaculate shot out in three spasms, thankfully missing her face. She was fine with him coming anywhere on or in her body but her face. Knowing it drove him crazy, she smeared it over her entire chest. The spark behind his eyes made her pussy clench.

"Dungeon," he said. "Now."

Different rooms in the house had different rules. Her art studio and her bedroom were off-limits. They could only enter at her invitation and everything happened on her terms. Lex was the only Master in his bedroom, as was Stef when they were in his room. In the rest of the house, they shared dominion over Sam, and they tended to just have wild sex.

In the dungeon, they played hard. Bondage was expected, as was the use of floggers, paddles, various toys, and other kinds of whips. Samantha liked moderate amounts of pain as long as it ended with orgasm. Lex and Stef were often in the mood to oblige. After all, they were the ones who introduced her to that need. They should be the ones who fulfilled it.

This was a reward. Even though she hadn't been at the door to greet them when they arrived home, both Masters were pleased with her.

She peeled herself from the leather ottoman and headed toward the stairs that led to the lower level. Lex and Stef would follow, but not immediately.

After punching in the code to unlock the door, she opened it up and turned on the lights. The dungeon looked a lot different than it had the first time they'd brought her down. For starters, she'd redecorated. The walls had been soundproofed, and the mahogany floor was now littered with soft mats. Kneeling on hardwood all the time was hell on the knees. It was great for a kitchen floor, but it didn't work for her as an option in the dungeon.

The attached bathroom had been completely remodeled. It now had a tub large enough for three and a shower in which they could all fit.

She'd also managed to have most of the equipment she hadn't liked replaced with things she enjoyed far more. The Y-table, which was one of her favorite pieces as long as she wasn't being punished on it, occupied one corner. A large St. Andrew's cross—she found it romantic—was mounted to another wall.

In the corner that had been cluttered with four kinds of spanking benches, a huge mattress stood on a raised platform. Eyehooks had been built into the frame every twelve inches, making it the perfect place for bondage activities. Because they were sunk into the wood, they didn't get in the way if part of her was hanging off the bed.

They had kept one spanking bench. It was a simplistic one consisting of a two-by-ten piece of wood on legs that supported her hips. A four-by-four piece formed a chest support that didn't interfere with access to her breasts. A final piece supported the other end. Nothing supported her head, which meant they had full access to her mouth.

Hooks and chains dangled from various places on the ceiling. Samantha knelt in the designated area in the center of the room, just below two heavy chains that connected to an exposed support beam.

Desire caused an ache between her legs, and she knew they would take their time seeing to it. Both of her Masters were sated for the moment. Since they loved to tease and touch her, she had no doubt she'd be begging in no time.

She folded her hands behind her back to resist the urge to touch herself and widened her knees so that she was spread wide. Masturbation and orgasms weren't permitted without permission, which meant supervision. Even when they traveled for business, on those rare occasions she didn't go with them, they wanted to watch her masturbate on video chat.

After an eternity, she heard them coming down the hall. The soundproofing worked two ways, but she'd left the door open. That was also protocol. She wasn't allowed to close the door to the dungeon. She could open it, but only her Masters could close it.

Her breath hitched as she heard the door close and the telltale *snick* of the bolts as they locked it. They came to stand in front of her.

"Have you been a good submissive?" Stefano asked the question that started each of their scenes. Samantha's first trip to the dungeon wasn't her favorite. Stefano had forced her to call him "Master" when she hadn't wanted to. She'd suppressed her anger until one day, about a year after she'd moved in, it had boiled over. That had been one hell of an argument. Stefano had apologized for days, and she had also admitted that she hated being called a slave. Since then they'd engaged in many conversations, gradually developing a protocol that worked for them all.

She couldn't lie. Unless they called to say otherwise, she was supposed to meet them at the door, kneeling and naked. It was the one requirement on which they both insisted. "No, Master. I wasn't at the door when you got home."

Stef looked to Lex, one brow lifted as he silently asked his brother's opinion. Perhaps he hadn't expected her to answer that way.

Lex lifted her chin until her gaze met his. "You have been a little neglectful lately. We'll discuss that later, after dinner. An appropriate punishment will be decided then."

"Yes, Master." They never failed to take care of her, but she'd failed six times in the past two weeks, and they had yet to punish her. That wasn't a great track record for any of them.

Lex released her chin. She returned her gaze to the floor.

"Other than that, have you been a good submissive?" Stefano asked again.

She recognized the edge in his voice that betrayed his impatience. If she had broken any other rules, she had no doubt he would have been ruthless in his punishment, in part for ruining his plans tonight. Of the pair, Stefano was definitely the stricter disciplinarian. Good thing she'd spent the morning at the spa and the afternoon researching Elysium. It had kept her out of trouble. "Yes, Master. I have been good."

"On your feet." Lex pulled her up as he gave the order. He regarded her with a brilliant smile, and then he blocked her vision with a blindfold. She loved not being able to see anything. It seemed to magnify her other senses.

Her Masters loved using the blindfold because it was the only time she couldn't tell them apart. Well, most of the time. Every now and again, one of them would say or do something to give it away.

They liked playing the anonymous twin games, and she liked to let them have their fun.

A motor whirred to life. Since they hadn't moved her, she guessed they were lowering the chains directly above her. A collar came around her neck. The soft, brushed leather caressed her skin, and the distinctive scent filled her nose, bringing with it the memory of multiple orgasms.

Each of her arms was lifted and cuffs were attached. A bar threaded through a ring on one cuff, continued through one on her collar, and ended after it passed through the ring on her other cuff. She heard the click of snaps locking into place and the whir of the motor pulling up the slack in the lines. Because it was hooked through her collar, they wouldn't force her to stand on tiptoe. Its sole purpose was to provide stability and support, which she would need when they really got going.

Soft leather encircled both her ankles at the same time. A spreader bar was slid through the rings on those as well. Now she was locked in position with her arms and legs spread wide. Her body was a blank canvas on which they could work their magic.

Fingers slid between the cuffs and her skin, one final safety check before they began. Other than to give orders, neither of her Masters would say much from now until the blindfold was removed. Sometimes she could tell their voices apart. It wasn't the sound so much as some of the subtle inflections or the way certain things were phrased. Still, they wouldn't take unnecessary chances.

One of them gathered her hair and secured it out of the way. Two sets of hands roamed her body, caressing every surface and exploring every crevice. The invasiveness only served to remind her how completely she belonged to them and how powerless she was in this room.

Lips nibbled each earlobe, sending shivers down her spine and through her breasts. She moaned and arched her back, searching for more contact, but she found only air. The lips had gone as well.

She ran her tongue along her lower lip in an attempt to lure one of her Masters close for a kiss. Nobody bit.

She listened intently, and she was able to discern the sounds of one person moving through the room. That mean the other one had his eyes on her. They wouldn't leave her alone bound like this, not after she informed them that having a closed circuit camera set up for viewing wasn't the same thing. The first time they'd punished her in this room, they'd left her bound to a table with a machine forcing her to have orgasm after orgasm. That had been the same night Stef had forced her to use his title. It had been the last night they'd ever done something that reckless.

Not having been in long-term relationships before, neither of her Masters was well versed in setting limits and boundaries. Communication was one of the areas they were still working on.

When they had remodeled the media room, the cameras were removed.

Something soft tickled across the back of her calf. It wasn't substantial enough to be the falls of a flogger or the flap of a crop. It moved up to the back of her knee. Samantha was ticklish there. Her knee involuntarily jerked, trying to escape the feeling, and she giggled. The tickle changed to a scratch, as if he was dragging the edge of a broken paintbrush over her skin.

The soft tickling alternated with scratching as the sensation explored around her thighs and ass, up her back, and down her front. He even stroked the soft thing over her freshly waxed pussy lips, something else that had occupied her time that morning at the spa. Thank goodness she healed quickly.

Because no pattern was followed with the stroking and scratching, she never knew what to expect. Every contact sent her nerves rioting. Breathing became difficult because she kept sucking in her breath. Cream seeped from her pussy with every caress.

Abruptly the instrument changed. The sound of falls swishing through the air was her only warning. They fell hard against the left side of her ass. She thought her nerves were on edge before, but now she knew they'd tricked her body. The next blow sailed through the air, but she was ready for the sting. Only it never came. The falls were softer than a tap, another caress when she expected pain.

They established a pattern this time. Soft blows alternated with sharp stings. Her body tingled. Her breasts swelled and her pussy wept. She needed more. They moved around her, aiming with strategy and care. The deerskin stroked her abdomen and breasts while the tougher leather caught her pussy and thighs.

Just when she thought she couldn't stand it anymore, she felt the press of bare skin along her back, ass, and thighs. A hard cock lodged against the curve of her ass, and a hand massaged lubrication into her anus. She guessed Stefano, but she had no way of knowing until he started fucking. Stef tended to be a little rougher, not that she was complaining. She liked it rough. She liked it gentle. She liked it fast or slow. Her Masters were good at pretty much everything.

He placed his cockhead against her tight ring of muscle, and then he gripped her hips with both hands. It was all the warning she was going to get. He thrust hard, burying his cock completely. She exhaled at exactly the right time, relaxing enough to avoid injury. His actions confirmed her assessment. Lex liked to ease his way in. Stef went balls out from the start.

"Stef." His name came out as a sigh, a sensual caress that revealed her heart.

He growled against the nape of her neck. "Vixen."

Behind his growl, she heard his smile. He liked that she knew him so well, that no matter how often he tried to act like he was half of a pair, she saw him as an individual.

His powerful thighs flexed behind hers as he withdrew and thrust again. In front of her, Lex continued alternating the floggers that caressed and stung, though he was careful to center his action on her breasts. Typical Lex, but it also made sure he didn't accidentally hit

Stefano. While her lovers could take a few hits, they didn't enjoy it the way Sam did.

A kaleidoscope opened in the darkness behind the blindfold as they worked their magic. Colors burst as heat traveled through her system, but it wasn't enough. She needed more.

"Lex." Another sigh, but this time it was wrapped in a plea. She needed him.

Stefano halted as the floggers fell away. Soon Alexei's belly pressed against hers. He guided his cock into her tight pussy, and she finally felt complete. Both of her Masters had claimed her. Sandwiched between them, connected to both her lovers, bliss washed over her and she lost any semblance of control.

"Yes," she whispered. "Please love me."

As they began to move in tandem, Lex pressed a kiss to her lips. "Always, Sammy. Always."

Stars exploded. She cried out with the first orgasm and they showed no sign of slowing down.

Later as she lay in the big soaker tub with her Masters on either side of her, each exploring her body with lazy caresses, Stef brought up the matter of her research.

"Samantha, what were you looking up so intently that you forgot we were coming home?"

He didn't sound upset, though he certainly had that right. Not only did both of them send her a text when they left the office, their secretaries each sent texts when the men actually left the building. Four texts should have been warning enough. It left her time to shower away the paint splatters that inevitably ended up on at least her hands, arms, and face.

She snuggled into his shoulder and pressed a kiss on his pectoral muscle where it stuck out above the water line. It was too enticing to resist. "Ellen called. Do you remember that place, Elysium, that you guys took me to last year?"

Stef nodded.

Lex rubbed her thigh, working his way closer to her pussy. "You want to go back? We can arrange some time off. It might only be a weekend, but I think we can manage."

She took a deep breath. "I want to buy it."

They both sat up and swiveled to look down at her, twin expressions of confusion marring their identical brows. Their handsomeness made her nipples perk up, which was amazing. After they'd taken her down from the chains, they'd moved her to the bed where they'd taken turns holding her down while the other one fucked her.

Stefano broke the stunned silence first. "You want to run a business?"

"It's not for sale. Last I heard, the Mehlbergs were in the middle of a nasty divorce." Lex frowned. She'd never once shown an interest in wanting to own anything, so his confusion was warranted.

She sat up and bit her lower lip. Her stance on that hadn't changed. She didn't want to be responsible for anything but seeing to her Masters' pleasure and painting to her heart's content. She had a perfect life, and nothing could induce her to tamper with that. "Let me rephrase. I want you to buy it. Ellen has talked to Sophie and Drew about investing already. She's on board. I think that's what Jonas was calling you about, so I assume he and Sabrina want to buy it as well. If we all invest, then we'll each own a quarter share."

Wheels turned as both men studied her. Finally Stefano cocked his head to one side. "Like Lex said, it's not for sale. Why does Ellen think they're suddenly going to change their minds?"

"Apparently they've stopped all cash flow to the island. The manager there can't even pay her workers. Ellen thinks the Mehlbergs are getting ready to sell at a very cheap price. They live in California, so they'd have to split the assets evenly. Ellen thinks Mr. Mehlberg is trying to devalue it so he doesn't have to pay his wife so much."

"That's not a reason to sell." Stefano took her hand between his. She rarely asked for anything but his attention, and she could tell he didn't want to deny her this thing. "Samantha, I'll buy you anything you want, but I can't promise this. I can promise to look into it. We'll call Jonas and Ellen and get the details. Okay?"

Samantha reached out her hands and cupped each of her lover's cheeks. "That's all I wanted to ask. I can tell you what I found out online, though you probably have contacts that can give you more detailed information."

Rolling to her knees, she kissed Stefano. He took over, plunging his tongue into her mouth until she purred with delight. When he broke away, she offered her lips to Alexei. He pulled her so that she straddled him, lifted her as he kissed her, and brought her down on his cock before he released her lips.

Whatever information she had found out could wait until later.

Chapter Ten

If she had an iota of talent in the kitchen, Sabrina had no doubt he would have her preparing their meal on her knees. With as much decorum as she could gather, she sank to the floor wearing only a chastity belt with a remote-controlled bullet vibrator stuck inside her pussy. The bathroom floor was tile, as was the kitchen, but the living area and the bedroom she had to pass through were both finished in bamboo. At least that type of wood would be easier on her knees. The textured tile dug in unevenly, hurting even when she wasn't moving. No doubt she'd have bruises on more than just her neck to show for tonight.

He didn't give her a pillow as he had at Mistress Hera's. She knelt on the kitchen floor, which thankfully was smooth tile, next to the island with the large marble countertop. She couldn't see what he was preparing, but that wasn't a concern. He was a damn good cook. Over the years her palate had evolved to match his favored flavor profiles.

Every time she sat back on her heels to relieve the pressure on her knees, he had her move. She followed after him, crawling around the kitchen on her hands and knees as he moved between the counter, sink, and refrigerator.

Every few minutes, he would hit the button on the remote to turn the bullet on. It would buzz away inside her until she was breathing hard, and then it would stop at a predetermined time. She watched the clock on the stove and estimated ninety seconds of torture for each round. It wasn't enough to do more than tease.

By the time dinner was ready, she vowed to never use her smug, superior smile and tone on anyone with a title.

He carried their plates to the table. Sabrina was surprised to see him with two. She thought he would feed her from his as he had done that afternoon.

Then he pulled out a chair and motioned to her. "Sit. I'll give your knees a rest while we eat. You're going to need lots of energy for tonight."

Relieved, she climbed into the chair without standing. He hadn't technically given her permission to stand. She didn't want to take the chance that he'd find fault with her and decide on another punishment. This was pushing her to the edge.

It didn't put her in the mood for conversation.

"What did you think of the tripod the other night?" Jonas cut into his steak, not even bothering to look at her as he posed the question.

Sabrina picked up her knife and fork. She had no opinion on the tripod. While she hadn't disliked it, neither did she feel the need to be suspended in midair again. "It was okay."

Now he looked at her. He studied her face as he chewed and swallowed. "That's not a very specific response."

She shrugged. "The harness dug into my legs and compressed my ribs a little uncomfortably."

He frowned as he masticated his way through another bite. "You didn't say anything."

He'd asked for her submission. She wasn't supposed to speak or do anything without his permission. It seemed logical to assume he wasn't looking to hear complaints or critiques. "I didn't know I was supposed to."

He set his fork on his plate and held a hand out in her direction. She put down her knife and placed her hand in his because it was expected. She wasn't sure she felt like holding his hand just then.

"Sabrina, you're supposed to tell me whenever something is uncomfortable or painful. Sometimes I'll expect some discomfort, but there's always a line. I don't always know what you're feeling."

She looked at her hand in his, at the perfect way they fit together. He surrounded her, cradled her without overwhelming her. Usually that was an accurate way to describe their relationship. She relied on him for so many things, most of them emotional and many of them physical. He was as necessary to her well-being as oxygen.

And he was pulling the rug right out from under her. She wanted to withdraw her hand, put it in her lap, and hide it in her other hand. Anything to assuage the uncertainty and turmoil within.

She didn't always know what she was feeling, but she knew when she was nearing the end of her endurance. It was close. If she could just hold out for one more day. Giving him what he wanted made her happy. Usually that meant getting what she wanted. She had to come to terms with the fact it wouldn't always be like that.

"I think I wouldn't have liked it very much if you hadn't flogged me. You're very good at that."

He flashed a brief smile. He knew he was accomplished with whips, canes, and floggers. He'd spent years honing his skills.

She scrambled to give him more of an answer. "I guess it's like exhibitionism. It doesn't turn me on, but it doesn't kill the moment either. I concentrated on you and forgot about the crowd and the fact I was suspended from three pieces of wood tied together at the top."

"The tie was for show. They were bolted together. I wouldn't take that kind of chance with your safety."

She opened and closed her mouth, stopping several trains of thought before she settled on a response. "I know that, Jonas. I trust you." It wasn't a lie. She trusted him. She just wasn't sure how much she trusted herself. Before she always had him at her back to push her forward and tell her she was all right. Now he was asking her to remove herself from the equation. Wasn't he?

Damn, it was all so difficult to sort out! She hated the way she felt so off-kilter. This was supposed to be a honeymoon and her birthday gift. She'd pictured lazy days at the beach and nights filled with sex. Well, she knew more than just her nights would be filled with sex.

Jonas became amorous when she fished down her bra for a stray Cheerio. The sight of her on the beach wearing a bathing suit would definitely give him ideas.

Things had started out that way, which just made the progression of the week that much more confusing.

He gave her a reassuring squeeze. "I wasn't thinking of getting one for home. I think you enjoyed yourself, but it didn't add anything new or special. Is that accurate?"

She nodded. He released her hand and went back to eating. She did the same. Several bites later, he smiled.

"It wasn't easy to flog you around all those straps. I prefer to have nothing in the way so I can concentrate on you."

That was so like something he would have said before they came to Elysium. Talking through a scene to find out what they'd both enjoyed and what they each felt needed to be changed had been a normal post-coital conversation. But this week, her issues weren't with the sex. That was as good as ever. Sabrina's heart swelled at this glimpse of the man she'd married. She returned his smile. "That works for me."

The tension broke, and they conversed amiably for the rest of dinner. Afterward he removed her collar, the belt, and the bullet. Then he brought her a shirt for their evening check in with the kids, which he confiscated the moment he closed the laptop.

He drew her to her feet and slipped his arms around her, pulling her so close she couldn't tell the difference between them. For the longest time, he held her. She realized how much she missed this simple act of affection and how much internal strength she drew from him. For the first time since that morning, she didn't feel like the world had changed and left her behind.

At last he kissed her on the forehead. "Remind me of your safe word."

"Onion." She'd never needed to use it, but this bit of normalcy also served to steady her nerves.

She expected him to release her, order her to her knees, and make her crawl to the bedroom. But his lips just kept moving across her face. He kissed her eyebrows and her temples. He used his lips to caress her cheeks and her eyelids. By the time he slipped his tongue into her mouth, she was liquid in his arms. He mastered her, taking over her will with just the power of his kiss.

This was the kind of surrender she loved. It felt natural that she would give herself over to his physical mastery. It wasn't forced or coerced. Though he didn't ask for it outright, he made his expectation clear, and she reveled in surrendering to him.

As he ended the kiss, he scooped her into his arms and carried her into the bedroom. She snuggled against his shoulder and inhaled his unique, utterly male scent. "I love you." It came out on a sigh of contentment.

He set her on the bed and pressed a kiss to her lips. "I love you, too, honey. Now hold out your wrists."

She eagerly obeyed. He flashed her a pleased smile and turned to the dresser. White PVC cuffs, the birthday gift from Sophia and Drew, sat out next to the floggers and crops they'd brought from home. The suite came equipped with everything, but if Jonas had the option, he preferred to use his own gear.

Sabrina didn't know why, but Jonas had always favored white lingerie and accessories where she was concerned. He said the color highlighted her innate purity. Whatever the reason, when she wore the color, he definitely took notice.

He buckled them around her wrists, but he didn't bother with the matching pair for her ankles. Then he snapped them together. "That's all you're going to get tonight."

She stared at the insubstantial bindings around her wrists. The material was bendable, but it didn't breathe well. Jonas had left them loose, not enough to slip her hands free, but enough so that they weren't suffocating her skin. They were lightweight and shiny, but they had no elasticity.

They'd hold her, but they didn't make her feel like she was bound. Sabrina liked heavier materials like leather or rope, something firm that made its presence known. She frowned at them even as she noted that the white did look good against her skin. It gave her a little more of a rosy glow.

Jonas stripped off his shirt and climbed onto the bed behind her. He arranged the pillows behind his back so that he could sit up comfortably. "Go choose two paddles from the dresser. You may also look in the cupboard in the living room if you'd like."

She hadn't expected this. When they role-played, one of his personalities, Armand, liked to spank her. Another was very into bondage. He liked to tie her up and fuck her until she passed out. Then there was the virgin who needed repeated lessons on how and where to touch a woman. Save Armand, none of them, including Jonas, spent so much time on her ass.

Because she knew what was on the dresser already, she headed to the living room to survey that selection. The large oak armoire had many more implements than Jonas had ever used on her. Some of them were meant for the male anatomy. She'd seen them at Ellen's and at Sophia's homes.

In the paddle section, she found nothing new. There were only three. One leather paddle was long enough to hit both cheeks at the same time. That wouldn't work in close quarters. Jonas was obviously expecting her to lie across his lap. The other leather one was the right size and shape, but they had a similar one in the bedroom. The last was small and round. It had an extra flap on it that would provide a loud sound to augment the small slap it would produce.

Frowning, Sabrina went back into the bedroom. Jonas waited patiently, his elbows propped on the higher pillows behind him. He didn't appear surprised that she returned empty-handed.

From the dresser, she selected a short rubber paddle. It stung, but it had enough bounce so that her skin didn't chafe, which meant she could handle more. Her hide wasn't as tough as she'd like it to be.

As her eyes roamed the rest of the selection—there was only one more paddle—they came to rest on her hairbrush. She'd set it there earlier and forgot about it. The hourglass handle was made from tortoiseshell, as was the oval head. It was hard and smooth. She wondered what it would feel like against her ass. On a whim, she picked it up.

Setting them down on the bed next to Jonas, she knelt on the floor. Something told her that he hadn't suspended her submissive role. In no way should she assume he considered them equals. That rankled, but she squelched the feeling. For a spanking from Jonas, she'd do just about anything.

"Ask for it."

This, too, was the man she'd married. Tension drained from her shoulders. "Please spank me with these."

He lifted the brush and turned it around in his hand, studying the smooth back and the boar bristles that kept her hair soft and tangle-free. "Interesting choice."

For the first time, she realized he could strike her with either side. She wasn't sure about the bristles, but anticipation coiled under her breasts just the same. "Do you approve? I could choose something else if you want."

Jonas shook his head. "Get your ass up here."

She assumed the position, her bound arms stretched above her head and her bottom in the air. Her legs were spread and her knees bent so that he could access every part of her. She liked this position immensely. Though she was vulnerable, she didn't feel exposed. This was the kind of submission that made her feel complete. All her worries and all those nagging doubts drifted away. Only Jonas existed.

The smooth head of her brush caressed her right cheek. Then it lifted and fell. The angle and the amount of force were perfect. He delivered a few more hits, and then he turned the brush around. As he had with the smooth side, he rubbed the bristles over her skin. It scratched the unscathed area over which he first tried it, sending complex signals through her nerve endings. It both chafed and tickled.

He explored this new toy, using it on her thighs and calves, even the bottoms of her feet, which sent her into a giggling fit. While Sabrina had scratched him in the heat of passion, he'd never tried scratching her before. His nails were always pared down too much to be effective.

"This leaves some beautiful lines on your skin." He switched hands and ran it over her back and shoulders with his left hand while he explored her pussy with his right. She was dripping wet, ready for anything he wanted to dish out. "And you like it, don't you?"

"Yes, Jonas. I like it." In the midst of congratulating herself for a good find, he'd switched the brush back to his right hand, and he pressed the coarse bristles against her exposed pussy. The sharp spines dug in like thick needles. It was a new sensation, and it took a minute to process the pain. She couldn't tell if it was radiating to other parts of her body or if it centered only in her pussy.

She went absolutely still, waiting for what he would do next. He eased the pressure slowly, and that's when the flood of endorphins released. She moaned loudly. Her pussy felt a little numb. The sensations had all gone subcutaneous. Then hot pain exploded. He'd smacked her ass with the bristle side of the brush. It felt like nothing she'd experienced before. It hurt, yes, but the pricking set off a firestorm that nearly blinded her with need.

She yelped, but that only seemed to encourage him. He hit again and again. Every few swats he flipped the brush, bombarding her with contradictory types of pain. The emotional upheaval of the past few days came to the fore, and her emotional dam burst. By the time he stopped, she was sobbing.

Normally when she broke like this, he held her in his arms until it subsided, but this time he simply extracted his legs from underneath her and removed the rest of his clothes. She felt his fingers at her back entrance, spreading cool gel.

"Take a deep breath, honey. Breathe out when I push in."

She thought it was a little heartless of him to ignore her breakdown, but she was too flustered to follow through on anything but what he told her to do. With the way her body and mind had short-circuited, she couldn't feel more than a pressure and a fullness when he pushed into her.

When he was fully seated, he pulled her up until she sat on his lap, her back against his chest and her legs draped on either side of his. Her bound wrists rested near where her empty pussy gaped, begging for attention it wasn't going to get. She was in the perfect position to masturbate, but she knew he wouldn't allow it. She let her head slump back against his shoulder.

With one hand on her chin, he turned her head and planted a searing kiss on her lips. "Let go, Sabrina. You belong to me. Your body belongs to me. Give me everything."

She did. The rest of her reservations fell away and she surrendered. As if he sensed her complete submission, he wrapped his arms around her body and held her, wiping the remnants of her tears with his thumbs.

"Just feel, honey. That's all I want you to do. Feel. Be. No thinking allowed."

She couldn't think if she wanted to, and she desperately didn't want to. His hands moved over her body, leisurely exploring her thighs, hips, and stomach. She wished he would have introduced anal sex through a role-playing scene. She would have gladly given him anything he wanted in a scene. Because this wasn't one, they weren't pretending to be other people, she felt like she had no point of reference, no way to understand the complex emotions simmering just below the surface.

Part of her felt broken, but she shoved it away, determined to give Jonas what he wanted. She closed her eyes, and a few more tears fell. Thank goodness she wasn't facing him.

He cupped her breasts and tweaked her nipples, rolling them between his fingers until she gasped. No matter where her brain might go, he knew how to bring her back, how to play her body perfectly to get the reaction he wanted. In minutes, he had her writhing again.

"I'm going to shift you forward, honey. I want you to grip the headboard. Hold on tightly. You're going to need the leverage." Gripping her hips carefully, he maneuvered them into position. When he finished, she was on her knees, and she clung to the headboard. He knelt behind her. His thighs were between hers, spreading her wide open.

She took a deep, shaky breath. Having him lodged deep inside her was intimate and comforting. It didn't feel like much of anything, not that she would tell him that, except a connection. She desperately needed the connection.

He withdrew and thrust back into her slowly. A need manifested, one that he wasn't fulfilling. It was a little manic and vague, but it wasn't going to be denied. Several thrusts later, it still hovered on the brink of being discovered.

"Harder," she breathed. "Faster. Please."

He increased the pace, but he was still being too careful. He was holding back, and she knew it wasn't with the intention of making her beg. His control was going to drive her nuts. He withdrew, and when he thrust again, she sank back, meeting him with as much force as she could manage.

His hips slapped her ass and upper thighs where they still tingled and stung from the spanking. That combined with the way his cock hit something significant to wring a cry of pleasure from her. Jonas got the message.

Not only did he pick up the pace, he slammed against her with abandon. Fucking her hard and fast, he threw off any pretense of mercy. The fingers of one hand dug into her hip while the other found her clit. He abused that whole area to a different rhythm, one at odds with the way he fucked her.

She was still a little tender from their marathon that afternoon. Her back arched to get away from him, but she only succeeded in making her position more perfect for him. Now when he slammed against her, his balls slapped her labia next to her empty hole with a light, soft thud.

It was enough to send her over the edge. She clung to the cliff with one shred of sanity. "Please let me come."

"Yes," he hissed. "Give it to me."

She did. Her whole body clenched and bowed. She left her shell for several seconds, floating above to see the beauty of their perfect joining. Yes, she was his. She belonged to him, and she never wanted to be anywhere else but in his arms.

He came hard, thrusting one last time and releasing jets of hot semen into her. She felt claimed in a whole new way, one she quite liked.

Later, after they'd cleaned up and slipped under the sheet to snuggle, Sabrina thanked him for the experience.

He stroked his hand down the length of her hair. "So you liked it?"

"Very much. But it didn't hurt or pinch or any of those things you thought it might do. I guess I'm not sensitive there, either." When they'd met, she had never experienced an orgasm. Through trial and error, they found out that she needed to be bound in some way, and she liked it extremely rough. She'd come a long way since then, but they had to start somewhere. This was no different.

He tilted her chin up and planted soft kisses over her cheeks and mouth. "Stands to reason. That's okay. I like that I don't have to be so careful with you. I can be as rough as I want and you like it."

"Yes. We're well matched that way." But she was beginning to doubt they were as well matched in other ways. Before doubts could assail her, she shifted until she lay on top of him. "I want to touch you."

He gave her one of those slow, sleepy grins that challenged her to keep him awake. She was up to the challenge.

* * * *

The next morning, he woke her with kisses that roamed her neck and breasts. By the time she opened her eyes, he had buried his cock between her legs. She loved when he woke her like this. In the past few years, this had happened too few times. It tapered off when she was pregnant and stopped completely until the baby was sleeping through the night on a regular basis. Then Rose learned how to climb out of her crib, and she made a beeline for their bed.

They really needed to start using the lock on their door.

She lifted her knees, wrapped her legs around his waist, and hung on for the ride. Jonas took her hands from his shoulders and pressed them to the pillow on either side of her head. Weakness spread through her body, and her legs fell away. With that one act, he rendered her completely pliant.

Immediately he picked up his pace, though he didn't pound against her pussy the way she liked. It was a slower climb to the top. Heat burned in her core at a slow simmer, and she felt even more helpless.

Above her, Jonas closed his eyes, purposely oblivious to her aching need. Shades of passion crossed his face. He murmured praises, telling her how good she felt and how good she made him feel. His heartfelt admissions fulfilled a different need, one that wasn't so easy to reach or define.

For the first time in days, she felt like she was giving him what he wanted. For most of their vacation, she'd felt lost, adrift in a sea of unclear expectations where she wasn't sure about anything he did. Knowing he was lost in something only she could give him sent her careening over the edge. She called his name. He pressed his forehead to hers and they came together.

She'd never felt so close to Jonas. Over the course of the week, she'd been terrified they were drifting apart. Something about having anal sex, having him claim her in such an intimate way, a way in which nobody had ever claimed her, made her feel like things were back to normal. Her emotional upheaval disappeared.

They spent the morning in bed, dozing between bouts of lovemaking. It was during one of those lazy times when her phone rang. The sound hadn't roused Jonas, so she scurried across the room with the intention of turning off the ringer. The caller ID showed Sophia, which made her hesitate. Sophia was one of her closest friends, and she was the only other Domme Jonas allowed her to see when she needed a session and he couldn't give her one. She didn't call unless she had something specific to say, so Sabrina picked up.

"Hi, Sophie. How are you?"

"Sabrina, I have to admit I'm a little shocked. You're buying Elysium?"

Chapter Eleven

Drew took his time prepping dinner. He wouldn't cook it until later, but he wanted to marinate the shrimp and scallops in his new concoction for at least two hours. The vegetables were all cut and lined up artfully on skewers. The bell peppers and two different summer squashes, fresh from his garden, were best lightly grilled. Sophia liked a little more char on her barbecue, but she loved his grilling too much to argue with him on this issue.

Of course that attitude didn't help when it came to his take on Italian foods. He'd learned early on that Sophia's entire family knew a hell of a lot more about that genre than he did. Over the past four years, he'd added a host of generational Italian cooking secrets to his repertoire.

His next cookbook, due out in six months, featured a wide array of recipes he'd picked up from the DiMarco clan. He'd featured his mother-in-law on several episodes of his show, and he'd named her as a contributing author. He hadn't asked her permission because he knew she wouldn't give it. Better to tell her after the fact when she couldn't argue. After all, he and his father-in-law had tricked her into signing the paperwork. It wasn't a bad philosophy. Flawed, yes, but it worked for him.

With a sigh, he threw his used dishtowel in the laundry. They should be ready for him about now. He headed downstairs, to the dungeon his wife had installed when he was out of town on a particularly tight leg of his last book tour.

Drew wasn't a submissive. He tended toward the alpha side, but he wasn't dominant either. Bondage was fun. He didn't mind restraining someone every now and again, and he did like to use the blindfold, but he wanted no part of the S/M portions. He'd tried it from both angles for Sophia's sake. He found out nothing he didn't already know. While he didn't mind slapping an ass or twisting a nipple every now and again, he didn't get a sexual charge from dishing out pain or receiving it.

But his wife did. She was a Domme, and there was no changing that fact, which he wouldn't even if he could. Sophia was one of a kind, and she was his. Because Drew liked threesomes, and so did Sophia, these kinks worked themselves out. He chuckled at his joke as he descended the stairs.

When they'd started out, the rule had been that they didn't begin a scene unless they were both present. He'd amended that after he'd realized how uninterested he was in watching or participating in the pain parts of a scene. Sophia was in the dungeon already. She had been for almost an hour, torturing Christopher, who couldn't climax without pain. Though they hadn't shared the rule with Chris outright, the man was bright enough to catch on to the fact that Sophia was never going to let him come unless Drew was present. No doubt he was listening for any sign that Drew had joined them.

Drew opened the door to the dungeon. Sophia called it a playroom, but Drew rarely felt playful in it. Whenever a sight like this one greeted him, he only felt the gravity of the situation.

Christopher was a handsome man. He had strong features and eyes so deep brown they appeared black. When they'd first met, Drew had thought he would become closer to Chris, and those eyes might look at him with adoration or another deep emotion.

They did, sort of. He watched Drew come toward him, the expression in his eyes nothing short of a bottomless desire. Drew was the only man Chris ever consented to having sex with.

Right now Chris was bent over a PVC structure that supported his hips and shoulders. A bar connecting the two supported his torso. His arms were bound together and secured to an O ring on floor. Each ankle was bound separately, spreading him open for whatever torment his Mistress devised, and his thighs were tied tightly to the supports. Having tried it out, Drew knew how the circular pieces of the structure dug into the body. It was part of the torture Chris loved.

Two steel lines were clipped to Chris's testicles, their weight stretching the sac so far that Drew's balls ached in sympathy. A series of metal rings covered his hard-on, and Drew didn't look too close. Sophie had a set of those that had spikes on the inside. He didn't begrudge another man his pain, but he didn't get off on it either. Another set of chains ran from the gag in Chris's mouth to his nipples. If the man turned his head either way, he was going to be hurting more than he already was.

Because Chris's skin was so dark, Drew had to look close to see the pattern of red welts covering the man's back, ass, and thighs. If he lifted Chris up to look at his front, he'd no doubt find a similar pattern there. Sophia had been pissed at a supplier this morning. She'd ripped him a new asshole, but that wasn't enough to appease her temper. It was good they had a session scheduled with Chris.

Even with a ball gag shoved into his mouth and his expression twisted with a combination of ecstasy and torment, he managed to give Drew a pleading look. He wanted to be fucked, badly.

"He's being punished." Sophia wrapped her arms around Drew's neck, focusing his attention completely on her. She knew that while this part didn't bother him, he definitely preferred to miss it. His lovely little wife could be positively ruthless, which is what brought Christopher back time and again, on his knees, begging for more. Drew could admit that he liked watching submissives beg at his wife's feet.

Truthfully Chris did fulfill something vital in Drew. Not only was he one of the only men Sophia consented to having in their bed, if Drew were to dig deep into his heart, he had to admit he liked having a submissive male at his disposal.

Drew brushed his lips over Sophia's. She liked soft and tender lovemaking, a contradiction to her harsh Dominatrix personality that he adored. Over that past few years, she'd let her luxurious dark brown hair grow longer. Even in a ponytail, it reached almost to the top of her corset. He grabbed it near the band and used it to pull her head back, exposing the long column of her throat. Nothing brought out his alpha tendencies like seeing her sexy body in Domme gear.

Sophia was easily the most beautiful woman in the entire world. Her Mediterranean skin tone meant she had a constant tan, though his penchant for seeing her on exotic beaches also contributed to that, and she was flawless. From head to toe, she was smooth and soft, completely feminine and physically perfect.

That wasn't all. She was intelligent, witty, and charming. He loved discussing a limitless list of topics with her. She always had an opinion to share about food, politics, celebrity gossip, and accounting. Drew had never realized how subjective topics involving numbers could be, but being with Sophia had opened his eyes in ways his math teachers only ever dreamed of doing. He liked her as well as loved her. She had become his best friend, confidant, cheerleader, and champion. He would do anything for her even though she rarely asked for more than his presence.

Her smile made his heart quicken, and that sharp inhale she took just now brought his cock to life. Nobody affected her the way he did. Not a single one of her submissives could bring that sultry twist to her lips.

"I want you first," he said, scooping her up in his arms. He gave her no chance to argue at the way he was changing the order of events in the scene, but that came as no surprise. He was forever revising the scripted scenes she went over with him before any of their playmates arrived.

She snuggled into his hold, settling her head against his shoulder for the short trip to the bed. It was to the side of Christopher. He wouldn't be able to watch unless he wanted to endure the pain of that clamp pulling at his nipple. Sophia smiled up at Drew, her eyes soft and dreamy.

He set her down before they got to the bed and turned her around so he could loosen her corset. As lovely as her breasts looked lifted up and squished together like that, he preferred her naked. She caught the stiff material as it fell, and Drew closed his hands over her mounds. She laughed at where his attention went, and she arched her back to press them firmly against his palms.

"What did he do?" He kissed her again, as soon as the question was out. The answer could wait. Christopher groaned, the whiny, begging kind that made Sophia hotter than she already was.

He moved his hands to her waist, where he unzipped her shiny, PVC micro-shorts and peeled them from her shapely hips. Releasing her lips, he bent to worship her breasts and stomach as he rid her of the rest of her clothing.

She tugged his shirt over his head. "He got mouthy."

Drew made a sound to show he was listening. Christopher was only a sexual submissive. He often needed discipline to remember his place, and sometimes he earned a punishment in the process. Drew knew how much he frustrated Sophia. If he could find another man who fulfilled Sophia's need to dominate who could handle the transition better, Drew would bring him home and gift wrap him for his wife.

With a soft pressure on her hips, he guided her backward to the bed, pushing until she sat down. Then he lifted one of her legs and parked it over his shoulder. Sophia gave that sexy little sigh as she ran her fingers through his hair. That sigh turned to a moan as he swiped his tongue along her folds.

One taste was all it ever took. Her flavor was his weakness. He opened his mouth wider, licking wide swaths, gathering her essence into his mouth. His moans matched hers. When she was close, he latched onto her clit and inserted two fingers into her cunt, expertly finding her sweet spot. She came in his mouth in a gush of creamy goodness.

Before she finished pulsing around his fingers, he climbed out of his pants and on top of her. She guided him inside and locked her legs around his back. Then she licked her juices from his face and kissed him with all the passion he'd come to expect from her. He braced himself on his elbows and watched her face as he moved his hips.

Her hands roamed his body, caressing his shoulders and back, arms and chest, and then wandering down to grab his ass. Her legs moved just as restlessly, rubbing against his hips and thighs or wrapping around his waist as she met his thrusts.

She went wild beneath him, her body bowing and her hands clutching at the sheet. He renewed his concentration as her velvety warmth tightened around him. She felt so good, but if he could manage to hold on for a few more seconds, she would come apart in his arms.

Her pussy spasmed as she cried out. Her entire body went stiff as he thrust once, twice more before that sweet bliss overtook him. He collapsed on top of her. He would have fallen to the side, but she latched onto him and pulled him down.

To the left, Christopher groaned. Sophia's eyes opened and she turned her head to check on him. For the first time ever, she didn't look thrilled to see him. Drew rolled to let her up. She moved slowly, deliberately, and he realized that she wasn't finished punishing Chris.

She bent in front of Chris and took his chin in her hand. "If I'm not pleased with what comes out of your mouth, I will untie you and send you home."

Drew started at her threat. She usually promised pain, bondage, or the agony of a denied orgasm. This was the first time she'd given such an ultimatum. From the look on his face, Christopher understood that his ass was on the line. She removed the gag, letting it swing and dangle from his nipples.

Chris winced. "I'm sorry, Mistress. Please forgive me. I have learned my lesson."

He sounded sincere. Sophia seemed satisfied because she reached for a low stool that she set near Chris. Then she propped her foot on top of it so that her pussy was bared to Chris. Wet with spent passion and the remnants of Drew's ejaculate, her pussy glistened.

"Clean me up with your tongue."

This got Drew's interest. Though he loved licking her pussy, he couldn't resist watching when a submissive did it. Chris parted his lips. He had great lips, strong and sensual, and he knew how to use them. Sophia brought her pussy closer. At first, she stayed still as Chris did his work. Then she thrust against his face and tongue as her passion reignited.

But she pulled away before things went too far. She touched a finger to Chris's lip. "Good boy. Now you're going to do the same for Drew."

At that cue, Drew slid off the mattress and approached Chris. He was already semi-erect from watching Sophia with a man's face between her legs. Chris opened his mouth, panting and pleading with his eyes because he didn't want to risk Sophia's wrath for speaking without permission.

Drew gave him what he wanted. He let Chris lick evidence of Sophia's orgasm from his cock until he was fully erect. Then he thrust forward and fucked Chris's mouth, not bothering to show any kind of mercy or consideration. Chris swallowed convulsively, trying not to gag as Drew fed him the entire length.

Sophia knelt next to Chris. As he pumped his hips, he heard little clicks, each of which produced another groan from Chris that vibrated pleasantly through Drew's cock. After a few minutes, Chris screamed and something dropped to the floor. Sophia stood up. She had that multi-layered ring in her hand. She set it aside.

"Do you want to come in his mouth or fuck his ass? Or we could fuck him at the same time."

She still had that sated smile courtesy of the orgasm he'd given her. He wanted to see her have another. He withdrew from Chris's mouth. "Let's fuck him at the same time."

With a nod, she gestured to the bindings on Christopher's arms. "You get the front and I'll get the back."

When he bent down, Drew noticed the steel lines were no longer attached to Chris's balls. He wondered if Sophia had jerked them off or taken them off gently. Chris's scream suggested the former.

The answer waited on the counter where he took the bindings. Sophia washed and disinfected everything after a session, so used accessories never went back in their places immediately. Waiting next to the steel set of four cock rings, which did have small spikes inside the rings, were the steel lines. The weights at the end had multiplied. Sophia had increased the load until gravity took over.

Drew neither winced nor shook his head. He knew Chris needed the pain if he was going to be able to climax.

Sophia helped Chris to his feet and led him to the bed. She climbed on and guided him to kneel between her legs. Chris waited obediently for Drew to roll on a condom and mount him from behind. Though he could have reamed Chris, and sometimes he did, Drew wasn't in the mood this time. If Chris had been mouthy to Sophia, he didn't get to have that kind of consideration. This was going to be all about Drew, and Drew liked to fuck slowly and thoroughly.

Christopher's ass was incredible. Tight, defined muscles flexed over one of the sexiest male asses Drew had ever seen. He spent some time caressing Chris's skin and luxuriating in the feel of those firm glutes. The fact that he put pressure on the welts and the parts where he'd simply been flogged made Chris moan and writhe all the more.

Below them both, Sophia fingered her clit as she watched their faces. She never got tired of watching him fuck. She brought her finger, glistening with cream, to her mouth and sucked it clean. He couldn't see the expression on Christopher's face, but Sophia scooped up more of her cream and held it for Chris to suck from her finger.

He handed Sophia a condom, which she took and rolled over Christopher's cock. From the hiss he issued and the way his hips jerked forward, he gathered that Sophia had grabbed Christopher's cock and urged him to place it at her entrance.

"Drew sets the pace, Christopher. Follow his lead."

This appealed to the alpha in Drew. He waited for Sophia's signal telling him that Chris was seated inside her, then he pushed his cock through that tense ring of muscle. Christopher matched the rhythm he set, thrusting into Sophia when Drew withdrew. He fucked Christopher, but he watched Sophia's face. He loved the way her lips parted and her back arched when she was about to come.

And Chris was incredible. He made growling sounds of pleasure in the back of his throat. They rumbled through his chest and grew louder when Drew pressed one of the welts left from his caning.

"Mistress, please may I come?"

Sophia laughed. Drew could tell she was close, but she wasn't going to let Christopher come until she'd tortured him a little first. She peeked around Chris and met Drew's eyes, and he knew she was trying to gauge how close he was. Not about to hurry things along, he shook his head. Her lips curled with a feline grin, and she raked her nails down Christopher's chest.

A shudder ran through the man, and his movements slowed down considerably. He was fighting the urge to climax. In a perverse turn, Drew thrust hard and fast, making sure he hit at least one welt with his hips or thighs each time he hit home.

Christopher cried out, shades of ecstasy mixed with his agony. "Please, Mistress. Please let me come!"

"No. Fuck me faster." Sophia reached up and caressed Christopher's face. It amazed Drew how she knew when to be cruel and when to give him a gentle reassurance. "Tell Drew how much you like it when he fucks you."

"A lot. I like it a lot."

From the sounds of it, Chris was losing his fight to stay in the moment. Sophia kept rubbing her hand against his face. She peppered it with kisses. "Christopher, you used to be so good with words."

In his daily life, Christopher was a corporate attorney. He had a voice that flowed like honey over velvet, and his persuasive technique consistently overrode Sophia's oaths that she wouldn't have him back because he was such a disrespectful son of a bitch until she brought him down a few notches.

"Drew you have an incredible cock and you fuck like a stallion."

Coming from anybody else, it might have sounded condescending or insincere, but Christopher meant it. The truth was evident in the way he met every thrust and the way he trembled with pleasure.

Heat shot up Drew's spine and his balls lifted. He came with a shout, burying his cock as deep as it would go. When he pulled out, he slapped Christopher's ass, hard. Sophia smiled up at him, but she spoke to Chris.

"Faster, Chris. Make me come."

Chris moved his hips obediently to the rhythm she dictated. Drew lay on the bed next to them, watching. He traced his fingertips lazily over Sophia's breasts. As she got closer, he angled his head between their chests and took her nipple in his mouth. She screamed as she came.

"Mistress?" Chris kept up the pace, knowing that if he stopped without permission she would completely deny him. "Please may I come?"

"Yes," She whispered, but Chris had waited so long, he climaxed before she finished speaking the word.

He gave a mighty roar, his eyes rolled back into his head, and his entire body shuddered.

Drew loved the raw pleasure on Christopher's face. He helped the submissive fall to the side so he wouldn't crush Sophia, and then he kissed his sated wife. He definitely had the best of both worlds.

Later as he put the shrimp on the grill, he heard the phone ring. Sophia sat in a lounge chair by the pool. When she answered she sounded half asleep.

"Hi, Ellen. How are you?"

Drew listened, but Sophia didn't do much more than agree and make tired mm-hmm sounds. Then she sat up straight, all evidence of lethargy gone.

"You want me to buy *what*? Don't get me wrong, it would be totally cool to own that, but I'm not rich, Ellen. I can't afford it."

It drove Drew nuts that she never considered his money at all. If she wanted to purchase anything, she only looked at her checking account. He'd added her name to his account, but she had never once used it. She'd only consented to having her name on it when he pointed out that it would make things easier if there was ever an emergency.

She laughed nervously into the phone. "Even if Jonas and Sabrina go in on it, I don't have enough money to buy it. A third or a quarter share is just out of my range."

He had hundreds of millions of dollars, enough to buy her a small island if she wanted. In a huff, he snatched the phone from Sophia's hand. "Ellen, she can too afford it. Go ahead and buy it." Then he hung up.

Sophia stared at him, an incredulous expression on her face. "I can't believe you did that."

There was no point in reminding her that she was fabulously wealthy. He set his jaw firmly, which was difficult because he noticed the fire it lit in her eyes. "Did what? Bought you something you want? It's my prerogative. Deal with it."

"Drew, you just bought Elysium."

Though he had never been there, he had heard of Elysium. It was an island devoted to adult pleasures. Then he couldn't help but laugh. He'd bought her an island. He kissed her on the cheek. "Happy Fourth of July."

Chapter Twelve

"I'm *what*?"

Sabrina's tone roused Jonas from the fringes of sleep. He'd heard the phone ring, and he was aware of her hurrying silently across the room to get it before it could rouse him. The sleepy intention of a smile slipped away as he went on full alert. She didn't sound upset or pissed, only shocked, so he ruled out problems with the kids.

He sat up as she turned to level an inquisitive and suspicious look in his direction.

"No," she continued, "I don't know anything about it."

At her continued frown, he shrugged. He didn't know anything about it, either. He didn't even know who she was talking to, much less what they were discussing. Because her tone had gone back to normal, his interest faded. He gathered his clothes and headed to the shower. Their flight left at ten the next morning, so this was their last day at Elysium. Whether they were open or not, he wanted to show her the Fields of Punishment.

He cleaned up quickly. When he emerged, he found Sabrina sitting in the chair near the slider wearing one of his cotton shirts. He liked the way it looked on her, especially with her sex-tousled hair, so he let her keep it on. He planted a kiss on her cheek. "Why don't you go rinse off and then we'll see if any of the restaurants survived to serve lunch?"

She caught his hand before he could turn away and opened her mouth to say something, but she was interrupted by a male voice. Alexei or Stefano, he didn't know which, spoke through the speaker on her phone. "Sabrina, what's this I hear about you wanting to buy Elysium?"

No words came to mind. This was one of the few times in his life when his mind went totally blank. Even when she'd shocked him five years ago by asking him to marry her without even introducing herself, he had about five ready retorts. It had been a matter of choosing the appropriate response.

She wanted to buy Elysium? He took a step back to wrap his head around that one. Then a thousand thoughts flooded his mind. She would have to travel a lot to run a business in the Caribbean. There was no way she could fit in another responsibility. Between working and being a wife and mother, she was tapped out.

She sighed heavily. "Lex, I don't want to buy Elysium. From what I can gather, Ellen wants to buy it. She wants to go in on it with Sophia and Drew, you guys, and us. I can't say I'm eager to buy a sex resort. The first thing I'd need to do is work on the advertising. I think more people would come here if they thought it was a honeymoon place instead of a meat market."

"That's actually not a bad idea. We could restructure it to be more relationship-friendly, maybe host 'meat market' weeks once every six months to generate more interest. Of course we'd have to call them something else. I also think we should sell some of the rooms like a time-share instead of as a hotel." As he talked, Lex sounded more and more excited by the idea.

Jonas lifted a brow at Sabrina. While she was the one who brought the money into the relationship, she wasn't one to make a large purchase without consulting him. She shook her head in a firm indication of "hell no."

"Lex. Calm down. Have you even looked into the business end of things? The Melbergs cut off money to pay the staff and purchase supplies. The manager is going to have a hell of a time trying to get people off this island. Do you honestly think a move like that isn't going to kill the business? I want no part of this." Sabrina fiddled with a strand of her long hair, drawing his attention to one of her best features. If he were to step back and be critical, he would have a hard time deciding what he liked best about his little woman. As he considered them, every feature stood out. Even the way his bulky shirt outlined the curve of her breast was sexy.

"Sabrina? Stefano here. I made some calls. Elysium is going to tank, but that's not a bad thing. If we let it go, we can pick it up for pennies on the dollar. That'll actually make it easier to rebrand it, which was a brilliant idea on your part."

Sabrina rolled her eyes. "Why are you guys so sold on buying it? What aren't you telling me?"

One of them sighed. Even odds on who it came from.

"Sammy wants it."

Lex consistently called Jonas's sister by that name, though both of them spoiled the hell out of Sam. They were trying to make this happen because his sister had asked for it. That made sense. Still, Jonas wanted to know Sabrina's opinion on the matter. Did she want to buy a share of Elysium? What did that mean about her opinion of their week here? He wasn't getting a clear read on whether or not she enjoyed her role as a submissive. His wife was usually so easy to read.

"So you're still researching?" Sabrina sounded relieved. "Can we talk about it in a few weeks when you know something for sure?" With her eyes, she threw a question at him, and he wasn't sure what kind of answer she was looking for.

"Yes. I told Ellen not to make any sudden moves. I think she was going to catch the next flight to the nearest island with an airport. That's another thing we'll have to consider. Elysium needs its own airport. That would promote privacy."

Sabrina shook her head. "I'm going to let you guys go. Continue looking into this. I'm not sold on the investment, but I trust you. Take care, Lex and Stef, and give my best to Sam."

She ended the call and rose from the chair. "Damned if I can't tell them apart in person, then they both have to get on the phone. They have the same voices, the same inflection, and the same way of phrasing things. I wonder if they do this with all of their business calls. It could drive people insane."

Jonas shook his head and guided her arms around his waist. "It's a good thing there's only one of me."

Resting her cheek on his chest, she hugged him and sighed. "One is plenty."

They stayed like that for a few minutes, enjoying the simple pleasures found in this intimacy. Then Sabrina peeled away reluctantly, an apology on her face. "I'm really hungry."

"Go shower," he said. "I'll find something for you to wear."

He selected a short, tangerine skirt made from a stretchy material that would be easy to move out of the way when the mood struck him. Then he grabbed a white corset-style top to go with it. Sabrina hadn't been too jazzed with this part of Sophia's present, but he had to admit their friend had excellent taste. It would provide the support Sabrina wanted, but in a way that revealed the swell of her breast and a bit of her nipple if he chose, and it left her shoulders and arms bare.

When he brought the outfit into the bathroom, he found Sabrina at the vanity, brushing her hair. He took the item from her hand and looked at it, remembering with more than a little bit of cocky pride how she had responded to being spanked with it. He glanced up to find her studying him, as if she was waiting patiently for him to use it on her. He curled his lip regretfully. Maybe later.

"Turn around. I'll finish for you." He loved brushing her hair. He couldn't remember how long it had been since she'd allowed it to happen. No more. She no longer got to call those shots.

She turned, offering him the gorgeous length that fell nearly to her waist. He started at the bottom and worked his way through her snarls. When they were gone, he spent some time watching her smooth, silky hair shimmer with each pass of the brush. In the mirror, he kept track of her facial expressions. She'd closed her eyes early on, and a contented smile played about her lips. He leaned around her and gave her a kiss. She parted her lips and yielded to him, her entire body softening, signaling him that she was his willing submissive.

If her stomach hadn't growled, he would have pressed his advantage again.

They found one restaurant open in the main dining room at Hades's Palace. As they walked along, he noticed how deserted the place seemed. Even the day before, he'd noticed there were fewer people on the island. It looked like Heather was following through on her plan to cancel all reservations. Part of him hoped Sabrina wasn't seriously considering purchasing a share of Elysium. It was a hot mess they didn't need.

Another part of him wanted her to want to buy a quarter share. It was a clue that he hadn't completely misread her, that a part of her yearned for this life. One thing for sure, she was much easier to read at home. He wished she hadn't insisted on waiting until Friday to talk things through.

At the time, he hadn't been totally comfortable with that arrangement. Part of him thought that if he didn't agree to those terms, she would refuse this experiment in full-time submission. It would give them a chance to discuss the experience as a whole instead of just dissecting the daily portions. From the way she held his hand and the carefree bounce to her step, he would say the week was a success. But there had been some tense moments when he'd sincerely doubted his plan.

She didn't protest when he steered her into a chair. If they hadn't skipped breakfast to stay in bed and make love all morning, he would have set her on the floor at his feet and fed her. It wasn't something he would do at home unless they were alone. He wanted kneeling at his feet to be a refuge for her, a place where she could retreat to when the stress of daily life became too great.

Really, that was his ultimate goal. He could see her being pulled in too many different directions. The demands of her job grew as she became more and more successful. Though she delegated a lot of the work, she bore the weight of responsibility like a lead cloak. Some days he wondered at how she held up. Add her quest to be the perfect mother and wife into the equation, and he was afraid she was going to snap.

He wanted to give her alternatives, let her know she wasn't alone. She would never be alone.

Perhaps if she did buy a share of Elysium, she could quit her job and focus on this. Co-owning it with four dominant people would make sure she didn't do more than her share. Ellen was just as type-A. There was no way she'd let Sabrina run the show. Alexei and Stefano had vast resources at their disposal. Sophia was much more laid back, but she also was the one most attuned to the nuances of Sabrina's moods. He'd sent his lovely wife to Sophia for a session more times than he could count.

"We need to think about souvenirs for Rose and Ethan. Maybe we should do some shopping today."

Sabrina's voice broke into his thoughts. He hadn't even thought about purchasing keepsakes for the kids. They hadn't checked out the shops, but they probably should if she was going to seriously consider an investment in this place.

He nodded. "We have some time. I didn't plan an excursion today. I wanted to see the Fields of Punishment."

It had been awhile since he'd been to the island. He and Ryan had come here on a dare in college. Ellen had goaded them, challenging their collective manhood. Both were studying to be Doms, and Ryan's mad crush on Ellen was still a secret.

When they'd returned, Ellen had been shocked to find they'd gone at all. She'd pressed her lips together until they were white, but all her anger had been directed at Ryan. Within two days, she had him on his knees calling her "Mistress." Jonas had been shocked at the time, but looking back, he could see all the signs he had missed.

He didn't want to miss those signs in Sabrina. She knew he'd visited here years ago with Ryan. She'd refrained from asking questions about his experiences, and for that he was grateful. He'd learned a lot from watching the Doms and Dommes at the Fields of Punishment. Back then, there had been a few teaching demonstrations. They hadn't been in the firelight and sexually charged like the one Heather had roped him into doing on the beach. There had been nothing romantic about them. To his way of thinking, that's the way a responsible instructor would run a demonstration. If the onlookers were too caught up in the moment, they would miss valuable information.

Damn. If he didn't watch it, he'd talk himself into teaching more than English and Brit Lit classes.

He looked for Sabrina's reaction to his plan, but she seemed to have none. She continued eating her lunch. He reached across the inches separating them and closed his hand around hers. "Honey, what are you thinking about?"

She lifted her gaze, looking everywhere else before she landed on him. "I think Lex and Stef are determined to buy this for Samantha. Only I can't imagine her running anything. She's a wonderful person, Jonas, but she can be a little flighty and she has zero business experience."

He wanted to be offended that she'd labeled his sister as an airhead, but he wasn't. Sam could run any business if she tried, but he couldn't see her wanting to try. Her life with Lex and Stef allowed her to concentrate on her art. Jonas couldn't remember a time when he'd seen his sister so continually and blissfully happy.

"They're not clueless. They'll have people run it for her." He gave Sabrina a reassuring squeeze.

"Yeah," she said dryly. "Ellen, Sophia, and me."

"Drew has built an empire from his cooking." He meant to be helpful, but she only frowned. "Ryan and I have minors in business."

"I know. But Lex and Stef think they know everything about everything. I can stand having them as stepbrothers because my mom is finally happy. I can stand having them as brothers-in-law because they're good for your sister. I'm not sure I can work with them."

Jonas threw his wrench into the gears. "I'm not sure you have the time to take on something else. You might want to consider what you're willing to give up."

The shock for which he was waiting never came. He'd never said anything to her about the way she tore herself into pieces trying to have it all. She set her fork on the edge of her empty plate, and when she spoke, he had to strain to hear her. "I know."

"You don't have to think about this until you get home. See what kind of information Lex and Stef turn up, talk to Ellen and Sophia. I'm not at all sure whether or not this is something I want you or us taking on."

His assessment seemed to comfort her. She smiled. "Shopping, and then the Fields of Punishment. I'm going to have to brush up on Greek mythology, I think. I don't remember those."

"It's part of the Underworld," he said. "Elysium is where exceptional souls get to spend eternity. They have to die as heroes three times to get there. The Fields of Punishment are where those who have been bad are sent to suffer eternal torment, a kind of Tartarus, if you will. It's the perfect place for masochists and sadists."

She nailed him with a worried look. "So it's like an outdoor dungeon?"

"From what I remember."

"And you just want to take a look at it?"

He thought they might do more than look, but he didn't have definite plans. If there was something that caught her attention more than other things, he might have her try it. "That's the plan. It's been twenty years. I don't know if they have anything you'll like."

She pressed her lips together, and he recognized that she was trying to hold in laughter.

"You're allowed to laugh."

Her smile grew and she shook her head. "I'm not into torture, you know. I can't think there would be anything there I'd like. Isn't that the point of the place, though, to punish naughty subs and slaves?"

Releasing her hand, he pushed back a lock of her hair. "You know that not every sadist or masochist is into having D/s relationships, right? Think about you and Sophia."

Sabrina drew back a little. They'd never discussed what went on when she had a session with Sophia. He treated it no differently than if she'd gone for a professional massage. "Sophia is just a friend. She wouldn't think of dominating me, but she does Domme for other people."

"Exactly. She flogs or whips or canes you, and then you go out to lunch. You'll find lots of that in the Fields of Punishment. Being submissive isn't for everyone."

He couldn't read the emotion in her chocolate eyes, and that unnerved him a little. Was that relief or upset or indifference?

She licked her lips. "I bet there's at least a St. Andrew's cross and a spanking bench. I like those."

He exhaled with relief.

Later, after they'd discovered the gift shops were all closed, he led her toward the Fields of Punishment. Things didn't look quite right there, either. Most of the stations were abandoned and marked off limits.

Sabrina looked around. Disappointment marred her chin with a frown. "It looks like Mistress Hera has had her staff meetings. I guess we were lucky to find an open restaurant. Good thing we're leaving in the morning."

He heaved a sigh. He'd wanted to show her the place in action. "It looks like they haven't done much to it. It had six stations when I was here before. I see eight."

Some of the stations were exactly the same. The single cross had turned into twin crosses, set up back to back so that someone being whipped could watch someone else receiving similar treatment. Jonas wasn't sure he liked that. The submissive's attention should be on her Master and what he was doing to her.

Sabrina must have thought the same thing. "I would want a curtain between them. Even if it's just a tree or a really tall bush, I think the areas should be separated."

"Yeah," he agreed. "Or turn them so that they're parallel. Voyeurs would like to see the masochist's face. Sometimes that's the best part."

A colorful bird landed on top of the nearest cross. It called a few times before flying away. Sabrina watched it arc across the clear sky. Her gaze came to rest on an object a little way down the path. "What's that?"

It was a circular object about six feet across. It had four beams radiating from the center. Each was sturdy enough to hold a person. Unlike the St. Andrews cross, it could be rotated into different positions. If he wasn't mistaken, it was also mounted on a hydraulic lift that would tilt it back or lay it down. "That's a Catherine wheel. It's just like a St. Andrew's cross, only it moves."

Sabrina stepped inside the area roped off to keep spectators at a safe and reasonable distance. She stopped in front of it and looked up at the smooth wood. "You could turn someone until they were hanging upside down."

"You could, if you knew what you were doing." Equipment like this should not come standard anywhere. "Leaving someone upside down for too long can cause all sorts of problems. I've seen people vomit on these things."

She looked it up and down, and then she peeked at the lift in the base. "Does it go in circles? That would be horrible. Not sexy at all."

Jonas shook his head. "No, not sexy. I know there's better equipment out there than this. I've seen some pretty fantastic stuff."

He looked around at the open sky. "Of course it wouldn't hold up outside like this. I think these stations need canopies or covers or something."

"If they like those rides at amusement parks that spin, they'd probably get off on that." She frowned. "Still, I wouldn't want to take the chance of somebody getting sick. It's a mood killer. A canopy, and maybe reorient it so that viewers are here by choice. Oh, and I think these all need to be farther apart. That way it's not so distracting."

It sounded like she was shopping for a sex resort, not like she was picking out which device she'd like to experience. He led her further down the path. A metal framework, bolted to concrete, came next. It featured a ladder-like construction and a host of O rings. Once it had been a wonderful piece of furniture. Now Jonas could see rust in some of the joints. Leaving these to the mercy of the elements bothered him.

"It looks like Mistress Hera concentrated all her energy on the food and the rooms. Perhaps this place needs a team to run it." He didn't mean to imply that Heather was incompetent. She likely replaced the equipment regularly. However, there were better ways to run a business, and frankly, there were better products available than these medieval-looking things.

He hated that he was starting to look at this place like a business prospect. It was supposed to be a paradise, a honeymoon, a chance to reconnect with his wife.

Draping his arm around her shoulders, he tugged her closer. It was a great position because it allowed him a great view of her breasts. "Let's walk through Persephone's Gardens."

Sabrina snuggled in and didn't argue with the change of plans. "I think I would have liked this if I'd been here with you twenty years ago."

Jonas shook his head. Twenty years ago, he wasn't half the man he was today, but a lot of that had to do with the woman on his arm.

"Twenty years ago, it would never have occurred to me to bring you here."

It had barely occurred to him to bring himself here, and when he'd come he'd spent the three days so overwhelmed that he hadn't tried anything. He'd simply gawked.

Sabrina looked up at him with wide eyes. "Yeah, you're right. I was fifteen and you were a hot and geeky college guy."

He smacked her ass for calling him geeky, even though he knew she'd meant it as a compliment. Whenever they role-played the virgin and the call girl, she delighted in whatever dorky getup he devised. There was an art to it, he discovered, and he'd quickly learned her preferences. Glasses, for example, turned her on, as did pants that were snug in the crotch. He made sure to always incorporate those elements.

She retaliated by squeezing a handful of his rear end. "You know what we've never played? The geek and the cheerleader. I wonder if my mom still has my old uniform anywhere. I wonder if it still fits."

"Mmmm." He savored that image of her in his head. "I think I'd prefer to get you one of those slutty cheer outfits, the kind with the low cut, bare midriff, and a skirt so short I can see the bottom of your ass hanging out." To illustrate his point, he slid his hand up her short skirt and exposed the lower portion of her ass.

"Okay, but then you have to go tech-geek. I want to see low-rise jeans that show off your hipbones, a shirt that has a witty saying about engineers, glasses, no shoes, and a few days' worth of stubble." She grinned wickedly, and he knew she was picturing him slouched down in a chair with some kind of electronic device in his hands. Maybe it was the remote control.

"I could have invented a new kind of vibrator, and I convinced you to come over and try it out. You might end up tied to a chair with your legs spread while I test my invention."

She shivered. "I think we have a plan. I'll be Cindy, the head cheerleader. You can be Alvin because I can't think of a better name for a geek."

"Kirk." He immediately went to Star Trek. "I'll make you call me 'Captain.'"

"More like you'll make me scream it."

She looked like she had more to say, but a round of applause cut her short. They looked around, but other than a few couples wandering aimlessly and looking confused, they saw nobody.

"What was that?"

"Shhh. Listen." She pointed toward a narrow path he thought led to the beach. Perhaps it was one of the excursions. Those were paid for in advance, so it was reasonable to assume those private vendors were still offering tours.

Why not see what was going on? He led her down that way. His plan to spend the afternoon at the Fields hadn't worked out. It was time for a new plan.

The path joined with another, growing wider as it led into an abrupt clearing. The hillside fell away, and he could see they were at the top of a natural amphitheater. Immediately his mind churned with the possibilities. This place was made for exhibitionists.

From their vantage point, Jonas could make out about fifty people in the audience and six onstage. They followed the path on its downward trajectory until they came to an entrance point halfway down. People were scattered throughout the lower half of the bowl, most in various stages of undress.

On the left side of the stage, one of the actors stood at a podium. In the center, three people stood behind three others who waited on all fours. The ones on their hands and knees wore headbands with ears. Some were floppy, and some pointed straight up. They were outfitted differently, but each wore a collar and a plug in their ass with an appendage to simulate a tail. The owners, standing behind their pets, each held a leash.

He looked at Sabrina to see if she understood what was going on. It wasn't a play, per se, but it was a show.

"Ladies and gentlemen, we are down to the final three. This is the last round of the Ninth Annual Prancing Puppy Contest." The announcer sounded a little sad, as if he knew this might be his last show at Elysium.

Sabrina's eyes widened. She leaned closer to him. "I've always wondered about puppy and pony play. I've heard of it, but I've never seen it."

That decided the matter. It wasn't his cup of tea, but he couldn't pull her away from a new experience. He could just hope it didn't ignite a longing he didn't want to quench.

The owners pranced each puppy around a ring, stopping at the judges table to be poked and prodded, fondled and petted. If anybody ever touched Sabrina like that, he'd punch them, and that would be only the beginning.

He watched her more than the show. From the way her jaw dropped open, he could see her shock. But then she bit her lower lip, a sign she was becoming aroused.

"I've been to a few dog shows. They do get a little personal with the animals, but I've never seen them take it to the climax." She shifted her knees urgently, and that was the final straw.

"Spread your legs so I can play with your pussy."

He reached for her knee to help peel her open, but she jerked from his grasp and looked around. "Jonas, it's a dog show, not a cat show."

Though he found her sense of humor funny, he didn't care for her timing and her refusal was insubordinate. Without warning, he flipped her over his knees, hiked up her skirt, and spanked her. Each smack echoed in the curved space. She didn't fight it and he didn't make her count the twenty blows. Though her cunt was wet and the breeze carried the scent of her arousal to his nose, he didn't pause to pleasure her. This was punishment.

By the time he stopped, so had the show. Everyone in the amphitheater watched them, even the puppies on stage. He set Sabrina back on the stone bench. From the top of her corset to her hairline, her skin had turned bright red. It wasn't the kind of color that came from being upside down. This reflected the level of her embarrassment. Though that hadn't been his intention, it was a natural byproduct of what happened when a submissive misbehaved in public.

"And that, puppies, is what happens when you disobey your owners."

The audience laughed and applauded. Sabrina fixed her gaze on a point close to her toes. Her chest rose and fell as she took short breaths. He recognized her effort to regain control through her breathing, and he let her work it out.

When she seemed to have regained her composure, he issued the order again. "Spread your legs."

She looked up at him, pain and uncertainty clouding her eyes. He hadn't spanked her harder than he usually did, so he didn't understand the pain. That level of intensity usually led her to an orgasm. She'd never had trouble sitting after that light of a spanking before.

He held his firm expression, and she spread her legs. The short skirt obligingly rolled up to reveal her gorgeous pussy. He lifted the knee nearest him and draped it over his legs, spreading her wider.

In the front of the amphitheater, the show resumed. Sabrina relaxed, and he realized she'd been mortified that they'd interrupted the show.

He nuzzled her neck. "Don't worry. I'm sure it was a welcome interlude. You take your spankings very well, my dear. No wiggling or wailing. Very dignified."

That didn't seem to make her relax, so he turned her face and captured her lips. They were soft and welcoming. She opened for him and met him with greedy enthusiasm. On the wings of a soft moan, she tugged at his shirt. Breaking the kiss, he laughed and disengaged her grip.

"Not yet, Sabrina. Be a good submissive and you'll eventually get your reward."

Her mouth turned down in an uncharacteristic pout. It looked too damned cute. If she knew how hard it made him to see that expression, she could use it to manipulate him. He used her breathing technique to get himself in line.

Then he made her sit with one leg over his lap, her pussy spread wide, until the show ended. Every now and again, he would stroke those sensitive folds. When people gathered their things to leave, he unzipped his pants and freed his cock.

"Straddle me. You're going to ride me until I tell you to stop."

She scrambled up, eagerly throwing her leg over him and sinking down on his cock with a speed he'd never seen. She rolled her hips, lifting up as she moved back and pressing down as she moved forward. People stopped to watch, and that seemed to fuel her energy. Faster and faster she moved, setting an impossible rhythm. His balls drew up and he came, pulling her down and sealing her to his body. Her pussy pulsed around him, evidence of her orgasm.

He kissed her. Over and over, he used his lips to express his appreciation for her performance. He was blessed to have a wife who not only indulged his need for exhibitionism, she got off on it, too.

When her heartbeat, thudding against his chest, slowed, he lifted her off him and fixed his pants. The stage called to him. Though nobody else was in the theater, he wanted to see her on that stage, naked and bound, completely at his mercy.

It would be a scene, not a show.

Chapter Thirteen

Sabrina followed Jonas up the center aisle to the deserted stage. It had no curtain or any signs warning people away. On the contrary, it seemed to invite people closer, as if the stage whispered, begging for more performers.

She hazarded a look around. Nobody was there. In the distance, they couldn't hear anything or anyone. Mistress Hera could have evacuated the island, and they wouldn't know. This amphitheater was truly hidden away.

The puppy show had been interesting. After doing some tricks and being felt up, one of them was awarded first prize. The audience applauded, and everybody left. Well, they left after she'd fucked Jonas as part of the encore. She'd liked feeling their eyes on her as she pleasured the man who meant more to her than anything else.

Steps on either side led to the stage, so Jonas headed right. Once on the stage, he positioned her in the center. "Stay here."

Then he disappeared backstage. She stood in the center of the stage of the abandoned amphitheater. The first shadows of late afternoon cast their darkness over the upper portion of the stadium seats. She was sure the stage wasn't very well lit either, with the shade from the overhang and all. Sunlight sparkled one foot in front of her. She was up for doing whatever he wanted as long as he didn't move her into the sunlight. If anyone happened upon them, she didn't want the glare to highlight the things she tried to hide.

No, she preferred to remain out of the spotlight.

Scraping and squeaking drew her attention to the opposite side of the stage from where Jonas had disappeared. He came out of the wing, and she realized there must be a passageway at the rear of the stage. He pointed to the audience area. "Face forward."

That meant she couldn't discern his mood from the expression on his face, and his tone held no clues. A few more noises, indications things were being moved, came from different areas of the stage. Curiosity was killing her. Sabrina wished she were the kind of submissive who misbehaved, but she wasn't, and he was too far back for her to gain any information peripherally.

Then she felt the magnetism of him standing directly behind her. That soft, subtle hint of heat and the seduction of his natural scent lured her closer, a helpless moth to his flame. She swayed, but he didn't steady her, so she doubted her senses. Perhaps she only craved the feeling of him standing next to her. Shifting her feet around, she was able to regain her balance. The moment she did, his hands landed on her hips.

"You didn't peek." He sounded pleased, and she was glad she hadn't given in to the urge to be bad just this once. Very few things made her feel genuinely whole like pleasing him did. And when she was at his mercy like this, she didn't have to worry about whether or not it was right to crave this outside validation, even if it was from her husband.

He moved his hands up her body, but the corset, made from heavy plastic and lined with soft satin, didn't translate the sensation, only the pressure. As if he knew what she wanted, he reversed direction, caressing slowly up and down her hips, lifting her skirt higher with each pass.

"Do you remember the night we got married, where I took you afterward?"

Those images were forever seared in her mind's eye. He'd opened her eyes to his exhibitionist lifestyle within hours of their vows, taking her to a private sex club so people could watch them consummate their union. In particular, she remembered that he'd stood behind her, his fingers exploring her folds as he whispered sexy and shocking things into her ear.

"Yes. Of course."

He cupped her mound, massaging it gently in his palm. "You were so beautiful that night."

His fingers parted her slit. She trembled, half in remembrance and half in anticipation. Sucking in a huge breath, she acknowledged his point. "That skirt was about this short. You barely had to lift it."

"I wanted to do so much more than just fuck you. I wanted to tie you in the center of the largest room so I could taste you, flog you, and fuck you all night."

She didn't doubt it. At the time it would have been too much. She'd known nothing about this kind of life. "Everyone would have known just how completely I belong to you."

He withdrew his fingers and held them at her lips. She opened and cleaned away her juices. "I love how perceptive you are."

Then he stepped back, and she whimpered at the loss of her anchor. She dropped her gaze to the concrete stage floor as she waited for him to return. Darkness stole her vision. Given the thickness of the blindfold and the way it carried his scent, she guessed he'd rolled up his shirt. It looked like he didn't have a bondage cabinet in his pockets today.

He circled her and adjusted the fit around her nose to make sure it didn't let in light or block her breathing. When he was satisfied, he brushed a kiss across her lips. She wanted more, but he pulled away.

"Lift your arms."

She lifted them, moving slowly because she wasn't certain as to what he planned to do. Cold cuffs made from rough leather closed around her wrists. They tightened and she felt the short pinch as he secured each buckle.

He tugged her skirt down and lifted each of her feet so she could step out of it. Similar buckles encircled her ankles, the metal rivets cold against her skin. She felt the push and pull as he secured a spreader bar to each cuff, making sure her legs remained spread.

"Blinded and bound." His hot breath seared her neck, and a series of nibbling bites sent shivers clear down the side of her ribcage. "Would you have let me do this on our wedding night?"

She honestly didn't know. If he'd tried this, she would have thought he was kinky, but she didn't know if she would have refused to continue with his game. In her opinion, this was less kinky than having sex in public. "I don't know. Not at the club with people watching. In private? I don't know. You were a good kisser and you were very persuasive."

"Were?" He growled.

She laughed at his chagrin. He was still a good kisser, and he had her tied up on a stage, so she would still call him persuasive. "Yes, you were. I don't think we'd be married if you weren't so accomplished."

He resumed his position behind her. "You're saying you married me because I was a good kisser?"

She could imagine him scratching his chin, trying to figure out why she chose that reason when her original reason had been to gain an inheritance. "Yes. You wanted sex as a condition of marriage. Twice a week. The only reason I consented was because you made my knees weak when you kissed me."

The zipper of her corset hissed, and the tight garment fell away. Those talented fingers returned to tease her pussy. "I knew it. I should have kept going. I could have had you right there in the conference room."

Then he would have realized much sooner that she didn't know how to have an orgasm. "No," she said. "I would have stopped you. Otherwise you would have known I was damaged goods. It might have ruined the deal."

"Don't." He was in front of her now, gripping her chin forcefully. "Don't you ever refer to yourself that way. You weren't damaged.

Nobody ever took the time to find the submissive woman hiding inside you who wanted to be tied up and flogged. That wasn't your fault."

His mouth covered hers, and he closed his will around her, forcing her surrender. His hands were everywhere, squeezing her breast, rolling her nipple, caressing her stomach and hips, and holding her ass as he ground his cock against her. She wanted him to take off his shorts, but he had her too dazed to hold any thought for more than a few seconds. Letting them all go, she focused on the way he made her feel—happy, whole, alive, and wonderfully needy.

Just when she thought he'd consumed her, he dropped to his knees and added his mouth to the mix. He ate pussy the same way he kissed, devouring her whole. He tongued her clit and pumped his fingers into her hole. Tendrils of heat chased tension all over her body. Her body swayed as her knees weakened. She fought to keep them under her because she knew the cuffs would dig in and leave painful bruises if she didn't.

"Please." The improvised blindfold was damp over her eyes. "Please. Jonas, please."

"Mmmm-hmmm." His permission vibrated through her tissues, and she came in his mouth.

His wet lips closed over hers as he tilted her hips forward and thrust his cock into her pulsating vagina. The musky taste of her juices flooded her senses, and she felt the breeze blowing across the wet trail his face made as he slathered his kisses and her essence over her neck, chest, and breasts.

Then he leaned back, leaving the places where he gripped her hips and where his cock met her pussy as their only points of contact. He thrust greedily four times, and then he withdrew.

The warm tropical air caressed her body like another lover, teasing her tender skin and tantalizing the areas that cried out for Jonas's touch. She inhaled a tremulous breath, both a reaction to her orgasm and to the emptiness he left inside her.

His hands closed over her breasts, and he pulled her body back, cradling her against him. "You belong to me, body and soul. There is no part of you I can't have."

"Yes," she agreed, whimpering in relief at his touch. "Body and soul."

One hand dropped and spread across her stomach. The other parted her butt cheeks and guided his cock to her anus. He hadn't brought additional lubrication, but she knew that didn't matter. Her cream was slick and plentiful.

Last night, he'd gone slow, working his way into her with the utmost care. It had been too gentle. Tonight he used a different strategy. With one thrust, he impaled her. Stars exploded in the darkness of the blindfold. Cold fusion rocked every cell up her spine and down to her toes. Moans echoed back to her, and she recognized the distorted sound of her own voice.

"Yes," she said. "Yes. Oh Jonas, like that." She was barely hanging on, and she knew he was intent on pushing her over the edge.

He showed no mercy, and she wanted for nothing. He fucked her with quick, hard thrusts. Each one sent a riot through her body, overloading her synapses. He didn't touch her clit at all. She didn't care whether or not she had an orgasm because nothing could possibly feel better than this.

But one built anyway. It detonated without warning, taking her completely by surprise. She screamed. Her entire body felt like it was falling, propped up each time he thrust home. The orgasm went on and on. Vaguely she registered the fact that he'd climaxed. His deeper shouts joined her higher pitched ones, filling the bowl of the amphitheater with their combined ecstasy.

She felt tugging at her wrists. It took a lot longer than usual. She knew she should stand up higher to help out, but her knees were useless. If his arm hadn't banded around her waist, she would have bruised her wrists and pulled her shoulders out of joint for sure.

Then she was on his lap. He held her, rubbing warmth into her trembling body, until she came down. She didn't know how long they sat there before she noticed he had pulled his shorts back on before he sat down with her.

She kissed his collarbone. "That was amazing. Thank you."

"Let's go back to the room and have dinner. You'll sit at my feet and I'll hand feed you."

His directive washed over her like a cold glass of water. She'd thought he had moved past the need to have her kneeling at his feet. She was also torn by her need to do this for him and her resentment at herself for even considering revisiting that scene. The way he'd punished her in front of all those people at the puppy show punched her in the gut with a wave of humiliation.

The magic of the night faded, leaving her feeling empty and cold. She reached for her corset, noticing almost nothing except the way her hand trembled and the way her rapid blinking wasn't going to hold back the flood of tears for very long.

His hand closed around her wrist, larger and impossibly stronger, dwarfing her slender limb. Ten minutes ago, the sight of his arm on top of hers would have made her feel safe and warm. She froze.

"No clothes. You'll walk in front of me with nothing hiding that luscious body."

Heat cracked the cold, but not the kind he was probably hoping for. Raw fury seized her so quickly she was a little afraid of it. "Jonas, I'm not going to walk around here naked. It's still daylight out."

He laughed, truly amused by her protest. "You don't have a choice. I make the decisions."

She tried to pull her arm from his grasp, but he tightened his grip. "Let go of me."

The back of the stage whirled through the background as he turned her roughly to face him. His eyes were dangerously narrow. She'd never misbehaved like this before, but she'd seen him pissed off at other people, mostly Ellen, enough to know this wasn't the time to mess with him. "You don't give the orders, Sabrina. Perhaps you need a reminder."

She shook her head in a feeble gesture, but it was all she had. "I'm not walking through this place nude, and I'm not kneeling at your feet while you feed me."

An explanation hovered just behind her refusal, but she couldn't give it voice. Too many conflicting emotions stole her reason. She felt like laughing and crying, screaming and curling in a ball to rock on the floor. This must be what hysteria felt like. She put her other hand over her mouth to hold it at bay.

"This isn't negotiable." His clipped tone contained a warning, but she fixated on the clue.

"You're right. It's not. Onion. I'm finished with this."

He let go of her wrist, lines of shock scrawled across his features. She'd never, not once in five years, used their safe word. He'd offered it every single time they played, but she'd never used it. "Sabrina?"

She snatched his shirt and jerked it over her head. It was long enough to cover more of her body than the skirt and corset combined. If he wasn't going to give up her clothes, she'd take his. She held out her hand. "Give me the room key."

He held up his hands. "Honey, using your safe word means we stop and talk. It doesn't mean you storm away pissed off."

Perhaps for most people, that's what it meant. But she wasn't most people, and they hadn't settled on any rules beforehand. That's probably where they'd gone wrong, but she was too upset to have a conversation. "I don't want to talk to you right now. Give me the fucking key and find somewhere else to have dinner."

* * * *

Jonas was at a loss for words. He still hadn't recovered from the way she'd used their safe word. It was a point of pride that he knew her limits so well that she had never needed to call a time-out.

This was more than a time-out. Right before his eyes, he watched his wife close off a vital part of herself as she grappled with emotions that vacillated through her face so quickly he couldn't identify them. He didn't want to let her leave before they talked it through, but she looked so fragile and lost, two expressions he never wanted to see on her face again, that he found himself fishing the key from his pocket and handing it over.

"Sabrina." He caught her arm as she turned to leave. She shook so badly he wanted to ignore her use of the safe word and wrap her in his embrace. "Talk to me. Don't keep this to yourself."

She shook her head, and he recognized that he'd pushed her too far. Only he didn't know exactly what was wrong. They'd shared something spectacular. He'd never felt closer to her than he had when he'd held her in his arms while she'd trembled with the aftershocks of her orgasm. He'd wanted to point out that this was the first time she'd climaxed without having any vaginal or clitoral stimulation. It was another step in her journey of sexual freedom.

Against his better judgment, he relaxed his grip and watched her slip away. They'd gained an audience during the show, which he hadn't seen the need to tell her about. She wasn't the one who got off from being watched. She'd repeatedly told him the audience was inconsequential.

Now he second-guessed everything. Her original objection to coming here had centered around post-pregnancy modesty. But he'd fixed that misconception, hadn't he? What had he missed?

He ate part of a flavorless dinner from the buffet in the only open dining area. Mostly he picked at the food and wondered if he'd given Sabrina enough time to think though her issues so she could talk to him. Each bite dropped into his stomach like a stone, sinking to the bottom and weighing heavily.

When he could stand it no longer—he estimated he'd given her about an hour—he returned to the room. She didn't answer his knock, forcing him to go to the front desk and have another keycard made.

Inside the room, he heard no sign of her until he got to the bathroom door. He knocked. Water swished, and he heard evidence that she'd pulled the plug. By the time she opened the door twenty minutes later, she was fully dressed, and she hadn't said a word. Her face and eyes were clear, so she hadn't been crying. That brought him some measure of relief, but not enough. Not nearly enough.

"Sabrina. We have to talk."

"I can't," she said, dropping her gaze, looking anywhere but at him. "Not yet."

The night dragged. She perked up when he called her mother's house to talk to the kids. Rose's smile and Ethan's happy squeals melted his heart. God he missed his children. He studied Sabrina to see if she was homesick, but he couldn't come to any definite conclusion.

She spoke to him, answering his questions with concise and polite responses. When they went to bed, she wore a silky nightgown and curled up as far away as she could get without going over the edge, but she didn't protest when he pulled her to him. It closed the distance, but it did nothing to diminish the gulf.

He held her all night, listening to her even breathing. He wanted to wake her up, somehow force her to talk to him, but he knew it would be useless. He could make her do a lot of things, but somehow it felt wrong to force this issue, as if doing so would irrevocably damage their relationship. Then again, what if allowing her to take this time was a mistake? If he knew what was bothering her, it would be easier to choose a course of action. He debated until he couldn't think straight, and he had no idea how long it was until he fell asleep.

The next morning was no better. She woke refreshed and in a good mood. She smiled and laughed as she packed to return home, commenting on some of the gifts they were bringing back for friends and relatives and how she planned to spend all day Sunday snuggling on the kids. Though her jokes were underlined in somber tones, he could chalk that up to her reluctance to leave or her eagerness to see the kids.

Heather met them at the dock to send them off. Sabrina thanked her for a lovely stay and wished her the best.

He didn't bother her with anything significant on the flight because he knew she would be mortified at the idea of discussing personal business where anybody might overhear.

The four-hour layover in Miami wasn't the right time either. His sister met them at the airport and took them to lunch at a private club in the heart of downtown. Sabrina even sanitized her answers to Samantha's questions about what they had done on the island.

"Was it everything you expected?" Sam's blue eyes sparkled with the excitement of conspiracy.

Sabrina shrugged. "I didn't know what to expect. The beaches were gorgeous, and there was a waterfall in the forest. We saw it when we went horseback riding."

Sam shook her head. "No, I meant the atmosphere. People were accepting? I heard it's supposed to be a beautiful BDSM paradise."

Sabrina shifted uncomfortably. Normally Jonas would enjoy watching her squirm, but on top of everything else, he couldn't stomach her uneasiness. "Yes. Whatever your kink, nobody blinked. They stared, of course, but only if you wanted them to."

Color bloomed on Sabrina's cheeks. Sam smiled at Jonas across the table. Every member of his family knew how easy it was to make Sabrina blush. His brash sister was almost never shy or embarrassed, which made her question stand out.

"Sam, are you okay? Did something happen?"

"Not really, no. Nothing new." She put her fork down, her salad half-eaten. "Sometimes I just get tired of having to explain why I have two boyfriends or correct people's assumptions that I'm a whore or endure the strange looks they give me. Lex and Stef just stare them down, but it bothers me."

Sabrina put a reassuring hand on Sam's arm. "If it helps, it wouldn't matter if you were just dating one of them. People would still make rude assumptions. It's not a reflection of you. It's mean-spirited and it stems from jealousy. They're both handsome and rich, a powerful combination, and they both fell in love with you."

Sam smiled brilliantly. "You're so good at putting a positive spin on things. I think that's one of the reasons I like you so much."

This was also a road paved with ways to make Sabrina uncomfortable. While her ability to accept a compliment had improved, she still suffered from embarrassment if anyone gushed, and Samantha was a gusher.

Jonas eyed his sister carefully. "Sam? Why do you want to buy Elysium? Running a business is a full-time job, not something you can fit in around your manic painting sessions."

Sabrina frowned at what she probably considered rude phrasing, but he knew she didn't disapprove of the question.

"I don't want to run it." Sam picked up her fork and speared some mixed greens. "I want Stef and Lex to run it. I just want some place we can go whenever we want, a place where I can walk down the street holding both of their hands and it's completely normal. I was going to ask them to change the Isle of the Blest area to housing for people in poly relationships."

"So you basically want a time-share?" Sabrina's incredulity was laced with exasperation. "You don't have to buy an island for that."

"There are no destinations anywhere that cater to the poly lifestyle. I checked. People who live in triads or more either keep their relationships secret or spend their time on the fringes of the kink scene. Well, what if they aren't into the kinky side of things? Then they have nothing." She pounded the table with her fist to emphasize her point.

Sabrina lifted her eyebrows at Sam's emotional display. "I understand where you're coming from. Elysium caters to people who want to be around others with similar interests. But it's still a business. Are you sure you want to take on that responsibility?"

Samantha shook her head, her long blonde hair shimmering in the sunlight. "Absolutely not. That's why I told Stef and Lex I wanted them to buy it. I just want to visit it with them."

"Well, they're looking at buying it for you." Sabrina looked to him for support.

"That's what it sounded like when we talked to them." Jonas threw his cloth napkin on the table. "If that's not what you want, you need to have another conversation with them."

Sam clasped her hands together gleefully. "Does this mean you guys are going to go in on it with us? Lex said he couldn't get a read on you."

Sabrina got a faraway look in her eyes, but it ended with a flash of pain. She shook it away. "I don't know."

It was an evasion that screamed reluctance, the kind that meant she was leaning away from investing. Jonas didn't care one way or the other. He only wanted to get at the root of the reason she'd used her safe word.

By the time they made it home, Sabrina's mother had arrived with the kids. Rose flew into Sabrina's arms, and he knew it was going to be nearly impossible to get her to talk. She fell asleep in Rose's bed, the book of bedtime stories on her chest, open to the page where she'd left off reading.

She didn't stir when he scooped her up and carried her to their bed. The next morning, he woke to Ethan's finger poking in his ear and calling, "Dada." In the past week, his fifteen-month-old son had learned how to climb out of his crib, following in his big sister's footsteps. He pulled Ethan up onto the bed and hugged the little guy.

"Our little monkey missed you." He looked over to find Sabrina smiling at the two of them. She snuggled against his side and caressed the side of Ethan's face. "Good morning, baby. Are you hungry?"

Ethan grinned and giggled, and Sabrina's face only lit up more.

Nothing in her behavior indicated anything was wrong, but he couldn't shake the feeling that something significant had happened right under his nose and he'd missed it. What if he'd lost part of his wife on that island?

Chapter Fourteen

A week had flown by, and Jonas hadn't forced her to talk. He hadn't pushed the issue at all. Every time they were alone, she introduced another topic, and he seemed more than happy to accept her evasion. The awkwardness between them was slowly disappearing in the face of their regular routine. She'd gone back to work Tuesday, after taking an extra day to soak up some love from her children.

Right now, the kids were corralled in a safe part of the yard with enough toys to keep them busy. Sabrina sat on a comfortable chair under a shade umbrella while Jonas prepared the grill. This would have been their first afternoon alone, but she'd invited friends over for an impromptu barbecue.

Ellen set an ice-filled drink on the table and settled into the chair next to her. They'd discussed purchasing Elysium in vague terms, both of them agreeing to wait on Alexei and Stefano to finish their investigation of the company. Her stepbrothers had advised them all to wait until they dug up financial reports on the assets and dirt on the Mehlbergs. The Morozovs smelled profit, and they were very invested in making this work for them all.

Sabrina wasn't sold on the whole idea. Part of her wanted to put the island behind her and never think about it again.

"Trouble in paradise?"

Sabrina frowned at Jonas's best friend. At times like these, she had learned to tread lightly. Ellen had become one of her closest friends, but Sabrina knew her tightest bond was with Jonas. Sometimes she didn't understand how the two of them managed to maintain a friendship with the way they argued, but they did. Not only that, but the arguments seemed to cement their commitment to their friendship.

Taking her cues from Ryan, Sabrina always stayed out of it. She secretly enjoyed watching someone stand up to Jonas. While she could and did disagree with him, she hated fighting. Arguments only made her want to cry, and that felt too much like manipulation.

"I haven't heard anything from Alexei or Stefano." She knew that wasn't what Ellen meant, but she wanted to open up the conversation so Ellen could take the out she offered. It worked with Jonas. "Have you?"

"You've been back a week. Usually people who have just spent a week having wild sex with their spouse are a little more happy and affectionate than you two." Ellen spooned a mound of ice into her mouth. The temperatures were in the high eighties, but there was a nice breeze, so it was a perfect day for a backyard gathering.

"We're not newlyweds, Ellen. We have two kids and we've been together for five years." She smiled to soften her dry tone. While she wasn't well versed at sarcasm, she was going up against an expert.

Ellen leaned closer. "You guys were all over each other before you left. Well, your version of it anyway. I haven't seen you hold hands or kiss once. You usually find some excuse to touch him every few minutes, whether you realize it or not. Yet I see that you've managed to put an entire yard between you all afternoon. Even when the kids were napping and you didn't have an excuse to be way over here, you didn't try to get close."

"Wow. You've been busy. It must be exhausting to spend the day dissecting other people's seating arrangements to come to that kind of conclusion." When she'd first met Ellen, she would have died rather than say something like that. I hadn't taken her long to realize how well Ellen responded to sarcasm. Of course, she expected a comeback.

She spotted Ethan pulling up grass and throwing it at his sister. Correcting that provided an easy out, but Ellen pounced on her when she sat back down.

"Sabrina, you're barely holding on. Jonas is miserable. What happened?"

Ellen was the kind of person who always pried, but she usually grilled Jonas. It occurred to Sabrina that he hadn't said a word to Ellen, and he usually told her pretty much everything. She didn't know what it meant that he'd kept it to himself. Had he forgotten it or filed it away as a meaningless incident? Part of her hoped so.

Then why did the heavy weight in her chest just grow larger?

"Ellen, I told you to leave Sabrina alone."

Sabrina looked behind her to find Jonas looming over her chair. If his clipped tone didn't give it away, his entire countenance exuded fury. She shot to her feet and put her hand on his chest, hoping to calm him down enough so that they didn't fight in front of the kids. Rose tended to cry when Jonas yelled, which was curious because he'd never raised his voice to their daughter.

But Ellen's hackles didn't rise. She looked away, making motions with her mouth as if chewing on what to say next. At last she swallowed and nodded. "I apologize. I didn't mean to upset either of you."

Sabrina felt bad. She hated the tension between Jonas and Ellen, and she couldn't help but feel responsible for it.

Ellen stood up and regarded them both somberly, worlds of sorrow in her deep brown eyes. "I just can't stand to see you like this."

Jonas's jaw set harder and he took a step forward. Sabrina moved at the same time, forcing him to put his arm around her to keep her from tripping over his feet. They'd touched plenty over the past week. He slept with at least one arm slung across her body. They snuggled together on the sofa with the kids. And he fucked her frequently, shoving her against a wall or down on the bed whenever he felt the urge. She craved those moments.

"Jonas, she apologized and she means well."

Ellen, of course, held her ground. Jonas wasn't violent, and neither of them were in the habit of backing down when they felt they were in the right.

He gave her a reassuring squeeze. "I'm going to start dinner. Call me if you need me."

The way he looked out for her made her heart patter a little faster. She smiled to let him know she was all right. In a way, she felt better than she had all week. Somehow his show of protectiveness eased her anxiety.

He sauntered across the lawn, and Ellen sat down. She sipped her melting mound of ice and they talked about the offer someone had made for the property housing Ellen's nightclub.

Later, Ryan cornered her near the gate to the swimming pool. She'd been in the water with the kids, conducting impromptu swimming lessons with six-year-old Jake, Ryan and Ellen's oldest, and coaching Rose and Emily, Jake's younger sister, on practice kicking. Mostly, they hung onto the edge of the pool and splashed with their feet, giggling maniacally with their three-year-old senses of humor.

Jonas and Ellen had taken the kids into the house for baths to wash the chlorinated water from their little bodies.

If she'd seen what was coming, she would have run. Ellen was the one who pried into people's lives. Ryan usually sat back and watched with a contented smile on his face. He didn't register as a threat, so he caught her with her guard down.

He was about the same height as Jonas, perhaps an inch taller, which meant Sabrina had to tilt her head back to look at him when he stood nearby. Though it was early evening, the summer sun glinted from his hair, highlighting the multitude of reds in his close-cropped cut. He handed her a bottle of icy water.

"It's not easy to be a submissive."

She froze, her gaze focused on the drink in her hand. The gate was locked. That safety measure registered in her mind, taking the place of Ryan's comment. "Thanks for the water."

She went to turn away, to head back along the flagstone path to the house, but Ryan caught her arm. "Sometimes it's easier to talk to someone who has been through the same thing. I'm your friend, too, Sabrina. I'm here for you and I'm a damn good listener."

Taken aback, she stared at him. On a normal day, she forgot he was a submissive. Ellen's dominance was hard to miss, but Ryan's submissiveness wasn't the first thing anyone noticed, if they noticed it at all. He was tall, broad-shouldered, and confident, not at all meek or mild. Laid-back, perhaps, but not a pushover. While he didn't tend to argue with Ellen, he still voiced his opinion.

He leaned against the fence, putting the sun to his back so that it no longer glinted in his eyes, and took a long sip from his water bottle. "I was with Jonas the last time he went to Elysium. That place blew our minds. We spent the whole time walking around and looking at everything. It definitely makes you question things, forces you to confront what you really want."

She continued to stare in silence. While she wanted to hear about what happened because Jonas hadn't said much about his previous visit, she didn't want to know about other women he might have met there.

"When I got back, Ellen was pissed. We weren't dating yet. Jonas and I had only gone to Elysium to show her we could handle the D/s lifestyle. Jonas had already figured out that he identified as a Dom." He shook his head. "It didn't appeal to me. At Elysium, I began to suspect for the first time that I was submissive."

Sabrina looked away. She studied the pattern of patio tiles on her side of the gate. Elysium hadn't clarified anything for her. At home she'd suspected she was more of a submissive than Jonas let her be.

She lived for playing the roles that cast her in that light. Even when he played the virgin, she liked it best when he took charge.

But actually living the part for five nights hadn't felt right either. Parts of it did, and parts of it didn't.

She felt Ryan looking at her, waiting for her attention to return to him. She looked up at him, giving him the signal to continue.

"As I said, Ellen was pissed. She had a crush on me, but she hadn't pursued me. She had thought I was submissive all along, but you can't force somebody to that realization. They have to make it on their own. They have to want it. The first time I knelt at her feet, I knew with every fiber of my being that I was doing it because I wanted to. She gave the order, but I wanted to fulfill it."

Sabrina didn't want to kneel at Jonas's feet. Did she? Confusion churned in her stomach, and she took another sip of water to calm it down. "It's not that clear to me."

It was the first time she'd admitted her bewilderment aloud, and she wasn't sure she was talking to the right person. But she couldn't seem to find the courage to talk to Jonas. The prospect terrified her.

"I know."

"I–I used my safe word. I've never done that before."

He put his arm around her and guided her to sit on the railing next to him. "There's a first time for everything. Using your safe word isn't a bad thing. It's there for a reason."

Sabrina shook her head. "I used it for the wrong reason. I used it because I didn't want to do what he said." She blinked quickly, trying to suppress tears.

Ryan gave her a measured look. She knew she was supposed to only use it if he'd gone too far and she couldn't manage the pain. He hadn't hurt her at all. Humiliation washed over her. Even though Ryan wasn't looking at her with any kind of distaste, she still felt like running away.

"How did he respond to that?"

She couldn't maintain even a semblance of a cool facade. "I didn't let him. He wanted to talk, but I refused. I told him to get dinner without me, and I went back to the hotel room and locked myself in the bathroom. I took a bath."

She thought her behavior sounded horrible, but Ryan didn't react as if she'd done anything wrong. He nodded thoughtfully, his blue eyes cloudy with sympathy.

"And you haven't talked since then?"

Sabrina shook her head. "I was hoping he'd forget about it. That we'd just put the whole trip behind us and things would go back to how they were before."

"It doesn't work that way." Ryan closed his hand around her fist. She hadn't realized she was squeezing so hard. "The longer you wait to talk, the harder it's going to be to start. You're both walking around here blaming yourselves, and neither of you knows exactly what's wrong."

Her shoulders shook, a tiny vibration she hoped escaped his notice. "How can I tell him what's wrong when I don't even know myself? I've thought about it for hours—days—obsessively going over every detail to find out what bothers me and what I liked. But it's like the more I think about it, the more it gets muddled in my head. I'm a problem solver, Ryan. I hate that I can't figure it out."

He put his arm around her shoulders and pulled her into his embrace. So much for him not noticing that she was falling apart. "Maybe that's because you need to figure it out together. What you're going through isn't easy, Sabrina. Ellen made me keep a journal so she could know what was going on inside my head. It might seem like it, but she's not a mind reader. Neither is Jonas."

It did seem at times as if Jonas read her mind. He frequently seemed to know what she wanted or needed before she did. Did she take him for granted? Was that part of the problem?

"This happened the last day, right?" She nodded, a small movement against the crook of his arm. "How did your other talks go?"

She sat up and cocked her head at him. "What other talks?"

"You guys talk after a scene."

Usually they did. Often it happened the next day or later that night after the kids were in bed, but Jonas usually asked her to talk about what she liked or didn't like. They often planned the next scene during these times. But she'd built the talk into the last day and then she'd refused to talk to him.

Ryan's mouth dropped open when she confessed that she was at fault. "I can see where he was coming from in agreeing to that. He wanted you to think about the experience as a whole, not parse it into scenes. But it sounds like you needed to write down your thoughts and feelings every day. It's a lot to process, especially because putting you in a constant submissive role changed your whole dynamic."

And he'd planned to do it all along, even going so far as to confide his intention to Ellen and Ryan. She marveled at her cluelessness. It hadn't been a spur-of-the-moment thing inspired by the presence of so many D/s relationships on the island. She set her water bottle on the railing and covered her face with her hands. He'd played a big card, one she'd never guessed was up his sleeve, and it had blown up in their faces.

More than ever, she dreaded talking to him. How could she face him knowing he'd finally come out and asked something from her that he really wanted, and she wasn't sure she had it in her to want to give it to him?

* * * *

Rose ran to him, her wet blonde curls bouncing in little ringlets. The wind ruffled her pink nightgown as she flew barefoot across the grass, heading toward the deck where he stood with Ellen. Jake and

Emily played in the kitchen. Ethan sat next to them with a small bowl of Cheerios. Rose had wanted Sabrina to braid her hair.

When she got closer, he could see that she was upset. Her lower lip quivered and she threw herself in his arms. He hugged her tightly and stroked her back. "What's wrong, sweetheart?"

She clung to him, and a single teardrop fell. "Uncle Ryan made Mommy cry."

Jonas turned to Ellen, rage boiling in his blood. He'd told her to leave Sabrina alone, so she'd sent Ryan to ambush her while she kept Jonas distracted with giving the kids a bath.

Ellen pressed her lips together. "Sometimes it's easier to confide in someone who has walked in your shoes. It's obvious she isn't talking to you, and you aren't talking to me and you won't let me talk to her. Something's gotta give, and I don't want it to be your relationship."

"It's none of your business." He regarded her incredulously, though he shouldn't have been surprised. Ellen never minded her own business. He loved that about her and he hated it, too.

"It is too my business. You're our best friends. We love you. If you think this is only affecting the two of you, think again."

"It's not a big deal." As the days went by, it was becoming less and less relevant. The rhythm of daily life had reestablished itself, sweeping them away in a tide of normalcy that seemed to be erasing whatever wounds he'd unknowingly inflicted.

Ellen shook her head. "Things like this fester. They blow up when you least expect it. Pop the boil now and save you both some serious pain later."

The sun would set soon, and parts of the backyard were already cast in shadows. He could just make out Sabrina and Ryan coming toward them along the flagstone path leading from the house to the pool. He wiped Rose's tears away. "Mommy's okay."

Rose lifted her head and studied him with a stoic expression Sabrina attributed to him. She often said that Rose was exactly like him. "Mommy's sad, Daddy. Are you going to fix her?"

That astute observation drove home Ellen's point. He glanced at her to see if she was gloating, but she just looked worried. He pressed a kiss to Rose's forehead. "Yeah, baby. I'll fix her. Why don't you go on inside and play for a bit?"

By the time Sabrina made it to the patio where he could see her face clearly, her eyes showed no evidence that she'd been crying, but she looked defeated and lost. He preferred tears and anger, proof of passion.

Ellen took one look at Ryan and disappeared into the house to pack up the kids.

Jonas kept his eyes on his wife. She offered him a hollow smile as she walked past him and went inside. When Ryan tried to follow, he put his hand on his friend's arm to stop him.

"What happened?"

Ryan shook his head. "You shouldn't have let her go so long without debriefing. She doesn't even know where to start. I'm not sure she knows what you want from her, and man, there's nothing worse for a sub than not knowing how to make your Dom happy."

Jonas was at a loss. He simply wanted her to be happy. Ever since Ethan's birth, she'd been headed down a dangerous road filled with more stress than she could handle. He'd tried talking to her. He'd tried letting her be. This was new territory for them. She'd never refused to talk to him before. He had no clue how to break through her wall. "Any suggestions?"

Ryan blew out a stream of air as if he thought Jonas should have figured it out by now. "If she won't talk, maybe she'll write. Give her a journal. Sometimes it's easier to write things down than it is to say them out loud."

Later, after the kids were in bed, he found her sitting at her vanity brushing her hair and staring into space. She didn't notice him approaching until he took the brush from her hand, and she didn't protest when he took over the job. He loved brushing her hair. Soft light reflected in a hundred different shades of brown. It was lighter now, after their week in the Caribbean, adding even more depth to her color.

In the mirror, he saw that she'd closed her eyes. He wanted to turn her over his knee and spank her with the brush, if only to recreate the night that had been so perfect before things had gone so horribly wrong.

He'd gone over it in his head a million times, and he couldn't pinpoint a specific moment that would have pushed her past her endurance. As Ryan had said, he should have made her talk to him all along. Now he had no idea what problem had ballooned and tipped the balance.

He didn't know how long he stood there brushing her hair. They'd both surrendered to the simple bliss of this ritual. Eventually, he set her brush on her vanity and kissed the top of her head. When she looked up, he captured her lips in a kiss meant to be searing but probably came off as more desperate than anything else.

She cupped his face in her hands and let him lead her to bed.

Chapter Fifteen

Jonas brushed her hair before bed the next night as well. Sabrina breathed a contented sigh and let this take her back to better days. The second time they got married, the first time having been a business arrangement and the second time having been for love, Jonas had begun brushing her hair. The calming strokes settled her stomach, as she'd been suffering from a lot of morning sickness at all times of the day, so that was significant.

On his end, this nightly ritual fed his need to touch her hair. It held an erotic appeal for him that she didn't understand. Not that it mattered. She didn't have to understand his attraction to her in order to reap the benefits.

Now things were different. The rules seemed to have changed, and those things mattered. She had to figure out what he wanted from her, and she needed to dig deep to find out if she could give those things to him.

When he finished, she expected him to lead her to bed and make love to her as he had done the night before. She needed to know he still wanted her, that he found her desirable. But he handed her something instead of taking her hand.

She stared at the spiral-bound notebook with the black cover. Eighty pages of paper. She opened it to the first page to find it blank. Glancing up at him, she sought an explanation.

"This is for you to write down whatever is on your mind."

She looked back down at the vacant white lines. They did not call her to spill her secrets. "Thanks, but I don't keep a diary. I don't have time."

"You'll make time. It's not a suggestion, Sabrina. It's an order."

Her head snapped up and she stared at him in shock. She thought they were past all that. "An order?"

"Yes. I should have made you do this before now. I should never have let you get away with pushing it off until the end of the week and then pulling this stunt where you refuse to talk until it's all bottled up inside you. That was my mistake and I'm sorry, but we need to move past it if we're going to figure out what went wrong so we can fix it."

His eyes were olive green, a reflection of the dark green shirt he'd changed into after his shower. They were as firm as the rest of his features, and his expression brooked no argument. She felt that place deep inside respond, and it took her by surprise because she was also angry that he'd given her an order outside a scene. Their conversation wasn't going to lead to a scene either, so there was no mitigating those conflicting feelings.

Yet he'd indicated a desire to fix what was wrong between them. She couldn't fault his motivation even though she hoped the problem would evaporate like dry ice. "What if I can't think of anything to write?"

"You will." He moved to lean on the vanity next to where she'd placed the notebook. With one firm tap, he indicated the blank page. "From the beginning, I've assumed a lot of things about you. Mostly I've been right, and that's lulled us into a false sense of security. Last week showed us both what a mistake we've made. In assuming I knew what you were thinking and feeling, I robbed you of your duty to figure out those things for yourself and communicate them to me."

She didn't know how to be that introspective with regard to her own feelings. Sure, she'd learned to embrace her anger, but that was easy compared to this. Exploring the reasons she loved and hated submission might wreck her marriage, and that prospect made it feel like someone had driven a dagger through her heart. "I seriously don't know what you expect me to say."

"I don't expect you to say anything. I expect you to write it down. I'm not grading you, honey. I'm not looking to critique or criticize. Nothing you write in that journal will be used against you. It's a tool to let me inside your head." He reached out and ran his fingertips along the side of her face. She closed her eyes to bask in the tenderness in his caress. "It's a way for you to tell me the things you can't say to my face. I'm not completely clueless, honey. I know I may not like everything you have to say, but we can't deal with it if you don't tell me what those things are."

Her mind wasn't working because feeling overwhelmed rational thought. He wanted her to write things in a diary so he could read them, which in her mind defeated the whole purpose of journaling. She should never have agreed to the anniversary trip. This can of icky worms would have remained closed. If she wrote down anything, it would be that expression of regret, but she didn't think he meant for her to lament anything. "Can I do it in the morning?"

In the morning, she would wake up in work mode. Her mind would be clear and focused on organizing her task lists for the day and week ahead. She would be able to concentrate and separate the subjective from the objective. She hoped. Perhaps writing while she was at work would give her even more distance.

"Can't I just e-mail you or text you?"

He shook his head. "I thought about having you e-mail or text me, but then I figured that would be too much too fast. This way limits the speed of response, but it forces us to each take the time to really think things through. When you're finished with an entry, put it in my top drawer. After I've read it, I'll put it back in your underwear drawer."

Sabrina had many drawers in their shared closet, but Jonas had only one stack of four. As he had been accumulating more and more clothes—her fault for shopping so much—she considered moving just to acquire closet space. Rose also had a thing for fashion and Ethan had more clothes than a baby could wear in a year.

She shook away that train of thought and nodded. Processing his request left her numb, so she climbed under the covers and turned off her bedside light. Jonas watched her for a moment, and then he stared at the notebook. She couldn't tell what he was thinking.

* * * *

Monday mornings were hectic, even during summer vacation when only Sabrina was going to work. Jonas made breakfast and made sure Sabrina ate. She had a tendency to forego food when she was upset.

He wanted to remind her about the journal, but he didn't want to push the issue too much. She was very close to a breakdown, but she wasn't close to a breakthrough. The notebook was supposed to be a safe space for her, one where she could say anything without fearing his reaction. He knew she wasn't physically afraid of him, but she was so terrified of his reaction, and possibly her own, that she had shut everything away.

Ryan's suggestion had been welcomed. Jonas preferred to have a conversation with Sabrina. He liked to see her expression and gauge her tone of voice. However, it was clear that wasn't going to happen. And he recognized that Ellen's prying had been from concern. She hadn't meant to upset Sabrina, and he had overreacted, his protective instincts kicking into high gear when he'd seen the distress in Sabrina's face.

He didn't have a chance to look in his drawer until the afternoon, when the kids were safely napping. His heart stuttered to see that black cover in his drawer. Part of him dreaded reading what she'd written. He carried it to the sofa on the far side of their bedroom and sat down.

I don't think I'm the kind of submissive you want me to be, and I'm terrified you'll figure out I'm not the wife you wanted.

Jonas stared at her messy handwriting. She'd jotted it down quickly, before she could rethink her message or her wording. Knowing her, she'd rushed it on purpose. If she'd taken her time, she likely would have talked herself out of being so baldly honest.

It crushed him that she thought she wasn't the wife he wanted. No matter what their D/s relationship turned out to be, he was married to her because he wanted to be. He'd pushed her because she was heading down a road filled with too much stress and unhappiness, but he'd pushed her too fast and too far in the wrong direction.

When he broke down their week, he could pinpoint the moments when she'd hesitated, when he'd coaxed her to follow his orders. But he couldn't identify any one thing she'd hated. Sure she'd resisted kneeling and being fed, but she'd ultimately accepted and enjoyed it. She hadn't loved the idea of wearing a collar or leash, but she hadn't protested it either. Had she changed her mind about exhibitionism?

He halted that line of thought. He'd been down that road, and there were no answers, only questions. He needed to address the main concern she'd put down. This problem required a slow, methodical approach to a solution. Sabrina needed to know that he didn't have buyer's remorse. He picked up his phone and called Ellen. She picked up on the first ring.

"It's nap time, so I know you're watching your stories. If you're asking what's going on, I'm not in a position to know that Sledge is really Sage in disguise and he/she is going to seduce Brock even though he's married to Sage's identical twin sister, Thyme. I'm not sure if that's a love triangle or a quadrangle. I haven't taken a math class in a long time."

Jonas laughed. Ellen's addiction to daytime drama was a well-kept secret. Jonas and Ryan both knew that disclosing that information would put their lives at risk. He'd told Sabrina, but she'd dismissed the notion without asking Ellen for confirmation. As for himself, Jonas didn't watch much television. It had taken him over a year to realize Sabrina didn't have one in the bedroom, but that was okay. He preferred to do other things in the bedroom.

"Summer afternoons are for getting some yard work done without having to stop a little guy from pulling up plants and handing them to me." Teaching Ethan to weed was definitely a work in progress. Rose hadn't yet developed a discerning eye, but at least she'd begun asking before she yanked. "Or relaxing with a magazine and an iced tea."

"Mmmmm." Ellen somehow laced a healthy dose of sarcasm into her murmur of agreement. "Ryan's napping. I woke his ass up last night at midnight when I got home and worked him over pretty well. He went to sleep smiling."

Jonas didn't miss pulling the late shift at her club. Ellen frequently worked until two or three in the morning, so getting home at midnight was a bonus. He also knew better than to ask about the scene because she'd give him more details than he wanted. While he didn't mind discussing technique or strategy, he didn't want a play-by-play accounting.

"But you can't be calling about that. Nope. This is your first moment alone and Sabrina's at work. Wanna talk about it?" She'd made the offer several times in the past week, but he'd refused.

Jonas took a deep breath. "I'm not sure what to say. Everything was going great, and then she called her safe word, demanded the key to the room, and told me not to come back until after dinner."

A loud snort came from the other end of the line. "And you let her get away with that? Calling the safe word is fine, but the rest of it? You should have paddled her ass."

If he'd felt that was the right thing to do, he would have. "You didn't see her, Elle. She was devastated, barely holding it together."

"That's the ideal time to push the issue, when she's the most vulnerable. Jonas, strong submissives aren't pushovers. If you let her raise those walls, it's going to be fifty times harder to break them down." She hissed vehemently. Jonas could picture her pacing the living room. She'd either paused or recorded the soap he'd interrupted.

However he didn't appreciate her rush to judgment. "Ryan wasn't nearly this resistant or closed off. He worshipped you. He wanted to be your submissive. He was a blank canvas." Though Ellen was his best friend, he'd known Ryan longer. Watching the two of them develop a relationship had been an exercise in caution, but he'd also witnessed the beauty of it unfold. It had seduced him. He wanted that with Sabrina. She deserved that kind of happiness.

She snorted. "That's bullshit and you know it. We had our share of fights and struggles, but I didn't let him go off in a huff without knowing there would be a consequence. He learned it was better to stay and talk it out or ask for his journal. I learned to take criticism, and it helped hone my technique. Twenty years later, we have a fabulous marriage and two wonderful kids. But that doesn't mean we don't still have disagreements." The heat went out of her voice and sympathy crept in. "Jonas, problems are just a part of everyday life in a relationship. The key isn't in avoiding them; it's in dealing with them."

"We didn't fight." He exhaled in exasperation. "A fight would have been easier. At least she would have told me why she was angry. But she wasn't angry, I don't think. Things were going great. I bound her from hanging restraints on the stage in a mostly empty amphitheater. We had a great scene. I was looking to keep the momentum, but she called her safe word. She's never done that before. I wanted to talk, but she refused. I can't exactly tie her up and beat it out of her after she's safe-worded."

Ellen was quiet. He heard her breathing, so he knew his cell hadn't dropped the call. After nearly a full minute, she spoke. "The first time is always the hardest, for both of you. Keep that in mind. Ryan didn't get much out of her either. She told him she didn't know what was wrong and that she'd used her safe word because she didn't want to do what you told her to do. She admitted that she'd used it incorrectly. He said she seemed frustrated and afraid. He didn't understand why she'd be afraid."

Jonas heard the censure in her tone. It was likely Ryan had been so bothered by his talk with Sabrina that he'd required a session. Ellen blamed him for this mess, which worked because it was his fault. And she wasn't finished.

"Journaling isn't an end in and of itself. It's a communication tool. Notice how I never say things to you like 'Ryan seemed to enjoy that flogging.' I always know what he got out of it, what he liked and what he didn't like, and I know the reasons why. It's not just a byproduct of my awesomeness. It's because I require him to tell me these things. We normally just talk now, but in the beginning, we mostly used the journal. Every now and again I find it set out for me on top of my bra collection."

When she took a breath, he spoke up. Otherwise he was in for a long lecture, and he hadn't called for a lecture. "I used a journal. She left me an entry this morning." He stared at her scrawled message, wishing she'd said more and knowing she'd revealed an uncomfortable feeling.

"Was it helpful?"

Ellen, he knew, had rules for the journal. It was neutral territory. Nothing in it could be used for punishment or in another argument. It was also confidential. Ellen shared a lot of things with Jonas, but she never told him the deeply personal and private contents of that journal. She wouldn't ask what Sabrina said, and she didn't expect him to tell her anything confidential.

"It's a start." His first task was to prove to her that she was the wife he wanted.

"You have a strategy?"

"Yeah. I think I went too fast, tried too much."

Ellen growled. "You *think* or you *know*?"

"She didn't say a lot." He wanted to get defensive, but he knew she was right. As he'd told Sabrina, he needed to stop guessing. "I *know* I need some time alone with her this evening."

"Are you asking me to babysit on my night off?" She purred too sweetly.

"I can return the favor, you know."

Ellen chuckled. "You're too easy. I would have settled for ice cream."

"I'll bring the kids over as soon as they wake up."

* * * *

Sabrina was tempted to skip lunch, but she knew Jonas would get mad at her if he found out. Whenever they fought or if she was facing a particularly stressful deadline, he became obsessive about making sure she had regular meals. She was contemplating lunch order options when her secretary buzzed to let her know she had visitors.

The only people in the habit of showing up at her office without an appointment were the Galens, and since they were the largest account Rife and Company had ever landed, she put up with it. If she had her way, she'd take Stephen and his father aside and give them a stern reminder about manners. Even a half hour's notice would be appreciated.

She'd known them since she was a teenager, and she'd spent six years on Stephen's arm. They were friends now, though not the kind she typically had over to the house. Jonas liked Stephen and Mr. Galen, but Sabrina thought that inviting her ex over on a regular basis was tacky. She'd kill Jonas if he had his ex-wife over for any reason.

Taking a deep breath, she squared her shoulders and went to the door. If the Galens wanted a meeting, they could talk over food. But it wasn't them. She opened the door to her office to find her sister, Ginny, standing there with Sophia. Sophia had married Ginny's best friend and business partner, Drew Snow, and now Sophia was as close to Ginny as she was to Sabrina.

She was three years younger and they had different fathers, but Ginny looked a lot like Sabrina. They had the same height, build, and coloring, though Ginny wore her hair a little shorter. It brushed the top of her shoulders, which was about twice as long as it used to be. People who didn't know them both often mistook them for one another.

Ginny spread her arms wide and grinned. "Surprise! We're taking you out to lunch."

Sabrina hadn't spoken to Ginny since her birthday dinner nearly a month before, and that was unusual. She was close to her sister. Though they lived almost an hour from one another, they tried to talk or email at least once a day. She returned Ginny's smile and hugged her tightly. Part of her envied her sister the right to wear jeans and a cotton T-shirt during the workweek. Even Sophia dressed casually.

"Perfect timing. I was just about to order in, but going out sounds wonderful."

They chose a place nearby. Ginny owned Sensual Secrets, a bakery and catering company. She was in charge of the bakery, and Drew oversaw the catering. Both were excellent chefs, and their company was very successful. Sophia now worked exclusively for them, handling all the finances so Drew and Ginny could focus on being creative.

Since it was Monday, the bakery was closed, which meant both women had the day off. Sabrina waited until after they'd ordered food to find out why they'd suddenly appeared at her office.

"So, what's this about?"

Ginny fluttered her eyelashes in mock innocence. "A girl can't miss her big sister? Since when do I need a reason to see you?"

"You don't. But it's not like you to just show up." Sabrina shot Sophia a look that reiterated the question.

Sophia smiled brilliantly. "Ginny wants in on Elysium. Drew talked to Stefano this morning, and he said the investment would be a good one, but he wants to wait until after the Mehlbergs' divorce is final to make a lowball offer."

Ginny grinned. "I said I'd go in on it if we made it more lesbian friendly. Lara and I spent a day there about six or seven years ago. It was nice."

Sabrina had thought the entire concept was LGBT-friendly. She cocked her head at Ginny. "What would make it more lesbian friendly?"

"Special events, like a lesbian week. And it needs to be green. More recycling and conservation. We could harness solar and wind power."

Buying into Elysium had been the last thing on Sabrina's mind, but it seemed to be the only thing on anyone else's mind. She wasn't sure she wanted to invest, and she and Jonas had yet to discuss it.

"That sounds great, but I'm not sure I want a piece of this. I have a job already. It sucks up most of my time." And having two kids and an iffy marriage sucked up the rest.

Sophia scrunched her nose, which did nothing to mar her beauty. She was easily one of the most exotically gorgeous women Sabrina had ever seen. She flipped her hand as if swatting away Sabrina's objection. "You hate your job. This will be more fun. Imagine the ad campaigns for a sex island. The slogans alone make it worthwhile."

"I don't hate my job." Sabrina felt her entire body stiffen. "I'm very good at what I do."

"You're one of the best," Sophia agreed. She bit into a piece of steaming hot bread that she'd slathered with butter. "But as one of the people who beats the stress out of you, I can say that I've never seen you this tense, and you just got back from a sex-filled vacation. Did you use my gift?"

Heat crept up Sabrina's neck, but she knew that wouldn't get her out of answering the question. "Yes. The corset fit very well and the cuffs came in handy."

Ginny giggled. "And did you use Ellen's gift? We all had a great time shopping for that."

Though Ginny's gift had been tame—she'd given Sabrina a pair of chairs that fit perfectly into the living room—Sabrina wasn't at all surprised to find out that Ginny had a hand in Ryan and Ellen's selection. Ryan probably had good intentions when he had suggested it, but her sister and Ellen both had a devilish streak.

The blush made it to Sabrina's face. She pressed the insides of her wrists against her glass of water, hoping that would help make the redness go away faster. Normally she just breathed through these moments, but this one brought back unpleasant memories of her trip and the way she'd run out on Jonas. He'd been devastated, and it had been her fault.

"Yes. Jonas quite liked that gift."

Something in her tone must have given away more than she intended. Sophia studied her in a quiet Domme way that Sabrina often found disconcerting.

She shifted her attention to Ginny, but her sister's frown didn't make her feel better. "Did something happen?"

Writing down her deepest fears had been all the emotional upheaval Sabrina could handle for one day. Behind every other problem and doubt was the fear that Jonas would wake up one day and realize he wanted something from her that she couldn't give. Her emotions became strangely calm as numbness washed over her.

She managed a polite smile. "Look, Elysium is a nice place to visit, but I'm not interested in buying it. If that's what you want, I wish you both the best."

Ginny whistled, drawing attention to them in this crowded restaurant. "Wow, Sophie. Did you notice how quickly she changed the subject?"

"Yes, and she did it so well, making it seem like she was going back to what we were talking about before." Sophia waggled her eyebrows in mock admiration.

A bit of the numbness eased away. Sabrina felt her smile warm up. "I love when you talk about me like I'm not here."

Ginny looked at her as if she'd just arrived. "Oh? Are you back now? For a second I thought Mom had come to lunch. Don't get me wrong, I love Mom, I just need a little warning first."

The feeling was mutual. Their mother had a difficult time dealing with Ginny's free spirit and the way she flaunted the rules of polite society. Melinda Morozov would hyperventilate if she knew Ginny was wearing jeans to an upscale restaurant, even if it was just for lunch and the dress code allowed for such things.

Sophia's expression had turned decidedly sober. "Seriously, Sabrina. You can talk to us. Or maybe you just want to ask questions?"

Understanding dawned. She'd been set up. She eyed her sister and her friend with harsh intent. "Jonas sent you, didn't he?"

Ginny and Sophia exchanged a puzzled look, and Sabrina realized she'd guessed wrong. She set down her fork and covered her eyes with one hand, punishing her head with a painful squeeze.

Sophia gently tugged Sabrina's hand away from her face. "Hey, that's against the rules. No hurting yourself. Now tell me what's wrong."

"I can't." Sabrina disengaged her hand from Sophia's grip and gave her a grim look. "It's between Jonas and me."

Ginny opened her mouth to ask a question, but Sophia waved her hand to halt the interrogation. "Gin, she knows we're here if she needs us. She said it's between her and Jonas. We have to respect that."

Ginny didn't look like she appreciated Sophia's interference, but Sabrina breathed a sigh of relief.

Monday ran late, as it always did. It seemed work just piled up over the weekend, a million small molehills could forge a mountain. Sabrina didn't leave the office until nearly five-thirty. As she battled rush hour traffic, she lamented her job and questioned why she kept it. After all, she didn't need the money and she could use the time.

The house was eerily quiet when she came in the back door. Rose usually hovered in the area between the kitchen and the laundry room where the door to the garage was also located. She did triple duty, keeping her father company as he made dinner, keeping Ethan from escaping out the slider in the breakfast nook, and keeping watch for her mother to come home from work.

Nobody greeted her. "Hello?" she called. "Rosie? Ethan? Mommy's home." Silence. She made it to the kitchen. It was vacant, and it bore no evidence of use. In light of the entry she'd left in that blasted journal, cold panic froze in her veins. "Jonas?"

She set her briefcase on the island and continued into the dining room where she came to a halt. The shades were drawn, but it wasn't dark. The room was lit with hundreds of candles. They lined the display shelves, sideboard, and the fireplace mantle. More covered the top of the table, and the air was thick with their perfume.

Only two places were clear of candles, and those had plates heaped with lasagna. She recognized Jonas's signature style in the patterning of the layers.

The man himself lounged in the opposite doorway, the one leading to the large foyer where he'd first convinced her that it wasn't wrong to want to be held down and that she wasn't doomed to a life without orgasms. He leaned against the wall with one ankle casually crossed over the other.

He wore jeans, the ones that made his ass look extra sexy, a green, silk button-down shirt that brought out the olive in his eyes, and a matching green-and-gold tie. His feet, as always, were bare. She had a hard time suppressing a smile at that small detail.

She wanted to tell him he looked amazing or that she was floored by the candles and the romantic setup. But that's not what came out of her mouth. "Where are the kids?"

"Ellen and Ryan's. They're having a sleepover." He pushed away from the wall and came toward her. "Take off your shoes and sit down. I'll pour the wine."

She stepped out of her heels, automatically losing three inches and any false confidence gained from having the extra height. He pulled out a chair for her and she sat down. Then he grabbed the bottle of wine from where it had been chilling on the sideboard.

He leaned over her as he poured, and she inhaled his clean, masculine scent. A wave of longing washed over her, and she desperately wished she knew what to say or do.

"Sorry I'm late. I hope you weren't waiting long."

He handed her the glass and smiled. "I know what time you usually get home on a Monday, honey. Try the wine."

Her hand shook when she picked up the glass, so she set it back down. "Jonas." Half-plea, half-cry, she whispered his name. She couldn't stand not knowing whether or not he'd read the journal.

He sat down at the head of the table, the seat next to hers. These were their usual spots. He took the dominant position, and she was always faithfully to his left. "I thought we would eat first, relax a little, and then talk, but I can see you're about to break."

If she shook any harder, she might shatter. She strove for a calm demeanor as she waited for him to continue.

He closed his hand over hers where they were balled together in her lap. "First, you are the wife I wanted." With difficulty, he lifted her left hand onto the table and held it there. She wasn't resisting him; she was just stiff with anxiety. He brushed his thumb over the white gold wedding band she never took off. "This ring does more than mark you as mine. It's a symbol of my promise to love and cherish you. I wouldn't give this to just anyone."

She looked at the larger diamond set in a nest of smaller diamonds and emeralds. It was a beautiful ring. It had belonged to his grandmother. Still, she couldn't stop her retort. "No, not anyone. Just the women you marry."

A dangerous light entered his eye, and she knew she'd crossed a line. She was pushing him, and he didn't like it. She jerked her hand away, and scrunched it in her lap with the other one. What did it matter when she'd crossed so many already?

"I've never given this ring to another woman. Helene kept her ring when she left. I didn't want it back." He exhaled loudly, a warning not to interrupt again, especially with an assumption she'd made. He'd never once told her that his ex-wife had worn the rings. "I gave you this ring because I felt you were the kind of woman my grandmother would have liked. She was a good judge of character. I didn't expect to fall in love with you, but I did. I don't regret it, Sabrina. Not a single moment."

She felt terrible. "I can't be what you want me to be."

"You already are." He sank to his knees next to her chair and took her face in his hands. "You're everything I want. You're my wife, the mother of my children. You're the first thing I think about in the morning and the last thing I think about when I fall asleep at night. I dream about you. I fantasize about you. I was broken, cynical and directionless, and you healed me. You gave me hope. You gave me the courage to choose a life path that fits me. You made me the man I am today, and I want nothing more than to make you happy."

He made her sound so much better than she really was. She trembled even more and wished she could cry, anything to make her feel a little better. "Jonas, I'm not submissive. I don't want to kneel at your feet or have you feed me by hand."

That wasn't exactly true, but it wasn't false either. She wished she could make heads or tails of her feelings.

He searched her eyes as if he knew there was more, but when she didn't add anything more, he nodded. "You are submissive, honey.

It's one of the things about you that I find attractive. I could see that it was becoming more and more difficult for you to deny that part of yourself. That's why I wanted you to try it. I thought Elysium was the perfect setting for us to explore a different dynamic, but I can see that I pushed you too far, too fast."

"I'm so confused." She heard the desperation, the supplication in her voice, which was surprisingly steady considering how badly her body quaked.

"I know, and I'm sorry. It's going to take some time to sort it out. We'll have to do it one element at a time. We'll use the journal. I'm going to ask you to write in it every day. We'll talk, too, especially after a scene." He pressed his forehead to hers. "It's not all smooth sailing, honey. We'll weather the storm together. For better or for worse."

Tremendous emotion welled inside her. She struggled to contain it because she couldn't release it. "Jonas, I need…"

He usually finished her sentence, especially when he knew she wanted time in the dungeon. This time, he didn't. "No more assumptions, honey. Tell me what you need."

"I need to cry. I've tried to let it out for over a week, but it just stays inside me. I can't stand it."

He stroked the side of her face. "Tell me what you need."

"The flogger. The four-footer. And the cat. Maybe more. I don't know what it's going to take. I just want to put myself in your hands and trust that you'll work your magic."

He pressed a kiss to her forehead. "That's my little submissive wife. Help me put out the candles, then go downstairs and wait for me, naked and kneeling."

Chapter Sixteen

Sabrina knelt on the soft rug in the center of the playroom Jonas had built in their basement and marveled at the fact she didn't mind kneeling naked. A week ago she'd balked at the order. Now she welcomed it. That was definitely a paradox for her journal. She wondered how Jonas would address that issue.

I hate kneeling at your feet unless it's for a scene. It's almost like if you don't subsume me with your power, I get angry. I feel cheated.

She used to think she had discovered the pinnacle of sexual expression and the secret to keeping their relationship strong, but now she saw the trail of her past spread behind her, a string of stepping stones that stalled and faltered more than they showed a strong, clear path.
Just when she thought they'd fallen away completely, Jonas had appeared, holding out his hand to guide her through the darkness, showing her that the path kept going, and they'd travel it together. That, more than anything, gave her a renewed sense of courage and hope.
The door opened, and Jonas came in. She didn't look up. He required that she keep her gaze firmly on the floor in front of her. He came closer, bringing the perfume of those hundreds of candles they'd extinguished together. She was sure the scent clung to her hair and skin the way same way it adhered to his clothes.

He stopped next to her, close enough for his jeans to rub her cheek, and he pressed her head to his thigh, a reassuring embrace and a show of power. "Remind us of your safe word."

"Onion." The word felt dirty and used, a piece of her humiliation. "We should choose a different one."

"Not during a scene. We can discuss it later." He hadn't rejected her idea, but he'd acknowledged the inherent plea. That made her feel a little better about her misuse of the word. Maybe they needed to discuss a "Wait-a-minute" word.

He stroked his hand along her temple, behind her ear, and down her neck, caressing her hair and brushing it away from her face at the same time. They stayed like this for a while. Sabrina closed her eyes and gave herself over to the inherent joy of being cherished by him.

Abruptly he twisted his hand in her hair at the nape of her neck and forced her head back. She lifted her gaze and stared at him in wide-eyed submission.

"I'm going to hurt you, Sabrina. I'm going to make you cry."

Her pussy tingled and heated, and a weight lifted from her chest. "Yes. Please."

"Then I'm going to carry you upstairs and make love to you."

Her lips trembled, but this time in anticipation, not fear. "Yes."

"Go bend over the spanking bench." He released his hold on her hair, letting go slowly, reluctantly.

She rose to her feet. The spanking bench was a padded affair, which made it bulky, and the plastic, non-porous padding reminded her of a doctor's office. Two legs jutted down, separated to provide full exposure. They were bent for kneeling, but high enough for him to fuck her if he so desired. If he wanted her to stand, they were situated on a pivot to move out of the way. She knelt on it, feeling split wide open to his view, which only made her pussy weep more. She missed having this reaction to his domination. It felt right, almost sacred.

She bent over the padded bench and placed her arms above her head so that he could bind her. She waited.

He slid his hand under her head. "Lift up."

She expected a blindfold, but he slid a towel under her head. While she appreciated the softness of the impromptu pillow, especially since that now meant she wouldn't be peeling her cheek from the plastic afterward, she didn't understand the purpose of the towel.

But he showed no sign that an explanation was forthcoming. Instead, he pressed a rope to her hand. "Hold this."

Normally he used cuffs. To those, he attached snaps that connected to the spanking bench and held her immobile. Sometimes he bound her with rope, but that wasn't his usual thing.

He pressed a rope to her other hand. "If you wrap them around your wrists or hands a few times, they'll be easier to hold. I'm not going to bind you, Sabrina. You're going to take this because you want it and need it. You're going to submit to me for the same reasons."

Forcing her submission hadn't worked, so he was asking her to give it. Somehow this seemed more difficult. It demanded more from her—active participation and willing surrender. It didn't diminish his power, but it did render him that much more difficult to please. She was being asked to prove herself worthy of his attention.

He moved around the room, mostly behind her. He hadn't instructed her not to look, so she remained still by choice. Soon she felt a feather-light caress on the bend at the back of her knee. It moved up her leg and over the curve of her ass to her hip. Then it continued up her side, across her back, and down the other side. It soothed and left her wanting, craving a firmer touch.

Up and down her body, again and again. Now she shivered from need instead of fear, the internal strife calmed, if not forgotten. In the periphery of her vision, she caught sight of a feather. It was long, and the edges were frilled, rendering it impossible to tell if it came from a real bird. She hadn't even known he owned a feather.

When he came around the top of the bench, he leaned down and bit her earlobe. The small sting roused her from the trancelike state she hadn't realized she'd fallen into. "You still doubt your submissiveness?"

She was naked and spread open, bent over a padded bench while he tortured her with a feather. All the while, she waited to be flogged. However she wasn't tied down. "I can get up and leave at any time."

"Any submissive can. Ropes don't prohibit you from leaving, Sabrina. Only your consent keeps you here. That's the way it's always been. That's the way it always will be." He brushed her hair away from her neck and gathered it together. While he preferred for her to wear it down, he always moved it out of the way before he flogged her.

Sabrina digested his argument. He frequently tied her up or held her down. She liked that display of dominance, but she took a step back and tried to consider it from his perspective. If she hadn't wanted those things, he wouldn't have done them. "Is that why you always make me beg?"

He laughed, a short sound that betrayed mischievous amusement. "No. I just like to hear you beg." He traced a leather rectangle down her back. She recognized the tip of the crop. "You beg so well, always with the right amount of desperation and deference. You still doubt your submissiveness?"

No, she didn't, but that didn't mean her doubts were gone. "Yes. I'm not as submissive as you would like me to be."

He brought the crop down across her ass, the thin rod stinging her unprepared skin. A low buzzing started in her ears, drowning out some of that doubt and spreading waves of painful pleasure. He drew the flap along the fresh line he'd made, and the tingling spread in small waves through her muscles.

"You liked that."

"Because I have a masochistic streak."

He whipped her twice more, laying parallel stripes above and below the first blow. Now he caressed her ass with his hand, playing his fingers across the stripes as if they were guitar strings. "Sophia doesn't require your submission." His forays grew, and he fingered her clit. "How is this different?"

"She doesn't touch my pussy." But she did like to rub and pinch the stripes and welts she put on Sabrina's body. Her hands were always cool, whereas Jonas was always hot. "But you're my husband. We're a little more involved."

His hand came down hard on her ass, a small punishment for the sarcasm lacing her tone. The correction shuddered through her body. She braced herself for the wave of shame and humiliation, but it never came.

"She ties me up. Always."

His fingers returned to her clit. "Why?"

Though Sabrina saw Sophia by choice, often scheduling the time and duration of sessions, Sabrina always instigated it. Sophia might offer, but she never insisted. Jonas never offered, but he often insisted. Sabrina could ask for a session, but it happened on his timetable. The quantity and duration where subject to his whim.

"Because she has no power over me. You do."

The crop—or had he exchanged it for a cane?—came down on the back of one thigh and then the other. Stars exploded behind her eyes. She sucked in a breath and wound the ropes around her hands one more time.

"Why do I have power over you and she doesn't?"

Smaller taps rained over the tender flesh surrounding her pussy and her anus. He definitely still had the crop in hand. She struggled to focus on his question only to find the answer right there. "Because I gave it to you and not to her."

He set the crop across her body and bent down until his cheek was on the padded bench and the tip of his nose touched hers. "That, my sweet wife, is submission. It can't be taken. It can only be given. It is your gift to me, and it belongs to me alone, for no other reason than because it's what you want."

"But this is a scene." Tears pricked the back of her eyelids. She blinked quickly to hold them at bay. "I only seem to have a problem submitting to you when we're not role-playing."

His hand moved over her back and up her neck. "This isn't a scene, honey. We're not role-playing. I am your husband, your Dom, and you are my wife, my submissive."

One fat teardrop fell. "But we're not doing this because you want it. We're doing this because I need it."

He caught her tear with the tip of his thumb. "That's my job, Sabrina. Your needs are always more important than my wants. I only pushed the issue of your submission because our scenes aren't enough for you anymore."

They weren't. She loved role-playing with him. She lived for their scenes. But he was right; they were no longer enough. What had been a nice break from reality had become a refuge that couldn't hold her problems at bay. The tears came in earnest now. Sobs shook her body.

"I'm sorry, Jonas. I'm so sorry."

"Don't be sorry, honey. Life changes. Your needs change, and that means my response to your needs has to change. I had the right idea, but the wrong execution." He lifted her from the table and carried her to a fold-down sofa where he held her in his arms as she wept.

Minutes passed, though they seemed like hours, and her crying subsided. He passed her a wad of tissue as he rocked her in his arms. She wanted to say something, to thank him for understanding, for loving her despite her insecurities, but she blurted something unexpected.

"I want to quit my job."

He stopped rocking her, but he didn't say anything for the longest time. She thought about taking it back, but the more she thought about it, the more she realized that working in advertising no longer made her happy. What had been a joy had become a burden. She wanted more time with her children, especially because they were young, and she wanted more time with Jonas. Though she tried to control it, she worked long hours and traveled for business several times each month.

It simply wasn't something she wanted to do anymore.

Finally he nodded. "Okay. If that's what you want. But please don't do it because you think I want you to buy Elysium. Owning a business isn't going to be easier than running a billion-dollar marketing division. I support any decision you make as long as you're doing it for the right reasons."

She threw her arms around him and slathered kisses all over his face. She couldn't remember the last time she'd felt so carefree.

"Jonas?"

"Hmm?" His eyes were closed and his hand rested on her hip.

"You didn't flog me."

"I never said I was going to flog you. I said I was going to hurt you and make you cry." He pinched one of the welts on her ass. She yelped, but he only laughed. "Now it's time to go upstairs so I can make love to you."

THE END

WWW.MICHELEZURLO.COM

ABOUT THE AUTHOR

Letting Go was my first published novel. It was a labor of love, full of characters I'd spent countless hours creating. Over the years, it's become the one I get the most e-mails about. Sabrina's journey is one with which so many women closely identify, and Jonas is the perfect man to balance her strengths and weaknesses. When fans first wrote asking for a sequel, I politely informed them that I was finished with the story. I had other stories to tell. But those readers planted a seed that grew, and I began to wonder how Sabrina and Jonas were getting along now that they had a few years and a couple of kids. I missed hanging out with them. Two years passed in real life, and I received many more e-mails. Scattered pieces came together, and *Stepping Stones* was born.

I am blessed to have a wonderful, supportive family and readers who appreciate and love my characters as much as I do. Don't stop letting me know your thoughts. If you haven't guessed from the way this one ended, I am planning more. Unless you think it's okay to leave things hanging like this…

For all titles by Michele Zurlo, please visit
www.bookstrand.com/michele-zurlo

Siren Publishing, Inc.
www.SirenPublishing.com